Glimpse Of Forever

Evanell

A Wings ePress, Inc.
Paranormal Romance Novel

Wings ePress, Inc.

Edited by: Diana Greenwood
Copy Edited by: Leslie Hodges
Senior Editor: Elizabeth Struble
Executive Editor: Lorraine Stephens
Cover Artist: Regina Brytowski

All rights reserved

Wings ePress Books
www.wingsepress.com

Published In the United States Of America

Wings ePress Inc.
3000 N. Rock Road
Newton, KS 67114

Dedication

To William, my husband,
without whose help my dream of writing
might still be nothing more than a dream.

* * *

I saw eternity the other night,

Like a great ring of pure and

endless light.

All calm as it was bright.

Ib. The World

Prologue

Denver, Colorado

Nine-year-old Jennifer scraped her knee as she struggled to reach the last branch to rescue her kitten from the top of the huge tree. Puffing with exertion after she had Mordora safe in her arms, Jennifer looked below and saw the new boy from next door.

"You must be Jennifer," he called, shading his eyes with his hand as he stared up at her.

She felt her face turn red and hastily tucked her red skirt between her legs. "Who told you my name?"

"Your cousin, Tyler."

Jennifer frowned, although Uncle Mac said she shouldn't because she might grow up with permanent wrinkles.

"Who're you?" she asked, although she already knew.

"Dirk. We just moved in next door to your aunt and uncle."

"I live here, too," she blurted.

"Yeah. I know. Tyler told me."

Jennifer frowned again. She hated sharing Tyler with anybody, except Kacy. Like her, Kacy was an orphan. She lived with her grandparents a few blocks away. They had been best friends since kindergarten, and both vowed they always would be.

"Can I come up and help rescue your kitten?" Dirk asked.

"Sure." Jennifer tucked her dress more firmly between her legs and squeezed them tighter together. Even though she thought they were beautiful, Aunt Rachel would give her holy heck if she let a boy see her new lace-trimmed underpants.

Dirk climbed fast, and Jennifer admired his agility. When he reached her, he leaned against a sturdy limb and hooked his thumbs in his Levi belt loops. "Tyler said you had unusual eyes, but he didn't say they were pretty."

People often teased Jennifer about her speckled green eyes, but nobody ever said they were pretty. "You like them?" she asked, uncertain.

Dirk nodded. "They remind me of my opal, Jeni."

Flustered, she resisted the urge to ask why and blurted, "Nobody calls me Jeni."

"Good. That's what I'll call you, then."

He had a nice grin. Even white teeth, too. She bet he brushed every morning and night, as Aunt Rachel said everybody should. His pale blond hair reminded her of Kacy's white-haired guardian angel. She'd only seen Rey once, but she'd never forget the jolly, wingless angel.

Dirk stood so close Jennifer could smell his skin—clean like pine-scented soap and shampoo. He looked a couple of years older than her, probably eleven or twelve, the same age as Tyler.

"Can I carry your kitten down?"

She nodded and cautiously extended Mordora, careful not to let go of her fluffy orange-brown pet until Dirk had a good hold.

"Why don't you climb down first and show me the way?"

"Okay." Grateful for his help and relieved he wouldn't see under her dress, Jennifer decided she might not mind sharing Tyler with Dirk after all.

When they reached the ground he handed Mordora back to her.

"Thanks," she said.

"You're welcome."

Her scraped knee stung. She looked down and saw blood trickling from the open gash.

"You're hurt." Dirk pulled a white handkerchief from his back pocket and squatted in front of her.

While he wiped her bloody leg, Jennifer struggled with her squirming kitten to keep her claws from scratching her face.

A few seconds later Dirk stood back up and stuffed the waded handkerchief back in his pocket. "It's stopped bleeding."

"Thanks,' she said again.

"Why don't you thank me with a kiss?"

Jennifer's young heart gave a funny lurch. She wanted to kiss him badly, but she'd never before kissed a boy. Did she dare?

Before she lost her nerve, she arched up on her tiptoes. He stood a head taller than her and she couldn't reach his mouth, so she aimed for his chin.

He caught her cheeks with his hands and placed his mouth on hers. It wasn't much of a kiss, just a peck actually, but Jennifer closed her eyes. And lost her young heart.

When they pulled apart, she felt dizzy. Woozy. Excited.

His expression turned somber. "Tyler said you were terrific, but I don't know if I agree."

"Why—not?" Jennifer hated the stupid warble in her voice. It sounded like she was about to cry.

"Because I think you're more than terrific, Jeni, I think you're perfect. And I'm glad I found you."

Jennifer blinked. "Found me? What does that mean?"

"We knew each other before. Don't you remember?"

Her heart pounded faster than she could play the scales on the piano, while visions of prior lives flashed in her young head. She gulped in awe. "I-I-I knew you before...?"

"Several times." Dirk grinned, and she wanted to hug him something fierce. He had remembered her as he'd promised!

"Will you do me a favor?" he asked.

She flashed a grin. "If I can."

"I like your long hair. Don't ever cut it."

Proud of her waist-long cinnamon-brown hair, she vowed, "I'll keep it long for you, always, Dirk."

When he grinned again, she worked up her nerve to ask, "Will you do me a favor?"

"If I can," he turned her words back on her.

"Will you marry me when we grow up?" She blushed at her daring, and expected him to tease her.

Instead he said, "You bet."

From his pocket he dug out a stone that resembled murky crystal, but as he exposed it to the sun, the stone reflected every color in the rainbow. "My guardian angel said this opal would guide me to you. Now that it has, I want you to keep it. If we're parted again, it will help you find me."

Dirk winked, and a delicious warmth curled around Jennifer as a vision—her special gift—showed them in the future, all grown up. Dirk sported a mustache, and in spite of her youth, she knew by the look in their eyes that they were deeply in love and very happy.

Music coming from a CD in her aunt and uncle's house played, "*Lay your head upon my pillow and make believe—*"

"That's our song," Dirk said. "When we grow up, we'll get married and you can lay your head on my pillow whenever you want to."

Mesmerized by her new neighbor and the visions she'd had, Jennifer didn't realize Aunt Rachel had opened the door until she called, "Jennifer, didn't you hear me? Kacy would like to talk to you on the phone."

"I'll be right there." Cuddling her precious kitten close, Jennifer backed away. "I'll see you later, Dirk."

"Yes, you will," he promised.

Budging Mordora's paws off her arm to protect herself from the kitten's sharp claws, Jennifer gripped the opal tight and smiled again.

Dirk smiled too and winked. "I think I'm going to be crazy about you, Jeni."

"I think I'm going to feel the same way about you."

Her happy heart sang merrily as she turned and skipped away, anxious to tell Kacy all about the boy she had known in previous lives who had just agreed to marry her. And then they'd live happily ever after, just like in all the fairy tales.

One

Twelve Years Later—London, England

Adrenaline pumped through Jennifer's veins as she dashed down the steep staircase of the bed-and-breakfast where she'd spent her first night in London. With her internal clock still on Denver time, seven hours behind London, she'd overslept. Now she had to rush to keep her appointment at Barings Bank.

At the front door, she opened her red umbrella, then stepped out into the August downpour for the short walk to Victoria Station.

"Good grief," she mumbled when a deluge swept sideways and soaked her gray Nike's and the bottom half of her navy blue slacks. Deciding to take a taxi instead of the tube, she hurried to the wet curb and held up her hand.

To her relief, the first taxi stopped.

"Where to?" the thin-shouldered, black-haired driver asked.

Because she was in a hurry, she ignored the weird sensation that shot through her as she climbed in and said, "Barings Bank."

While the taxi merged with busy London traffic, Jennifer rummaged in her backpack until she found Kleenex to blot her wet slacks. When they no longer dripped, she stuck the soppy Kleenex in an empty pocket of her backpack, rezipped it and gazed outside.

Attached Victorian houses, with bed-and-breakfast signs dangling from chains near their front doors, lined both sides of the narrow street. All had small front yards, or gardens as the Brits called them, with tiny patches of grass surrounded by colorful flowers that helped ease the gloom of the rainy August day.

Excited to be in London again, even though it felt strange to be here by herself, Jennifer admired the old historical buildings that came into view when the taxi left the residential area and the road widened.

As they often did, her thoughts turned to Dirk. *Don't go there,* she admonished herself, but her heart never listened when Dirk came to mind. How she would have loved to share London with him.

Tears threatened. Even though he'd been gone more than three years, she still missed him terribly. She touched the opal, now hanging on a chain around her neck, while her thoughts reverted to the day he'd given it to her—twelve years ago. The youthful vision of him, all grown up with a mustache, flashed. Dirk hadn't ever grown a mustache, so she'd never seen him with one, except in that long ago vision. And except for one brief time in a hotel room, the day they'd eloped, she'd never laid her head on his pillow.

Jennifer swallowed and glanced at her watch. Half an hour till her appointment. She drew in a calming breath and forced her thoughts in a different direction, away from Dirk. Last year Kacy had traveled back in time with her guardian angel and decided to live there. But she'd promised to write a journal and leave it in the Barings bank vault. Jennifer hoped to locate and claim the journal. Not only did she want to know how Kacy had fared in the past, Jennifer intended to write a novel about time-travel and reincarnation. Kacy's journal would provide vital information.

"Is this your first visit to England?" the cab driver asked, jarring her thoughts back to the present.

Staring at the back of his oily black-haired head, Jennifer had the distinct impression she'd seen or met him previously. "No," she said, and in an attempt to appear friendly added, "About a year and a half ago I came here with my best friend."

"Have you ever wondered what London looked like before the invention of cars, paved carriageways, electricity and all the modern-day things that make a big city teem with activity?"

"Many times," Jennifer admitted. "Actually, I'd give just about anything to experience England as it was a hundred and fifty years ago." *Where Kacy is,* Jennifer thought, but didn't mention it.

"How long would it take to decide to step back in time?"

Although Jennifer thought his persistence odd, she said, "About half a heartbeat."

The cab driver braked to a stop.

A chill crawled up her spine. Suddenly anxious to get away from the weird man, Jennifer unzipped her backpack again. "How much is the fare?"

"This ride is free, Miss Quinlane."

Too shocked to ask how he knew her name, Jennifer gaped as he turned his head and she recognized him—Sevil, the black-eyed wizard in her most recent vision. The wizard who had shape-shifted and jumped to the rooftop, taking Miranda, the girl who resembled her, with him.

Wary, Jennifer clutched her backpack to her chest. Her hands trembled. She gripped the pack tighter. *Why would a wizard pose as a cab driver?* And why had she had a vision of him and Miranda spying on two other people named Drake and Prudence, all of whom lived in the past, judging by their old-fashioned clothes and the carriages they rode in?

"I know your deepest wish," the wizard-cab driver rasped, "is to see your friend Kacy, again. I can turn that wish into reality."

Before Jennifer could utter a word, a putrid fog that smelled like rotten sulfur filled the inside of the cab. She gagged and fear shivered through her as she clapped her hands over her mouth. Was she about to be asphyxiated?

The cab door opened and a strong wind swept inside. She recoiled, and shrank back against the seat, but the wind curled around her, spinning into a whirlwind and knocking her backpack and umbrella off her lap. Blindly, she groped for them. But to her astonishment the wind twirled her outside, along with the awful smell, and propelled her up into the rainy sky.

Never in her life had she been so terrified. Her heart pounded. Her skin burned. Her body trembled. And, as she hurtled through space like an out-of-orbit satellite, she feared the noxious fumes might make her barf. Round and round she whirled, higher into the sky. Would the petrifying experience never end? Would she die before it did?

In desperation, she reached for the opal at the base of her throat and prayed it would do as Dirk promised—guide her to him.

A sudden strong force expelled her from the whirlwind. In the blink of an eye, the thick, smelly mist disappeared. With a loud resounding whoosh she started to fall, skimming tree tops with frightening speed.

Panicked, she reached out and snagged a limb, halting her plunge back to earth. Before she caught her breath, lightning struck the limb and snapped it in two. Branches scratched her face and hands as she groped wildly for something else to hang on to... and failed.

The ground rushed up to meet her. She hit it hard and saw a million tiny stars. Then everything went pitch black.

Two

Cottage in the Woods

Moist, dank smelling earth greeted Jennifer's return to consciousness. Flat on her stomach, she saw insects skirting over the scum of a stagnant puddle next to her nose. Gross.

Cold and wet, with a headache pounding like hoof beats against her temple, she forced herself to roll onto her side. Every bone and muscle rebelled. In addition, her legs were trapped by unfamiliar petticoats and a long, pale green dress. Where had these soaking wet clothes come from?

To Jennifer's surprise the hoofbeats were real. Through gnarled tree trunks she saw a white stallion with a hatless rider galloping like a demon toward her. She raised one shivering arm. The effort cost her, but the rider waved back. Dazed and shivering, she lowered her arm.

Moments later the stallion halted a few feet away and the blond, mustached rider jumped down and knelt beside her. "You're alive."

So are you! Jennifer drew in a sharp breath and forgot to release it. *Dirk, with a mustache.* Too stunned to utter another word, she groped for the opal, but she blacked out before she found it.

~ * ~

The next time Jennifer opened her eyes she lay on a lumpy mattress in what appeared to be a one-room cottage. She inhaled the pleasant odors of burning wood and candle wax. Across the room, a fire crackled in the inglenook fireplace. The flames of two candles on a narrow table, cast eerie flickering shadows on the smoke-stained walls.

Dirk sat in a chair beside the bed. He had removed his red blazer, unbuttoned the top buttons of his white shirt, and rolled his sleeves up to his elbows. And she was so darn glad to see him, she didn't know what to say.

He eyed her as though he couldn't quite believe what he saw either. His slow perusal felt intimate, almost as though he touched her.

She smiled, then grimaced as tingles of excitement mingled with her wounds.

Concern shadowed his blue eyes. "Are you in pain?"

"Yes. I'm cold, too. Please hold me and warm me."

Exposing a gentle smile, he bent over and tugged his black boots off. "I do not wish to hurt you further."

"You won't."

"If you are certain...?"

"I am."

He shifted his tall, lean body onto the bed, slid under the coarse blankets and gathered her close.

Jennifer relaxed, not realizing until then how tense she'd been. Her bruised temple rested against Dirk's warm chest. He smelled like she remembered, clean, piney and sexy. If this were a dream, she hoped she never woke up. Feeling safe and secure, she closed her eyes. The steady beat of his heart lulled her back to sleep.

~ * ~

Early morning light draped the cottage in shadows, the next time Jennifer awakened. Alone in bed, she looked around the room. The cottage had one door, two windows and was sparsely furnished with only the bed, a small table, two straight-backed wooden chairs, and a sofa that had seen better days and faced the fireplace.

Her rescuer stood with his back to the fire, his eyes trained on her. Disappointment swirled through her as the fog cleared from her brain. He couldn't be Dirk—unless he'd been reincarnated. Although he smelled like Dirk and had the same tiny mole under his left eye, she couldn't be fortunate enough to find him again in this lifetime, could she?

Embarrassed by her plea to be held last night, she said, "I should've known it was too good to be true."

The stranger arched his blond eyebrows. "What?"

"I thought you were someone I knew."

He did a double take. A wavy lock of pearl-blond hair fell over his forehead.

"And now you think I'm not?" he asked with a clipped British accent.

"No. He isn't English. You obviously are."

He frowned; his fierce glare all encompassing.

Unnerved by his close scrutiny, Jennifer reached for the opal. It was gone. Where? The opal bound her to Dirk. Without it she felt she had lost him all over again. Upset, she battled the sting of tears.

The stranger, fully dressed again in what Brits called riding pink, cleared his throat. White, skin-tight jodhpurs hugged his muscular thighs and the white shirt beneath his red blazer looked new, if a bit old-fashioned. His cheeks and chin were cleanly shaven, his mustache neatly trimmed, his blond hair, except for that errant lock, combed into sleek waves. Even his black, knee-high boots boasted a military shine.

"Last eventide I summoned the village physician. He said to keep you warm, ensure you ate and allow ample bed rest."

Eventide? Still a little groggy, Jennifer knew something wasn't right, but she couldn't put her finger on what was wrong. Every inch of her body felt bruised and battered, her throbbing head like it might explode.

She sucked in her quivering bottom lip as the blue-eyed man approached the bed. He moved with the easy grace of a panther. When he leaned over, his piney scent filled the space between them. His sheer size should have frightened her. It made her feel safe instead.

"I really wiped out, didn't I?" she choked out.

His mustache twitched and his eyes twinkled, but he didn't smile. "I beg your pardon?"

When she didn't reply, he asked, "Can you move your limbs?"

Limbs? "Ye-s," she said over the enormous lump lodged in her throat. Who was he? And where was she?

Fighting dizziness, Jennifer closed her eyes.

"Are you all right?" His soft words warmed her cheek.

She opened her eyes. He was kneeling on the floor beside her, his elbows propped on the lumpy mattress, his face mere inches from hers.

"Yes," she managed. "I'm fine. I think."

Worry creased his forehead. "Do you not know?"

"At the moment I'm not sure of anything."

"Should I summon the physician again?"

"No, that isn't necessary."

Gingerly she slid her arms out from under the covers. They were bare. Then, to her mortification, she realized she didn't have a stitch on.

"Where are my clothes?" she blurted.

Amusement sparkled in his blue eyes. "Over there, by the fire, drying."

Her face flamed. Had she lain in his arms as naked as the day she was born? And who did those cumbersome looking clothes belong to? What had happened to her navy slacks, red sweater and windbreaker? Confused, she touched her bare throat. Where was Dirk's opal?

Jennifer licked her dry lips, then remembered she'd missed her appointment at the bank. Ignoring her naked mortification, she looked for a phone, but didn't see one. Everything in the cottage looked old— antique, actually.

"I need to get dressed," she said.

"You speak like an American."

Surprised by his sharp tone, she eyed him warily and resisted the urge to comment on the strange way *he spoke.*

"I have to get up. I need to go to the bank and apologize for missing my appointment."

He rose from his knees and towered above her, his amusement replaced by a frown.

"You cannot go anywhere."

She felt intimidated by his height. Buck-naked under the covers and flat on her back, didn't help. "You must think all my ducks aren't quacking."

He arched his blond brows in surprise. "I beg your pardon?"

"Forget it," she mumbled. "Do you have a cellular?"

His brows arched higher. "A what?"

Did he have a hearing problem? Not about to ask and risk embarrassing him, she said, "Never mind."

Clutching the coarse, musky smelling blankets to her bare chest, she forced herself to sit up and managed not to wince.

"Do you recall what happened?" When she didn't answer, he said, "You fell from a tree, and you're fortunate you have no broken bones."

"How do you know I don't?"

"I examined you whilst you slept."

How much had he examined? She wasn't sure she wanted to know, but the words popped out before she could stop them. "Before or after you undressed me?"

A wicked gleam blazed in his eyes. "Both."

Heat swam up her neck. She didn't know what to say.

"I intended to lend you my shirt. However, the physician thought it best not to disturb you."

Jennifer's face burned. To avoid his probing gaze, she looked around the cottage again. Her concern returned to her appointment at the bank. How could she get there? Her backpack was in the cab, so she didn't have any money.

Worried, she stared beyond Dirk's look-alike. Helplessness washed through her. What was she going to do?

~ * ~

Drake shoved his errant lock of hair off his forehead while Miranda stared blankly at the wall behind him. He didn't know what to make of her dazed expression. Nobody except her would do something as lunatic as climb a tree to spy on him. Why had she done it? What did she expect to see? Dash it, he never knew what to make of her. Trouble. She was always in it, one way or another.

Still, he did his best to ignore her bedeviling antics because he felt an affinity with her. Like him, she was second born and often ignored because her older sister claimed the limelight, as his brother, Albert, had always done.

Miranda and Prudence had been Drake's charges ever since his deceased wife's parents died five years ago. His father had arranged for him to assume responsibility for the two cousins when he arranged Drake's marriage.

Silently he thanked the Almighty that Miranda's bones were all still intact. He had confirmed that while she lay unconscious in the woods, before he carried her to his hunting lodge. There he removed her wet clothes and examined every inch of her. He found a number of scratches, bumps and bruises. That nasty one on her temple had already begun to purple.

Never before had he noticed how unusual her green eyes were. Lord, they were pretty. When had she turned into a beauty? Small and shapely, with extremely long hair, she possessed an enchanting oval face, complete with adorable dimples and freckles.

He stared at her delicate hands and ringless fingers. Why had she removed his betrothal ring?

Although he had agreed to wed her some six months ago, he shunned personal involvement. Helen, his dead wife, also Miranda's cousin, had soured him on women and he intended this marriage to be in name only. Miranda wanted to be his duchess, but Drake vowed she would never be his wife in the biblical sense. Up until last evening, he had considered her a child. Now he knew she possessed the body of a full-grown woman.

In spite of his celibate vow, concern for her injuries mingled with desire unlike any Drake had ever known. When had she become an enchanting temptress? A grin tugged at his mouth. The little minx would likely be shocked if she knew his lusty thoughts.

To wipe the grin away, he smoothed his mustache. He had tried to be a kind, benevolent, impartial guardian to both sisters, but often found himself dragged into one of their frequent altercations. Their most recent was Miranda's decree that Prudence could not attend the wedding. Drake had sided with her. Past experience had taught him Prudence would undoubtedly attempt to upstage the bride.

Not pleased that the sisters didn't get on and with no remedy in mind, Drake decided the silence between him and Miranda had lasted long enough.

"Is your pain unbearable?"

His question chased the dazed look from her lovely eyes.

"No. Not at all," she said quietly—more quietly than Miranda usually spoke.

He expected her to complain about her injuries, even to cry and rant and rave. That she did none of those things puzzled him. "Are you hungry?"

She glanced at the cold food on the table. Servants from his mansion had delivered the meal while she slept.

"I guess I should eat to regain my strength. Maybe, I should get dressed first, though. Are my clothes dry?"

Drake nodded and went to fetch the clothes. He'd never waited on anyone, except his mother when he was a small boy. Unfortunately, she hadn't appreciated anything he ever did.

Now, although he was a duke, servants didn't attend him at the hunting lodge, other than to deliver food. This is where he came to be alone. And Miranda had invaded his privacy. But for some reason, that didn't disturb him. He was enjoying her company.

When he offered the clothes, she stared at them as though she hadn't seen them before. "Is something amiss?"

Instead of replying, she shrugged and accepted the clothes. "Would you please turn your back?"

The blankets had slipped, and even though he'd had a good look at all of her last night and again this morning, the sight of one creamy shoulder heated his blood anew.

Careful to keep his tone neutral, he asked, "Do you need assistance?"

"No." Her blush deepened. "Certainly not from you. I don't know you. Should we introduce ourselves?"

Too shocked to comment, Drake could only stare. *Had she injured her head when she fell? If so, how much damage had been done?*

Three

Recognition

To Jennifer's discomfort, Dirk's look-alike stared as if he expected something from her. Always self-conscious about her freckles, and afraid he might comment on them, she decided to take the offensive. "Does it hurt?"

He looked perplexed. "What?"

"Keeping your upper lip so stiff."

Dirk's clone didn't reply. He merely glared.

Embarrassment stole through Jennifer. She wanted to give him a bad time because she was attracted to him. Good grief. As if she didn't have enough problems. She had no idea where she was, or how badly she'd been injured. Besides missing her appointment at the bank, Catharine, her roommate back in Denver, and Aunt Rachel and Uncle Mac had expected Jennifer to call last night. If they called the London bed-and-breakfast today and discovered she hadn't returned, they'd be alarmed.

Bombarded by questions, Jennifer closed her eyes. Why had the wizard-cab driver created that noxious fog? Dropped her from the sky? Brought her here?

She opened her eyes... and saw Dirk's clone still staring.

"Who are you?"

He frowned. "Who am I?"

"You shouldn't frown," she said.

"Frown?" Now he looked baffled.

Rattled herself, she asked, "Must you repeat me?"

"Must you startle me with statements that make no sense?"

"If you'd been through what I have, you probably wouldn't make much sense either."

"Had I been through what you have," he muttered, "I bloody likely wouldn't be alive to discuss it."

"Isn't bloody a swear word?"

"Cease your demmed prattle and tell me your name."

"Jennifer," she blurted, startled by his barked command. "Jennifer Quinlane. And you are?"

He shook his handsome head, apparently deciding to treat her to a dose of her own medicine. "Perhaps," he said softly, "you should guess my name."

Suddenly it struck her who he must be—Drake, the other man in her latest vision. Had the wizard Sevil brought Drake to the future? Or had she misinterpreted her vision?

Confused, Jennifer massaged her throbbing head with one hand, pressing the coarse blankets against her naked chest with the other. Why hadn't she recognized him sooner?

She cleared her throat. "I'd guess Rake, I mean Drake. Come to think of it, Rake better suits a man who would make a girl his mistress with the dual intention of marrying her sister."

"What?" His shout thundered through the cottage.

"Never mind."

Drake's glare held her gaze with hypnotic intensity. "Tell me what you meant by that insipid statement."

"It wasn't insipid," she retorted, "and I didn't mean anything by it. I merely repeated a conversation I heard."

"You eavesdropped?" he blasted.

"No. I didn't," she defended, indignant. "The conversation was paraded before me. I couldn't help seeing and hearing it."

He folded his arms across his broad chest. "Where did this alleged parade take place?"

She hesitated, unwilling to be accused of pipe dreaming. "Where it occurred isn't important. You see I have a special, extraordinary gift. Sometimes I have visions of other people."

He steepled his blond eyebrows like inverted V's. "You expect me to believe you possess the Gift of Sight?"

"Yes," she reluctantly said. Usually she guarded her secret with a vengeance because she hated to be ridiculed or teased. Only her very closest friends and relatives knew about her gift.

"Did your extraordinary gift allow you to see yourself being struck by lightning before it occurred?"

"No, and I didn't get hit by lightning."

"You certainly did." He started to pace. "It knocked you out of the tree. Out of your mind too, it seems." He paused to demand, "Why the devil did you climb a tree?" Without waiting for an answer, he paced again. "Such behavior is unbefitting for a young lady—even one pretending to be an American."

Unbefitting behavior? Pretending to be an American?

His pacing made Jennifer dizzy. She closed her eyes and drew in a deep, steadying breath. "This can't be real. You must be a figment of my imagination."

She opened her eyes and stared into his ever so blue ones as he stepped closer.

"Do I look like a figment of your imagination?"

She pulled the blankets up to her chin. "No. Maybe you're a hallucination. Or a dream. Yes, that must be it. I'm dreaming."

He sat on the edge of the bed and seized her bare shoulders. "Do you feel this?"

She clutched the coarse blankets tighter, unable to deny the yearning ignited by his touch. Why did he affect her like this? Nobody else, except Dirk, ever had.

"Yes," was all she could say.

"You are neither dreaming, nor hallucinating."

"Then what the heck is going on?"

"That's what I would like to know."

A sneaky suspicion threaded its way through Jennifer. Had she, like Kacy, somehow traveled back in time?

Logic insisted it couldn't happen.

But the possibilities stared her in the face.

Although Drake's riding clothes were fashionable in her time, as well as in the past, the clothes he'd given her weren't. Besides, he looked, acted and sounded old-fashioned. Also, her vision of him had been in the past. She'd stake her life on that.

The wizard-cab driver's statement flitted through her mind. *Your deepest wish is to see your friend, Kacy, once more. I can turn that wish into reality.*

Had Sevil created some kind of time warp inside that noxious, foggy whirlwind? If so, why was she here, instead of with Kacy?

Nervous, Jennifer swallowed. Her sixth sense told her Sevil must have plunked her smack dab in the middle of the nineteenth century. Excitement mixed with trepidation. *She had traveled back in time!*

But how far? And how could she find out without sounding like she came from la-la land? Would she see Kacy? If so, when? And how could she get back to her own time?

Jennifer hated the idea of being trapped inside a horrible, smelly fog again. Kacy had described a colorful, spiraling time tunnel, and said it was a pleasant experience.

Drake interrupted Jennifer's thoughts when he raised his hand to her face and gently caressed her cheek. Her erratic pulse started to race again, and her insides quivered as she inhaled his piney outdoors scent. Why was he tormenting her? Making her want something she couldn't have?

As though he sensed her silent questions, he jerked away and stood up. "You are either quite serious young lady, or quite mad. Before we discuss which, I suggest you get dressed."

"Yes, I guess I should," she agreed, anxious to confirm her conclusion.

He turned and faced the fireplace.

Jennifer stared down at the lace-trimmed chemise, whalebone corset, petticoats and pale green, mud-stained dress. She couldn't imagine where these clothes had come from, or what had happened to hers, but if Sevil could shape-shift, and bring her back in time, he could probably change her clothes, too.

When she remembered Dirk's opal was gone, she almost burst into tears. Where was it? She never took it off; not even to shower. Had Sevil stolen it?

Battling tears, Jennifer set the cumbersome underclothes aside and slowly, painfully slipped the green, puffy-sleeved gown over her head. After buttoning the lacy jabot on the bodice, she said, "I'm as dressed as I'm likely to get without help."

Drake turned and eyed the corset, chemise, and petticoats still on the bed. Then, without a word he picked her up and carried her to the small rough-hewn table, so narrow not more than two people could eat at it, then only if they staggered their plates. After he plunked her on a chair, he took the one across from her, picked up a fork and stabbed a piece of cold gammon, what Brits called ham.

Feeling half-naked without underpants, a bra or slip, Jennifer tried to tuck her feet under the long dress. It didn't work. Giving up, she let them dangle in the cold cottage air as an idea struck. *A newspaper would give her the date and confirm she'd been hurtled into the past.*

"Is there a news agent nearby?"

A frown puckered Drake's handsome forehead. "A what?"

"I didn't think so," she mumbled, then asked, "Can you tell me how far we are from London?"

He looked startled at the quick change in subjects.

"We're in Kent." He lowered his gaze and took another bite.

Kent? Although Great Britain was smaller than Colorado, Kent was a fair distance from London. But Havenhurst, where Kacy might be, was in Surrey—and hopefully not all that far from Kent.

Jennifer dragged air into her lungs, and as casually as she could manage, asked, "Do you know the Earl of Havenhurst?"

Drake's head shot up, his scowl narrowed on her. "Yes."

"And his wife?"

His scowl deepened. "Why do you ask?"

Jennifer uttered a silent prayer that she was in the same time Kacy had decided to live in.

"I think I know her."

"Surely you jest."

"No I don't. Why should I?"

Drake's razor-sharp stare nearly made her cringe. "If you know her, what is her name?"

Jennifer decided to gamble that Kacy had used her own, and not assumed Catharine's, after they switched places.

"Kathryn Cassandra Rose."

Surprise flickered in Drake's eyes. "Miss Rose married the Earl of Havenhurst, therefore, her surname is now Banes."

Excitement shot through Jennifer, almost obliterating her aches and pains, and the terrible loss of Dirk's opal.

"Would that make her the tenth Countess?"

"It would."

Jennifer's breath caught in her throat. She'd done it—*actually traveled back a hundred and fifty years to the time Kacy had chosen to live in!*

More questions bombarded Jennifer's brain. How long will I be here? When will I see Kacy? What year is this? Has Kacy delivered her baby yet?

Swallowing a gulf of emotion, Jennifer wistfully said, "I haven't seen the Countess in over a year. I miss her so."

Drake's brow arched in suspicious disbelief. "How well do you know her?"

"Very well." Not wanting to create problems for Kacy, Jennifer chose her next words with care. "We met when we were children, and we've known each other most of our lives."

Drake's handsome features relaxed a little. "The Earl and I studied together at Oxford."

When Jennifer realized he expected her to say something, she forced a smile. "I love Oxford. Kacy and I were there shortly before she met the Earl."

"When was that?"

Jennifer prayed the time zones ran parallel as Kacy had said. "Around Easter, about a year and a half ago."

Jennifer didn't expect Drake to smile, but he did, and his blue eyes twinkled. "Their marriage was rather unexpected. Clay invited me, however, he didn't spare time to invite other friends."

"Have you seen Kacy recently? If so, how is she?"

"I saw the Countess at the twin's christening in the spring, and again during the Season. Each time she looked supremely happy."

Twins. Kacy had twins? Startled, yet delighted too, Jennifer asked, "The twins, were they boys, girls, or—?"

Eyes still twinkling, Drake said, "One of each."

Unable to camouflage her excitement, Jennifer grinned. The possibility of seeing Kacy and her babies made her feel giddy. And the fact that Drake had seen them in the spring indicated that time here had elapsed the same as in the future.

Jennifer stared at the familiar mole under his left eye, then at his hair, so blond it looked pearl-white, and at his mouth, sensuous and tempting. Being in the nineteenth century alone with him made her tremble. Could he be Dirk? Had he died in the future and come to live in the past? Taken over someone else's life? If so, would he forgive her for losing the opal?

Her heart dived when she thought about the opal. She looked away, shaking with despair.

When she dared another glance at Drake, a glimmer of amusement still shimmered in his wonderful eyes. Fascinating blue eyes, so like Dirk's.

"Kacy's eyes are blue, too." Not knowing why she made that inane statement, heat crawled up Jennifer's neck.

"The Countess has lovely eyes, however, they're no more lovely than yours."

Jennifer's heart did a flip-flop, then threatened to quit altogether.

"Have you nothing to say?" he teased.

"Look Mr.—?" When he didn't fill in his name, she said, "I don't even know your last name."

His amusement gone, he hiked a brow. "Do you not?"

"No. In my vision Miranda only called you Drake."

He looked confounded, and his voice sounded strained when he croaked, "You had a vision? Of Miranda?"

Jennifer nodded. "Yes, the same one you were in, along with Prudence and Sevil."

Drake rammed a hand through his wavy hair, his eyes troubled. "Who is Sevil?"

"A wizard."

"How do you know he's a wizard?"

"Miranda called him one. And he did unusual things."

"Such as?"

Jennifer shrugged. "Magic."

"What kind of magic?" Drake pumped.

"At the end of my vision he shape-shifted. Then he jumped clear up to the top of a roof, and he took Miranda with him."

Drake looked startled. He folded his arms across his broad chest, his food apparently forgotten. His frown had returned. "Tell me more about—this vision."

"It wasn't much," Jennifer hedged, not ready to repeat everything she'd seen and heard. If she said Sevil had promised to take Miranda to the future to see Catharine, Drake would probably think she was crazy. Suddenly remembering Miranda wanted Sevil to make a switch, *apparently with her*, Jennifer almost gasped out loud. But she expected Miranda to return soon. Even though they looked alike, Jennifer couldn't pretend to be Miranda. Other than what she'd seen in the vision, she knew nothing about Miranda's life, or what was expected of her. And Jennifer had no intention of being treated like a nineteenth century lady whose activities could be curtailed or restricted. She'd come back in time to see Kacy, and she intended to, just as soon as possible, then hopefully she'd return to her own time.

"I consider myself a patient man," Drake said, "however, I'm impatient to hear about your vision."

Jennifer licked her bottom lip. "I saw a man and lady, who called each other Miranda and Sevil, spying on you and another lady through a window. They called you Drake and Prudence. You were preparing to go out for the evening and I think that upset Miranda because she's apparently engaged—betrothed to you."

"What did Miranda and Sevil say?" Drake pumped again.

"She said you ignored her and doted on Prudence. Sevil said he convinced you to let Miranda take the Grand Tour last year, then arranged your marriage as he promised. But now Miranda wants more."

"More what?"

Jennifer stared at the food on the table. She hadn't been very hungry, now she felt even less so. "Miranda doesn't want Prudence to be your mistress."

"I see," Drake said, but he didn't look convinced. He looked doubtful.

At a loss for words, Jennifer picked up her fork and stabbed a piece of cold ham. When Drake remained quiet, she reminded, "You haven't told me your last name."

"Edward," he said.

"Mr. Drake Edward." Jennifer said his name dreamily, then cautioned herself not to get carried away. He might not be Dirk. Even if he was, Miranda intended to marry him. Jennifer's mouth went dry. That reminder bothered her. *If he was Dirk, he was her husband, even though their marriage had lasted only a few days.*

More questions flitted through Jennifer's mind. Deciding she needed to talk to Kacy before she said much more, Jennifer asked, "Is it possible to travel to Havenhurst from here by train?"

Drake shook his blond head. "There's no line between Kent and Surrey."

"I guess I'll have to return to London." But she didn't have any money. Dare she ask him to loan her some?

She shoved her long auburn hair behind her shoulders. Her coiled braid had come undone, probably inside the whirlwind, and her hair needed attention, but she didn't have a brush or comb. Besides, it would be rude to fuss with her hair at the table.

"Are you going to eat?" Drake asked.

She nodded, knowing food would help her regain her strength, and nibbled on a lavishly buttered crust of bread.

"How well do you know the wizard, Sevil?" Drake asked.

"I don't know him at all, but..."

"But what?" Drake prompted.

"It occurred to me that he might be the Saucerman, also dubbed the Jumping Man, who started to terrorize England during Queen Victoria's reign. When he shape-shifted, he filled the description I read."

Drake's mustache twitched. "He shape-shifted?"

"Yes. At the end of my vision he changed until he resembled a creature from outer space."

"Outer space?" Drake's gaze narrowed. "What exactly did he look like?"

"He wore a slick white, one piece jumpsuit, had his head enclosed by a clear globular bubble, and he grabbed Miranda with paws that terminated in sharp metallic claws, before he jumped to the top of the roof where I think Prudence lives."

"Sharp metallic claws?" Drake's eyebrows shot up. "Surely you do not expect me to believe such a preposterous tale."

Jennifer shrugged. "Believe whatever you wish. It's no skin off my nose."

Drake leaned across the small table. She inhaled his piney scent while he stared pointedly into her eyes. "How well do you know Miranda?"

"Not at all. I never saw her before my vision."

"Why then, did you have a vision that included her?"

Jennifer didn't like feeling intimidated, not even by the man who took her breath away; the man she might have loved in other lives, and been briefly married to in the future.

She leaned back. "If I could answer that, I'd be a genius, wouldn't I?"

"It does not take a genius to fabricate tales."

"True," Jennifer conceded, "however, I don't fabricate."

"That remains to be proven." Drake squared his shoulders and glared.

Miffed by his superior attitude, she retorted, "I don't have to prove anything to you. I don't even think I like you."

His features froze. Now he looked astounded. Offended. Insulted. "You don't like me?"

"I'm not sure." Already she regretted her outburst. Last night he had taken very good care of her. He'd even climbed in bed to warm her when she complained about being cold. She refused to dwell on the fact that in this time, sharing the same bed not only soiled her reputation, it could ruin her beyond repair. "I don't know you well enough to make a judgement."

When Drake frowned again, she said, "You really shouldn't frown. Those wrinkles between your brows might become permanent fixtures." Then she added softly, "And it would be a shame to mar your handsome face with premature wrinkles."

She knew her off-hand compliment startled Drake. For a few stony seconds he stared without speaking. Finally he said with polite formality, "I suggest you eat, young lady."

Having learned to eat like a Brit, she held the fork in her left hand and the knife in her right, cutting cheese and ham, then forking them backwards before she raised them to her mouth. As she chewed, guilt kneaded its way through her. She should probably tell him she came from the future, and that's where Miranda had gone.

But even if she did, would he believe her?

How could he, when she scarcely believed it herself?

Four

Reactions

Drake's reaction to Miranda, alias Jennifer Quinlane, annoyed him. He didn't trust her, or any ladies, except his grandmother. Helen, his deceased wife, had created the distrust. Other ladies had fed its growth. In spite of that, this new Miranda stirred him as no lady ever had.

Had the lightning created a serious change? Or had she staged an elaborate charade? Unable to determine which, he decided to call her Jennifer, if only to keep peace. Lord knew he did his best to please her when they shared the same roof. Most often, he gave her whatever she asked for. When Prudence complained that he spoiled Miranda, he usually consoled her with a new gown or bauble. He knew he took the coward's way out, but he disliked dicey confrontations.

Now he wondered why Miranda wasn't in London, shopping. She had pleaded for permission to charge at London's finest shops to complete her trousseau before they wed, and he had agreed, to keep the peace.

He looked across at her. Her eyes weren't actually green as he'd always believed, but green with wee brown spots. Or were they brown with green spots? Telling himself the color of her eyes shouldn't fascinate him, he lowered his gaze. The neckline of her soiled gown exposed a tantalizing glimpse of soft cleavage, and he enjoyed the view.

After she ate a few bites, she set her knife and fork side by side across the center of her plate. Her table manners had improved, remarkably. Still, he was surprised she hadn't eaten much. Miranda usually consumed every tasty morsel on her plate, and demanded more, then wasted most of it.

Absorbed in his thoughts, he didn't realize she intended to stand. But she did. And her legs gave out. As her backside hit the floor with a thump, he jumped to his feet and dashed around the table like an eager swain.

She looked up, a dazed expression on her lovely face. "I can't believe I'm so weak."

"You shouldn't have attempted to stand with swollen ankles," he said, worried. "You might have injured yourself."

Her grimace seemed to say, *'I'm already injured.'* "Do you enjoy telling people what they do wrong?" she asked.

Pricked by guilt, he picked her up and cradled her against his chest. "Where do you hurt?"

"In about a gazillion places."

He hiked a curious brow.

"Gazillion? That's an inventive word."

"Yes," she said. "In other words, I hurt everywhere."

Their gazes held while he carried her to the bed.

Having her here was unique. No other lady had ever been inside his hunting lodge. Five years ago, he had refurbished the lodge in order to avoid Helen. He hadn't thought about his deceased wife for a long time. The marriage had been arranged, but they were unsuited and it had been a miserable match. Even so, Drake regretted Helen's death.

When he had seen the burning crofter's cottage, with her mare and Albert's stallion tethered outside, Drake had dashed inside the burning inferno and found them unconscious in the rumpled bed. He carried his naked wife out first, then went back for his naked brother. The roof collapsed before he made it outside a second time, and falling timber knocked him down. With his back burning and pain throbbing in his right leg, he crawled the rest of the way, dragging Albert as best he could.

Only after he had them both out of the blazing inferno, did Drake discover he had arrived too late; Albert and Helen were already dead. Apparently they had inhaled too much smoke. Exhausted himself, Drake passed out.

When he came to, Olvan, his trusted older friend and head groom, had arrived. A quick examination confirmed Drake had broken his leg.

His grandmother summoned the physician to Stonemeade. While he treated Drake's burns and set his leg, Albert's widow, Alisha, jumped from the attic window. Drake heard her scream as she plunged to her death. Never had he felt more helpless. Second-born, he hadn't expected to be the Duke. Now he would carry the title, as well as the scars and slight limp he had earned on that horrible day, to his grave.

Drake shook thoughts of the past away. In his arms he held the only lady who had ever truly fascinated him. And that confounded him. He told himself her appeal wouldn't last. Sexual attraction always paled after a few months.

But the nagging hunch that he felt more than sexually attracted persisted.

His body was reacting to having her in his arms. Grateful for the distance that separated their bodies at that crucial juncture and kept her unaware of his aroused state, he placed her on the bed before he did something foolish, like kiss her.

She reached up and touched his mustache.

"Does it tickle Miranda when you kiss her?"

Her touch was his undoing. Although he considered the question impertinent, Drake followed impulse. He sat beside her and bent his head, intending to teach her a lesson.

Instead she taught him one, meeting his lips halfway. Hers were warm and inviting. He wrapped her tighter in his arms and deepened the kiss. When her lips parted, he accepted the open invitation. His tongue delved inside and explored the satiny recesses, while her sweet flowery scent filled his nostrils and weakened his brain.

When she twined her arms around his nape, desire raged through him like a fire out of control. He crushed her against his chest. Passion and desire escalated. Her ardent response aroused him to a fevered pitch. He lay down, taking her with him. One hand moved to explore her heaving breasts.

Her quiet sigh brought him back to his senses.

He ended the kiss abruptly. Releasing her, he stood. He hadn't believed her capable of wielding such power. Had she cast some kind of spell to make him forget himself so completely?

"I trust that answers your question," he said, irritated with himself for allowing passion to briefly rule him.

She touched her kiss-swollen lips. "I apologize. I shouldn't have asked such a personal question." Her cheeks flamed and she lowered her gaze, her fingers still on her tempting lips.

To Drake's knowledge, Miranda had never apologized for anything. That she did so now, perplexed him. If she could change this much from a fall, she might possess the makings of a proper wife and duchess after all.

"I have a problem, Mr. Edward." Her cheeks still pink with embarrassment, she stared beyond him.

Hearing himself called by his middle name sounded odd. Although he'd never given Miranda permission to call him by his Christian name, she always did. He had withheld his surname, Castlebury, and kept from mentioning his title, thinking that might force her to end the charade.

"Do you wish to tell me about your problem?"

"No, but I guess I must. You see, nature's calling."

Puzzled, he asked, "You hear someone calling?"

"No." She shook her head, still avoiding his gaze, her cheeks turning a deeper shade of pink. "I need to go out."

"Why?"

"I need to use…" she hesitated, sighed and finally said, "the necessary, or whatever it is you call it."

Understanding dawned and he felt like a dunce.

"You need to visit the privy?"

"Yes. I hope you have one," she said bluntly.

"I do." He walked to the fireplace and seized his black umbrella from behind a stack of logs and a bucket of coal. Then he gathered her shoes and stockings, returned to the bed, and offered the umbrella. "Use this as a cane until I arrange for crutches."

After she accepted it, he knelt on the floor and took her dainty foot in his hands, intending to put her stockings and slippers on. "Your foot is cold," he said in surprise.

"Yes," she agreed. "They both feel like ice cubes."

"Ice cubes?" he asked, rubbing her feet to restore some warmth.

She nodded and in a small voice said, "I can do that."

"Relax and allow me to perform this simple service."

Dash it. Why did he enjoy touching her, and taking care of her in this personal fashion? Perplexed at himself, he continued his ministrations.

She didn't relax. Not at first. Befuddled, Drake continued to rub until each foot warmed. By then she had closed her eyes, and she looked thoroughly relaxed. One by one, he slid her silk stockings onto her feet, rolled them halfway up her shapely calves, then realized they wouldn't stay and rolled them back down to her ankles.

Her faint perfume filled his nostrils again, and the shared intimacy nearly made him groan. Knowing she wore nothing beneath the green gown, he forced himself to concentrate on her satin covered slippers, appropriate for evening wear, but unsuitable for an outing in the woods.

When he finished his task he scooped her back up in his arms.

As he stepped outside she said in a subdued voice, "I'm sorry to be such a bother."

"You need not apologize."

"I suppose your outhouse smells horrible."

He wanted to laugh, but controlled the urge. People did not discuss the privy, or how it smelled. Well, most people, that is.

"On the contrary," he said, "my privy is quite new."

"I hate having to be carried to the john. In America we call it the john," she said in a rush.

Where had she learned so much about Americans? At the finishing academy where she had constantly written and begged him to let her leave and to marry her? Or last year during her grand tour of Europe?

Not yet ready to insist that she own up to her true identity, he said, "I don't imagine men with the name of John appreciate the association."

"I imagine you're right." Suppressed merriment danced in her expressive greenish-brown eyes.

He reached the new structure, completed only last week.

"Can you open the door?"

"Yes. I'm not completely helpless." She said that with a degree of self-disgust, and he grinned as she reached for the latch.

He stood her on her feet and settled his hands on her waist while she balanced herself with his umbrella staff. "Can you manage now?"

"Of course." She wobbled, but the umbrella helped support her, and she giggled as she hobbled inside.

He walked away to allow privacy. At the moment she seemed to have no clue about proper behavior, but he thought it refreshing. Actually, he found the changes in her quite to his liking. Although she seemed familiar, almost like a cherished loved one, she also seemed like a stranger. When would she revert to her normal self-centered ways? If she didn't, would he continue to enjoy her company?

A noise near the new stable drew his attention. Olvan, his devoted head groom, who had been with Drake all his life, opened one of the double doors, and called, "Mordora be about to foal."

"I'll be there shortly," Drake called back.

Mordora, an excellent specimen of pure cinnamon-coated horseflesh, had been mated with Quicksilver, Drake's favorite stallion, and he expected a colt as fine as its sire. Breeding, which had begun as a hobby, had become a lucrative business. Men from all over the British Empire, as well as Europe and America, now vied to purchase horses from him.

Miranda—he must remember to call her Jennifer—opened the privy door sooner than anticipated. Drake tried to ignore the odd emotions she stirred in him as he hurried to pick her up. When he did, she smiled, her cheeks dimpling. He'd never before seen her smile like that. Truth be told, he didn't even know she had dimples. This smile, sunny and bright, sped past carefully erected barriers and made itself right cozily at home. The impact nearly made him stumble, but he caught himself in time, he thought, to save face.

"Am I too heavy?"

"No," he said, confounded by his clumsiness. He expected her to pursue her question, if only to embarrass him. Any other lady would. He had discovered that after he became a duke. Not even the scandal created by Helen and Albert's adultery, plus Alisha's suicide, or the year of formal mourning, kept ladies from prying into Drake's life to get his attention.

"Mr. Edward?"

"What?"

Jennifer smiled again, and he nearly stumbled again. Her smile dissolved to concern. "I am too heavy."

"No, you're not. You weigh next to nothing."

"Do you have sore legs or ankles, too?"

She looked worried, so he explained. "An old leg injury occasionally bothers me. If you put your arms around my neck, that might help."

Draping her arms around him, she held his black umbrella aloft, and stared him in the eye. "When did you injure your leg?"

"Five years ago."

"What month?"

"October."

The color drained from her face. "How?"

Not about to remind her he'd broken it while trying to save the lives of her adulterous cousin and his oversexed brother, Drake said, "I do not wish to discuss it."

Concerned by her pale complexion, he hastened inside the lodge. As he carried her to the bed, odd shafts of pleasure slid through him. She truly didn't weigh much and she smelled like a lady really ought to smell. Sweet and womanly. Better than anything he had smelled in a very long time. Once again his body reacted. The plain and simple truth struck him. He fancied her! That stuck in his craw and knocked some sense back into him. He would not allow desire to rule him.

"Miss Quinlane?"

"Yes?"

"You shouldn't frown. It might leave permanent fixtures between your lovely brows."

"Touché." Her laughter echoed through the lodge and made him want to laugh too, but he resisted. Life was not a laughable matter. Sooner or later she would realize that, whether she continued her charade or not.

He set her on the narrow bed. When she slid her arms from his shoulders a pang of regret crept through him. Maybe he should have kissed her again while he held her in his arms. When would he have a better chance?

Determined to control himself, he said, "You should rest whilst I'm gone."

He reached the door before she asked, "Where are—that is, will you be gone long?"

Hearing the quiver in her voice, he glanced around and saw her crestfallen expression.

"No. I'm not going far," he said gently. "Only to the stable. My mare is about to drop a foal."

"May I go with you?"

"Foaling is not a sight for a young lady to witness."

"Please," she pleaded. "I don't want to be left alone."

"The physician said you need bed rest."

On that discordant note Drake closed the door behind him with a decided thud. He had no intention of allowing Miranda or Jennifer Miranda, as she had been christened, to get too close or involved in his private life.

Why then, a small voice niggled, did he regret the disappointment he'd seen in her colorful eyes?

Five

The Foaling

Jennifer cushioned her head on the only pillow on the bed, thinking it so thin it didn't deserve to be called a pillow. The cottage had cooled and she spread a scratchy, musky smelling wool blanket over her as she thought about Drake's leg injury. Five years ago, also in October, Dirk had broken two bones in his ankle. After the bones healed, sometimes he limped, especially in damp weather. Could there be a connection between Drake and Dirk? Were they the same man? How could she find out?

While she stared at the rough timbered ceiling, blackened by years of smoke from the open fireplace, a vision flashed. It was so clear Jennifer could have been out in the stable with Drake, his reed-thin companion and the pregnant mare. If somebody didn't do something quick, both mare and foal would die.

Recalling a movie she'd seen about a difficult foaling, Jennifer scooted off the bed. Ignoring her aches and pains, she grabbed the wooden handled umbrella for support and snooped around until she found a bottle of whiskey and a clean bowl. Then she stumbled outside, praying she wasn't making a mistake.

In the stable, Drake and a man with a weathered face and crooked nose, glanced up from the mare they were bent over. The odor of soiled straw and fresh animal dung assaulted Jennifer's nose as she hobbled closer. The cinnamon-coated mare lay on her side, her swollen belly supported by dirty straw, her black eyes tortured.

"I think I can help and I'm not at all squeamish," she said. "I've seen animals and women give birth." She'd seen them on closed circuit TV, not in person.

"You haven't recovered from your fall," Drake objected.

She held up the whiskey. "This might help the mare, but first we need to get her on her feet."

"Why, lass?" the older man asked.

"The foal's head is trying to come out first. If it does, the legs could get tangled up inside. Then both mother and baby will be in deep trouble."

Drake slanted her an annoyed look. "We know that."

"Th' lass means well," the aging man defended her.

Drake gave him a disapproving glare, but the older man didn't so much as blink.

"Wha' good will come frum getting 'er on 'er feet, lass?"

"Please, just do it," Jennifer pleaded. "We're wasting valuable time."

The thin man nodded and looked pointedly at Drake until he nodded too, although with apparent reluctance. Together they prodded, nudged, shoved and urged, and finally got the mare off her side, up onto her feet.

Jennifer leaned her head against the mare's, talking low and soothingly as she offered the whiskey she'd already poured in the bowl. "Drink this. It'll help you relax."

She saw surprise in Drake's eyes as the mare obeyed, slurping as a human would, not lapping like a cat.

"We want to help you," she said to the mare. "Please trust us." With another quick glance at Drake she asked, "What's her name?"

"Mordora," the gaunt man said, when Drake didn't reply.

Jennifer gulped. *Mordora. The same name as my cat, who's so old now she ought to be put to sleep.*

She smiled at the man with the Scottish burr and kindly green eyes. "I'm Jennifer Quinlane."

"I be Olvan McDougal."

"Pleased to meet you." She turned her attention back to the mare. "She needs to walk. The whiskey should dull her pain. If we're lucky, the foal will turn on its own. If not, one of us might have to help."

Mordora didn't want to budge. It took all three of them to get her to take one step, then another. But after that she bent to her front knees, then rolled onto her side and kicked her feet in the air as though that would relieve her misery.

Unmindful of the pretty green gown, Jennifer knelt on the soiled straw and stroked Mordora's head. "How long has she been in labor?"

"Over an hour," Drake said.

"Foaling usually only takes thirty or forty minutes," Jennifer repeated what she'd heard in the movie. "Is this her first time?"

"Aye," Olvan said.

Jennifer ran her hands gently down the length of Mordora's slick, sweaty nose. As she did, another vision flashed. She saw Mordora with her frisky colt, romping in a green meadow in sunshine. The next instant she saw the position of the colt still inside Mordora.

Stroking the mare's cheek, Jennifer crooned, "It won't be long now, Mordora. Soon you'll have a beautiful colt, the exact color as your own cinnamon coat."

Jennifer felt Drake's eyes on her, but she kept her attention on the mare. "Don't push yet, Mordora," she cautioned. "You're wearing yourself out, and it's not doing any good."

Mordora grunted and pushed anyway. She tossed her head, snorted, and tried to roll over, but Jennifer urged the mare's head onto her lap and held it firmly there. "Stay put, Mordora," she said sternly. "We're going to have to help you."

She looked up at Olvan, whose hands and arms were considerably smaller than Drake's.

"The foal's head keeps pushing down and drawing back. One of us must reach inside, find the front legs, and pull them out. Who should it be? You or me?"

"Ah'll do it," Olvan volunteered.

"Pour some whiskey over your hands and arms first," she suggested. When Drake started to object, she added, "It will cleanse and lubricate them and make their journey easier."

~ * ~

She sounded so confident, Drake tamped down the urge to disagree. He couldn't help thinking how often Olvan resisted his suggestions. Now the stubborn Scot agreed with everything she said. He sloshed the costly whiskey along his bare arms, then rubbed it all over with his hands.

Drake tried to observe Jennifer Miranda with detachment, but he found it nigh on impossible. So absorbed was she in the mare's misery, her own injuries seemed forgotten. Which was not at all like the Jennifer Miranda he knew. He had not thought her fond of animals, but she stroked Mordora as though she adored the mare.

Olvan worked his hand inside the birth canal, and groped around.

"I found 'em," he said.

"Are the hoofs pointing up or down? "Drake asked, needing to know whether they were the front or hind legs.

"Down," Olvan grunted.

"The front hoofs." Jennifer's eyes were closed as though she could see inside Mordora's belly.

"Hang on and pull," Drake ordered. "I'll hold Mordora down." He flattened his body across the mare, grateful for his size and strength, and certain he'd exert considerable brawn before the foaling ended.

"Push now, Mordora." Jennifer wrapped her arms around the mare's head to help Drake keep her still.

Mordora bore down and as she did, Drake felt her swollen belly heave, contract then shudder. "Hang on tight, Olvan," he grunted.

"I be hangin' on tight," Olvan gritted through clenched teeth.

"Push," Jennifer urged. A few seconds later, "Push again, Mordora." She petted the long nose. "That's a good girl. Come on now, once more."

She stroked the mare's sweaty head and soothed, "It's almost over, dear. Push. Yes. That's right, Mordora. You're doing fine. Just fine."

The huge distended abdomen heaved, contorted and contracted. Mordora kicked. Her hooves grazed Olvan's cheek. Drake grabbed and held the hooves as the old Scot's elbow slid from the birth canal. Thankfully, his fist remained planted inside.

Mordora started to fight then.

"Hold her," Drake ordered.

Jennifer's eyes met his, and they communicated without words. *'I will,'* she promised.

'As will I.' The silent communication forged a pact stronger than words. Something flashed in recognition. For one brief moment Drake had the peculiar notion that he had known and loved this new Jennifer Miranda in a prior life, but he didn't believe in past lives. A sharp pang stabbed his chest as awareness of her increased tenfold. Somehow he knew her thoughts. Like his, they centered on concern for Mordora and the foal, and Drake realized he had no problem thinking of her as simply Jennifer.

Mordora grunted. The foal budged inside her. Drake prayed Olvan could hang onto the slippery feet. Mordora snorted, kicked against Drake, jerked her head against Jennifer's arms, and fought to pull away from Olvan. But they all hung on.

"Pull," Drake grunted.

And Olvan did. The foal's cinnamon colored hoofs came out. With a loud sucking noise, the head and front quarters quickly followed. Then came the wet body, smattered with birth fluid and blood. Last, as nature intended, came the hindquarters and back feet.

"He's awesome!" Jennifer looked awestruck, and Drake found it difficult to keep his eyes off her.

Befuddled, he slid off Mordora and wiped perspiration from his brow with the back of his damp, sweaty arm. His intended patted

Mordora's sweat-slick neck, resting her own cheek against the long, cinnamon one.

Where had that flash of recognition that indicated he had once loved her, come from? Was it some sort of wishful dream?

With a rueful shake of his head, Drake ordered himself to concentrate on what must be done, rather than the odd emotions she now stirred.

"You can relax, Mordora," Jennifer murmured. "It's over, and you have an awesome colt." Her eyes, bright with the wonder of birth, locked with Drake's. "Isn't he beautiful?"

"Yes." Her lovely eyes looked like liquid pools, and he felt he could drown in them.

"How ye ken it be a colt and not a filly, lass?"

"I saw it in a vision, Mr. McDougal."

"Ye have the Gift a' Sight, then?"

"Yes."

Olvan looked as though he believed Jennifer implicitly, while Drake marveled at his own emotions. Was she different now? Or had he merely failed to notice how captivating she could be?

"Ye helped calm th' mare," Olvan said.

"I think Mr. Edward's whiskey did more than I."

Raising his wiry gray brows, Olvan exchanged a puzzled look with Drake, but the trusted Scot said not a word about the name she had called him.

The mare stood and walked away. The colt scrabbled about, trying to gain his feet. Mordora shied further away. Apparently she wanted nothing to do with her baby. It made Drake wonder if his own birth had been a difficult one, and that's why his mother had harbored little love for him. How often had he heard her say she had produced an heir and a spare, and no one should expect more from her? She certainly hadn't given anyone any affection, least of all him.

Jennifer interrupted his gloomy reflection.

"We can't let Mordora reject the colt. That happens sometimes when foaling is difficult. We might have to help them bond."

Drake had no idea what that meant. "Bond?"

"If they don't connect as mother and offspring, Mordora might not be willing to feed the colt. Maybe we should push him close and urge her to clean him, too."

At any other time, Drake wouldn't have given credence to such a suggestion. Yet bond and connect described exactly what he, Olvan and Jennifer had just shared.

With a nod at Olvan, they dragged the colt over to Mordora.

She ignored her baby and Olvan said, "Ah think he could be fed by a stable lad."

"I've heard that when foals are fed by humans, they grow up thinking they're human, too," Jennifer said. "You don't want that to happen, do you?"

"Ah dinna think we do," Olvan agreed.

"Mordora needs the colt," she added. "Otherwise, she won't be able to rid herself of her milk."

Without a word, Drake forced Mordora's nose close to her colt. When she tried to shove him away, Drake pushed the colt closer and held their heads together. To his surprise, Mordora sniffed the colt. Then she licked him. Once, twice and again. Motherly instinct took over. She kept licking him.

"You did it." Jennifer's pretty eyes sparkled with warmth and something Drake thought might be hero worship. He wanted to bask in it, but then he felt vulnerable. Turning his head, he watched Olvan rake the soiled straw into a pile.

"What will you name him?"

Drake shifted his gaze back to Jennifer. "You did."

"Me? What name did I give him?"

He grinned; he couldn't stop himself. She looked so delightfully startled. "Awesome."

Her smile lit up his heart, and he almost forgot she was Miranda, temporarily without her memories. He remembered in time to keep from moving closer.

After the foal gained his feet, Mordora snorted and walked to Jennifer. When she held out her hands, the mare sniffed, licked her palms then laid her velvety nose trustingly on them. Jennifer's long hair, strikingly similar in color to Mordora's cinnamon coat, cascaded over her shoulders and blended with the mare. Drake didn't know when he'd seen a lovelier sight. For the first time in his life he wished he were an artist so he could capture the scene on canvas.

"I ken ye be wantin' to wash yer hands, lass," Olvan broke the silence.

"What I'd like is a bath," she admitted softly.

Olvan glanced at Drake. "Are ye of a mind to make the lass's wish come true?"

Drake nodded. "I'll go fetch a tub."

"An' ah'll heat water whilst yer gone," Olvan said.

"Should I walk you to the lodge before I leave?" Drake asked Jennifer.

"Thank you, no. I think I can make it on my own."

Ignoring a stab of disappointment, he went to saddle Quicksilver. The fact that he came to the hunting lodge alone, and allowed only Olvan to accompany him, galled his grooms and stable lads. They would be scandalized if they knew a duke saddled his own horse. Olvan alone understood, and knew Drake didn't always bow to custom or ceremony.

He led Quicksilver from the stable. Outside he found Jennifer leaning against the wall, apparently too exhausted to take another step. Biting back the chastisement she deserved, he swept her up his arms. She swung his black umbrella that she'd used as a crutch behind him, and wound her arms around his shoulders. Damn, they felt as though they belonged there. With purposeful strides, Drake carried her toward the lodge, Quicksilver trailing behind them.

"I'm glad you're strong," Jennifer said.

Curious, he raised a brow. "Why?"

"Because you needed great strength to hold Mordora down. And," Jennifer said more softly, "a girl wouldn't want to be rescued by a weak man."

She glanced up at the cloudy sky. Strands of her long hair swirled across Drake's bare arms and grazed his cheek. To his amazement he enjoyed the silken feel. For a man who craved his solitude and went out of his way to be alone, it surprised him that he now enjoyed Jennifer's company so much.

They reached the lodge. "Can you open the door?"

"Of course."

He released Quicksilver's reins and ordered, "Stay." Then he carried Jennifer inside and set her on the bed.

"Thanks." Her gaze held his, and desire threatened to claim his control.

He smoothed his mustache to keep his hand busy. "I should thank you for your help in the stable."

"You needn't thank me. I wanted to be there."

When he merely stared, she added, "You rescued me yesterday, like a gallant white knight. If you hadn't found me, I might still be in the woods, lost, alone, frightened, and in extreme pain. I don't know what to do to show how much I appreciate your taking care of me."

He groaned inwardly over what he really wanted. "Rest is what you may do. Stay inside and do not wander about while I'm gone."

She gave him a saucy grin. "You must be an easy man to please if that's all you want from me."

Although he could think of number of things he wished from her, he had better sense than to mention, or even dwell on them. She was his charge, and he was honor-bound to protect her from himself, at least until they wed.

"The physician left some tablets. You may wish to swallow one to ease your pain."

Her grin spread, creating a twinkle in her unusual eyes. "Sounds good to me."

To keep from touching her, Drake fetched a jar of water and a clean mug. After he filled it, their hands brushed when he handed it to her.

She gazed up at him, her eyes a mystery of emotions. Before he could think of a suitable comment, she swallowed the tablet then said, "Thank you."

"You are welcome, Miss Quinlane."

"I like it better when you call me Jennifer."

He thought he heard a hint of laughter in her voice, but couldn't be sure because he hadn't spent enough time with her to judge the varying inflections in her voice. *Not yet,* that is.

Why had he added that silent codicil to his thoughts? He had not planned to spend a lot of time with her after they wed.

Unable to think of a quick comeback, he left. If his luck held, she wouldn't regain her memories before he returned.

Six

Distractions

Drake's grandmother, Lucilla, who lived in the dower house near Stonemeade's mansion, followed Drake inside.

"I have bad news," she breathlessly announced, "Boyden's horse threw him, and he lays abed, paralyzed from the neck down."

Concerned about his cousin, Drake said, "Send word that I will call on him soon."

His grandmother smiled. "I'm sure that will be appreciated. May I go with you?"

"Certainly."

Shortly after he became a duke, Drake had named his married cousin, Boyden, his heir. If Boyden failed to recover, the responsibility of providing a healthy heir would fall back to Drake, and he might be forced to bed Miranda—Jennifer. Oddly, that fact no longer bothered him. It now held enormous appeal.

As soon as his grandmother left, Drake's secretary, Josian, extended a letter. "Who is it from?" Drake asked.

"Miss Miranda's governess. Apparently she dismissed Miss Tippstend three days ago, and put her on the train to Yorkshire where her sister lives. With the Grand Tour behind her, and the wedding a mere fortnight away, Miss Miranda said she will be busy with fittings, and is no longer in need of a governess."

She'd been busy snooping and fell from a tree, Drake thought.

He marched to his study and dictated a letter to soothe Miss Tippstend's ruffled feathers and assure her a generous stipend for her services would be provided. He had intended to dismiss her himself, and engage a strict matron companion-chaperon who would ensure Miranda never strayed into another man's bed. The chit could have the title she coveted, but he'd make damn sure she was a faithful wife and proper duchess, and obeyed him in all matters.

Remorse for those thoughts attacked. She had given him no reason to think she might be like Helen. In truth, she had gone out of her way to avoid gentlemen callers, using the excuse that she wanted only him.

~ * ~

By the time Drake returned to the lodge, pouring rain created muddy puddles and soaked his jacket and trousers. The clean clothes he'd brought for Jennifer were protected under his jacket, and the crutches a servant had found in Stonemeade's attic, protruded beneath his arms.

As Quicksilver cantered into the stable, Olvan grabbed a brush to brush him down.

"I ken those be fer th' lass." He nodded at the crutches.

"Yes," Drake said, dismounting. "Can you shorten them?"

"Aye, Yer Grace."

"I've told you not to call me that."

"Aye, ye have." Olvan's doleful expression emphasized his reproach. "I ken ye dinna remind the lass she be yer intended."

"I saw no reason to do so," Drake said, unaccustomed to Olvan's censure, and not liking it one whit.

"Ye be not a deceitful lad."

"I'm hardly a lad," Drake said, though he knew the Scot would likely call him one to his dying day. "And deceit has nothing to do with it.

When Miranda regains her memories, she'll remember we are to be wed."

"Wot if she dinna regain 'um?"

That question had plagued Drake all the time he'd been gone. Should he postpone the wedding? Or allow the plans his grandmother fussed over to proceed? Not pleased with his indecision, he reminded himself his betrothed might be playing a game.

To Olvan he said, "Then I'll tell her at the appropriate time."

With a curt nod, Drake strode away, through the rain, still protecting the clean clothes beneath his soaked jacket.

Inside the lodge, he eased the door shut... and found the bed empty. Disappointed and worried, he tossed the bundle on a chair, then smoothed his dripping mustache. Where had Jennifer gone? And what would become of her if she had no memory of who she was or where she lived?

Disturbed and concerned, he shook his wet jacket off, then stomped across the lodge. He found her on the worn, brown settee. She lay with one arm draped over her forehead; the other poised on top of the coarse blanket that covered her. Asleep she looked at peace, lovely and serene. Also deathly still. Alarmed, he knelt to feel her wrist, and found it warm.

He relaxed and inhaled. Her sweet-smelling breath caressed his cheek. A web of desire tangled around him. Slowly, without actually intending to, he lowered his mouth to hers.

He meant it to be a gentle kiss. But to his surprise she curled her arms around his neck and kissed him back, once again with passion and ardor to match his own. Her mouth was warm and giving, moist and demanding, too. Need, raw and urgent, welled inside him. She tasted as sweet as she smelled, and only by sheer force of will did he keep from giving in to the temptation to ravish her.

"Your mustache does tickle." A quiet chuckle escaped her as their mouths parted a mere inch.

He raised his head, expecting to see laughter in her luminous eyes, but they were closed.

"Don't leave," she whimpered, trying to draw him back. "Please don't go away. I can't bear to lose you yet."

Drake didn't know what stunned him most—her plea, or his willingness to stay close. He held her until her breathing evened out and he knew she was sleeping soundly.

Tension crept into his muscles before he straightened. The fire had burned low and the lodge had cooled. Naked from the waist up, he tended the fire, imagining his intended's lush, bare curves pressed against him. Closing his eyes, he pictured her face at the height of passion. He could almost hear her whispers urging him on.

Lord. What was wrong with him? Yesterday he'd had no intention of bedding her. If not for the freak accident that might leave Boyden permanently paralyzed, Drake wouldn't be entertaining the notion now. At least that's what he told himself. He had kissed her again because he had been curious. However, he would not allow demmed curiosity to become a habit or get the best of him. If he had to bed Jennifer to beget an heir, he would. Otherwise, he would treat her as he always had, providing the baubles that seemed to amuse and delight her, and ignoring her antics when she did something that displeased him.

Another thought intruded. An irritating one. Where the devil had she learned to kiss like that? Suspicions merged with jealousy. Had Miss Tippstend failed to control her more often than she admitted? Or had Jennifer-Miranda managed to escape the finishing academy and indulge in flirtations prior to her Grand Tour? Angered by the jealous images those thoughts provoked, Drake vowed to engage a suitable matron-companion as quickly as possible. Annoyance mingled with his anger. That would necessitate an unscheduled trip to London, but he would take Jennifer with him so he could keep an eye on her.

In the next breath he realized he didn't want to share her, not even with a companion-chaperon. He wanted her all to himself. Would he feel this way when—if her memories returned?

Because he hadn't taken time to clean up at home, Drake tossed more logs on the fire, then sloshed water from one of the hot kettles into a basin to wash his grime away. Afterwards he changed from his soiled togs. Then he cleaned his rifle and sharpened his hunting knife.

The rain ceased. Servants delivered a copper tub and food. Olvan brought the shortened crutches. Still Drake's betrothed slept. His gaze was constantly drawn to her. Why did he suddenly find her so lovely to look at? And why did the thought of her kissing another man rankle? He raked his hand through his hair. The hoyden had always frustrated him. Now she enchanted him. She worried him, too.

Like the anxious father of a newborn babe, he checked her a dozen times. But she was nothing like a newborn babe. Nay. Jennifer-Miranda had grown up. Now she was all woman. And she presented an inviting picture lying there with long strands of hair dangling off the old settee, her elegant features relaxed in sleep.

With little else to occupy his thoughts, he decided to examine her injuries. If her ankles were still swollen, the crutches would not yet be of much use. The moment he stood her arms began to flail. She mumbled in her sleep and jerked the bed cover over her head.

In two hasty steps he reached the settee, gripped her shoulders and shook her. "Wake up."

She threw her arms around him, dislodging the bed cover. "Tyler. They're awful. Please make them go away."

Stabs of jealousy pricked Drake's ego. Had Tyler taught her to kiss? "I'm not Tyler. I'm Drake," he groused.

Suddenly wide-awake, she stared at him. "Yes. Of course, you are."

"Were you having a nightmare?"

"I think I still am."

"You think I'm part of a nightmare?"

"No, not you. Those snakes up there." She nodded at the ceiling, her hands clenching his shoulders.

He glanced up. "There are no snakes on the ceiling."

"Of course there aren't. They're flying. Look out!" She grabbed his head, pulled it down to her chest and yanked the bed cover over them both.

Drake thought he might suffocate. *But it would be a pleasurable way to die.* With his nose buried in her lush breasts, he inhaled the intoxicating scent of her faint perfume. The heat of her body transferred to his, and he became immediately and fully aroused.

He needed air and raised his head. The bed cover slid down his back. In an attempt to calm the panic in her eyes, he wrapped his arms around her. But calm for him was out of the question.

"You didn't see them, did you?" she asked breathlessly.

"No."

"They're still there. You'd better keep your feet off the floor. It's covered with huge bugs that have gaping jaws and sharp, jagged teeth."

Sprawled atop her, she fanned his desire as she wiggled beneath him.

"There isn't room for you to lie beside me," she said. "You'll have to stay where you are. But don't worry. I'll protect you."

Engaged in a full-scale battle with lust, Drake didn't know whether to be amused or insulted. He gazed down into her greenish-brown eyes, and smiled. "You think yourself capable of protecting me?"

"Yes."

"From what?"

"The flying snakes and monstrous bugs. Can't you see them?"

"No."

"Look more closely," she implored, the panic in her eyes escalating.

Although reluctant to move from the enticing position, Drake struggled to stand up, then looked around his lodge. "There are no snakes or bugs, Jennifer."

"Are you sure?"

"Positive."

"Can you see that tiny blinking light in the corner?"

"No."

"Am I hallucinating?"

"One would assume so."

She sighed and ran a hand over her eyes. "Do you think that tablet the doctor left could be responsible?"

"Possibly."

"Forgive me." She closed her eyes. "I'm disorientated. *Disoriented.* No, in England you say disorien*tated,*" she corrected herself again.

Relieved she believed him about the bugs and snakes, Drake kept his tone mild as he asked, "What other words do the English use that are different from those used by Americans?"

"Well, there's dodgy, grotty, blimey, stroppy, chap, bloke and old sod to name a few. And some words are pronounced differently. For instance, when Brits say privacy, the first syllable rhymes with priv, as is privilege. When we say privacy, it rhymes with pry. We say controversy, Brits say contrauv-a-see. We say itinerary, Brits say eye-tin-a-ree. Also, we say aluminum. Brits say ahl-u-min-nee-um."

Puzzled, he wrinkled his forehead. "Aluminum?"

"Oh, you may not have heard of that yet. It's a new type of metal some people use in the States."

Drake resisted the urge to scratch his head like a schoolboy. Where had she picked up such odd bits? When he didn't comment, she asked, "How are Mordora and Awesome?"

Pleased she cared enough to ask—he didn't think she would have before her fall—he said, "They're fine." Then he gave in to his curiosity. "Does Tyler have a mustache?"

"No."

Long ago Drake had mastered the art of keeping his voice and expression devoid of emotion, and he did so now. "Who is he?"

Her expression turned wary. "Why do you want to know?"

Was her dodgy comeback an attempt to evade his question? Had she kissed the man, or worse, been intimate with him, and couldn't think of a plausible answer? Or, had she forgotten? "How long have you known Tyler?"

"All my life. He's my cousin."

Miranda and Prudence had no cousins, or any other living relatives, which was why Drake had become their guardian when Helen's aging parents passed on. Abandoning the subject of Tyler, Drake asked, "Do you know the name of our sovereign?"

"Of course," she blurted. "Queen Victoria."

"And the President of the United States?"

Her finely arched eyebrows creased in a frown. "Certainly."

"Then kindly tell me his name."

~ * ~

Jennifer blinked as her mind scrambled for an answer. To stall him, she asked, "What year is it?"

He wrinkled his brow. "You do not know what year this is?"

"No."

"1855."

So who was President before Lincoln? American history had been Jennifer's college minor and she'd memorized all the president's. James Buchanan was before Lincoln.

"Pierce," she said, "Franklin Pierce. A democrat. He won a smashing victory over General Winfield Scott. His platform advocated slavery and tariff for revenue only."

Drake's beginning smile narrowed. "Do you condone slavery?"

"Of course not." She knew England had abolished slavery about thirty years before the U.S. "I don't approve of the mastery of some men over others anymore than I approve of husbands being lord and master over their wives."

Ignoring the astonishment in his eyes, she added, "I predict slavery will soon be abolished in the U.S."

"Do you expect large plantation owners to agree?"

"Not peaceably. The North and South have been in disagreement for years. Daniel Webster's impassioned Seventh of March Speech in 1850 made the Washington politicians recognize that the South has certain inalienable rights, but I suspect the Union will be divided and there will be a horrible, bloody civil war in the next decade."

Drake looked thoroughly astounded. "Where and when did you learn such things about America?"

"I—I like to read." She didn't want to mislead him, but didn't yet dare admit that to her it was history. "Also, I saw some things in my visions."

"Did you?"

She nodded, then a new vision flashed—one of Drake with a young captain, arranging to ship horses to the colonies during the Civil War.

In an attempt to discourage anymore discussion on that subject, she nodded at the clothes spread over a chair.

"Are those for me?"

"Yes. I brought a clean gown and some bedclothes."

"How thoughtful. Thank you."

His nearness did strange things to her insides, and being the object of his intense scrutiny increased her nervousness. She glanced at the copper tub placed before the fireplace, then at the three kettles Olvan had hung above the fire to heat water.

"Do you wish to bathe now?" Drake asked.

"That would be nice." Smiling, she swung her feet to the floor, tested her weight, and sank back against the sofa with a grimace. "I can't believe how weak I am."

"You're fortunate to be alive," he muttered, plucking her off the sofa and cradling her against his chest. "I'm still amazed the fall didn't break every bone in your body. You're so thin you look as though you starve yourself."

"American girls don't think they can be too thin," she said.

"You're not merely thin," he taunted, "you're scrawny. A strong wind could unseat you if you were riding."

"I'll have you know that where I came from thin is in; fat is out. Thin is fashionable. All the styles are designed with thin people in mind. Furthermore—"

"Beauty is in the eye of the beholder. And," he added with a wicked, teasing gleam, "you have ample flesh in all the right places."

Reminded that he'd seen her without clothes, Jennifer tried to sound stern, but failed miserably as she accused, "You were baiting me."

"Teasing," he corrected gently.

Jennifer thought she detected fondness in his smiling gaze. All too clearly she remembered the kisses they'd shared, and her responses. No other man, except Dirk, had ever made her want him the way Drake did. She wondered again if he could be Dirk. But if he were, why didn't he remember her?

Although he had reached the shiny, copper tub, he still held her. She looked away and saw her reflection in a small mirror on the wall beside an old clock that apparently no longer kept time.

"Why didn't you tell me I look a fright?" she gasped.

"You cannot expect to look the height of fashion after what you've been through."

"I guess you're right." She glanced down at the floor, then said, "May I ask a favor?"

"What would you like? The moon on a silver platter?"

Delighted by his sense of humor, she grinned.

"Nothing as elaborate as that."

"What then?"

"I'd be happy to borrow a comb or brush."

~ * ~

"It will be my pleasure to indulge you." While they stared, Drake realized he didn't want to set her beside the tub. He wanted to keep her in his arms. Was he becoming besotted?

With the resolution of a man thoroughly disgusted with himself, he lowered her to the chair, then stalked away to fetch a brush from the small chest where he kept a comb, brush, soap and straight razor.

When he offered the brush, an invisible spark leapt between them. Surprise changed her greenish-brown eyes to a darker hue. She licked her lips with the tip of her pink tongue, and he found it impossible to look away.

"Th—thank you." She sounded breathless.

He tore his gaze from her tempting mouth, feeling a bit short of breath himself. "You're most welcome, my lady."

While she brushed her hair, he filled the tub. A new surge of desire spiraled through him as he imagined her naked and in her bath. In an attempt to ignore those erotic images, he seized the crutches and offered them, careful to maintain his distance.

She accepted the crutches with a smile so warm it threatened to melt his insides. "I'll go out whilst you bathe." He cocked a brow in question. "Unless you require assistance?"

"I'm sure I can manage on my own." She propped the crutches against her chair. "Thanks for these." Then she flicked her long hair behind her shoulders, gathered and twisted it into a thick rope. Using a piece of ribbon she had apparently removed from her chemise, she coiled her hair in a crown and secured it on top of her head. Finished, she raised her eyes and saw him staring.

"Does it pass inspection?"

Gloriously so, he nearly said, but caught himself in time and only nodded. He had never watched a lady prepare for her bath, and the thought of seeing her naked again sent another rush of primal lust soaring through him.

She glanced at the dried mud and splotches of Mordora's blood on the skirt of her pale gown, then folded her hands primly on her lap, and waited for him to leave. He didn't because he couldn't move, but finally he found his voice again.

"Can I get you anything else?"

"No, thanks." The tremor in Jennifer's voice shifted his stare into her eyes. Were they green or brown? He still couldn't decide. Not a man who generally wasted time thinking about ladies, let alone the color of their eyes, he chided himself for his fascination and the throbbing in his lower extremities.

"Are you certain you don't need help to disrobe?"

"I can manage, unless you have a lady's maid in your immediate service."

His mouth went dry. He didn't want a maid to assist her. In truth, he didn't want to share her with another soul. And he disliked the possibility that other men might have already sampled her.

Dash it. He smoothed his mustache. He would not allow the minx to lure him into a situation he did not feel ready for.

Lord, who did he think to fool? His body was beyond ready.

With that unsettling thought, he jerked his glance away and stalked outside. Surely the rain-cooled afternoon air would calm the turbulence inside him.

Seven

The Bath and Supper

Drake told himself he wouldn't spy, but as he strode by the lodge's front window, he glanced inside to ensure Jennifer hadn't fallen. She had already disrobed and stepped into the copper tub. He caught only a fleeting glimpse before she sank into the water, but that naked peek incited another onslaught of unwanted lust.

So why didn't he walk away? Because, like the veriest dunderhead, he couldn't move. While she lathered her arms, he convinced himself he had her best interests at heart. She had fallen from a great height, suffered numerous scratches and bruises, and might need assistance.

Her magnificent crown of hair, highlighted by the fire behind her, made her look like an elegant, desirable princess, and his body continued to react while she lathered her legs and feet. Annoyed at her allure, he tried to recall her faults, but couldn't. She hadn't displayed any here at his lodge.

Just when he thought he had mastered his lust, she stood up. The fiery desire ignited moments before returned with a vengeance. Honor demanded that he leave. But his feet refused to obey and his eyes remained fastened on her, as though held there by a polar magnet.

Supported first by the side of the tub, then by the crutches, she stepped awkwardly out. As she patted herself dry, he battled desire. And guilt. He had no right to ogle her before they wed. Still, he did.

She folded the towel, placed it on the chair, and sat on it. Getting dressed didn't look easy, and he sensed her pain from her slow, clumsy progress. Even so, he couldn't stop ogling and he fought the urge to go inside and help. At least she had the good sense to leave the corset off and wear only drawers, chemise, and petticoat beneath the clean blue gown.

Finally she finished dressing. He heaved a pent-up sigh, stepped away, and leaned against the rain-wet lodge. Moisture seeped through the back of his shirt. He ignored the cold and counted slowly to one hundred, twice, before he strode back to the door and knocked.

"Come in," she called.

When he stepped inside, she still sat on the chair, but she had draped the damp towel over the side of the tub nearest the fire to dry. Tidiness wasn't a virtue he would have attributed to her, but it pleased him that she didn't expect someone to pick up after her here at the lodge.

"I need help with the buttons in back," she said. "Would you mind?"

He stifled a groan, and with unusual gruffness, ordered, "Lean forward," as he crossed the lodge.

Her smooth flawless skin beckoned his touch. He clamped his teeth together and willed his hands to be steady while he buttoned the gown.

Some strange words, put to music swirled through his mind. *Lay your head upon my pillow.* Where had he heard that refrain before? And why did it linger as he backed away and watched Jennifer untie the pink ribbon holding her hair on top of her head? Her long copper strands tumbled down around her shoulders and arms.

How could such a simple act render him useless?

He recovered enough to stride to the fireplace where he tried not to watch her brush her tresses. But his eyes kept straying from the flickering embers to her. She had the longest hair he had ever seen. It fell below her hips, and he wondered how she kept from sitting on it. Why had he never noticed its luxurious length before? How long had he been an unobservant nob?

When she gathered her hair at her nape and tied it with the ribbon, relief flowed through him, but desire still tormented him.

She caught his gaze on her and tilted her head. "You shouldn't go out without a coat. You might catch a cold."

Startled that she had the nerve to chastise him, he also felt flattered she cared enough to notice what he did. Although the late afternoon had taken on a chill after the storm, the cold had bothered him not at all. Watching her had heated his blood and kept him quite warm.

"You are not to worry about me."

"You might as well tell me to stop breathing." She gave him a lopsided smile. "I can't help it, Drake. I'm a worrier, and you're not invincible. Nobody is."

Touched by her concern, he searched for something to take his mind off the temptation threatening his control. His gaze settled on the table. She hadn't eaten since morning, and only a few morsels then. Carrying on with her charade, he asked, "What do American ladies like to eat?"

She smiled. "This one isn't fussy. I like almost everything. What kind of food do you enjoy?"

He stared at the platters of cold roast beef, cheese, bread and wine on the table.

"Well prepared," he said dryly, wondering if she would scoff when she saw what his servants had brought. "Shall I carry you to the table?"

"I'd like to use the crutches and see how I manage."

Having expected her to use her injuries as an excuse to appear helpless, he blinked. To his surprise and slight disappointment, she managed the crutches remarkably well.

He turned his back to her while he changed his shirt.

~ * ~

Jennifer watched, unable to tear her eyes away from his strong biceps, his wonderful muscles, the smooth skin on his arms and shoulders, or the scars that lacerated the middle of his back. She wondered what had caused them as he hung his damp shirt on a peg by the fire to dry.

After he buttoned his clean shirt, he sat down, across from her.

More hungry than she wanted to admit, Jennifer sampled everything, relishing the taste and flavor of every bite.

"Do you like the food?" he asked.

"Yes. It tastes delicious. Thanks." She curved her lips in a smile, and warmth snaked through her when he smiled back.

Her attraction radiated way down deep inside, and kept her on edge. Irritated at herself for being so hugely drawn to him, she said, "Stop looking at me like that."

He flexed his brow, but the potent expression in his eyes didn't change. "Why?"

"Because it makes me feel like you want to devour me."

"Perhaps I do."

She flushed, but didn't bat a lash. "Is that a promise or a boast?"

Drake laughed. She hadn't heard him laugh yet, and it made her smile again.

"Where would you start? Not with my feet, I hope, because then I couldn't walk."

"Where would you have me start, little minx? With your lips?"

His voice sounded husky. Her breath caught in her throat. In his eyes she saw undisguised hunger. It matched hers. Suddenly afraid she might say or do something foolish that would keep her from seeing Kacy, or getting back to her own time, Jennifer frowned. She didn't belong here. Drake was engaged—betrothed to Miranda. And Sevil, the wizard, could return her at his whim.

When Jennifer didn't say anything more, Drake looked at her untouched wine. "Are you not thirsty?"

"Wine usually gives me a headache and I don't want to make the one I already have worse."

"I had hoped the wine would ease it." When she didn't comment, he asked, "Would you like something else to drink?"

"Water. If it isn't too much trouble."

He stood and walked to a corner where he fetched a jar of water from the shelf. Jennifer wondered if he had ever waited on Miranda, and hated the jealousy that thought provoked.

"I don't drink much," she said, "but if you have something besides wine, I'd appreciate a few drops in my water."

Drake set a glass full of water on the table. "What do you have in mind?"

"Something to help me relax or dull my pain. I don't dare take any more of those tablets the doctor left. I don't want another bizarre hallucination."

"I have brandy, whiskey, scotch."

"I left the whiskey in the stable," she reminded, "but I'm not fussy. Anything will do."

Drake fetched a bottle of scotch. Dusk had fallen outside, and the lodge lay in semi-darkness. The only light came from the fire, and Jennifer smiled when he lit a candle before he poured two fingers of scotch in a small snifter, then carried it and the bottle to the table.

"It's a sin to water this down. Drink it straight."

"Won't it sting my throat?"

Drake grinned. "It may. However, it will also make you feel better quickly."

She reached for the snifter. Their fingers touched. Her hand trembled, and an almost overpowering urge to reach up and touch his cheek struck her. When he covered her hand with his, her heart pounded.

"Drink," he ordered. Without giving her a choice he urged the snifter to her lips.

She swallowed the scotch in one long gulp. Then blinked and thrust the empty snifter into his hand. Grabbing her water, she drank the contents without pause.

"Wow!" she said. "That has some kick."

Drake grinned while he poured another finger of scotch, then collected the lighted candle before he sat down.

"Although you slept a good part of the day, you still look tired, and that nasty bump on your temple has black added to the purple. Are you in pain?"

"Not as much as I was this morning."

She dabbed the corners of her mouth with a white linen napkin. "I probably shouldn't drink any more. Drugs and booze don't mix very well."

Drake hiked an eyebrow. "Drugs and booze?"

She shrugged. "That's what I call pills—tablets, and strong drink." Without waiting for him to comment, she changed subjects.

"May I ask some questions about Miranda and Prudence?"

"Feel free," Drake said, a strange look in his eyes.

"I understand they're sisters, but how do they relate to your life?"

"As my charges."

"How did that happen?"

"I assumed responsibility for them shortly after my marriage to their cousin, when her parents died."

You're married? Confusion set in. "Miranda said she intends to marry you. How can she if you already have a wife?"

"My wife is deceased."

"I'm sorry," Jennifer said, a little startled by her relief. "I had no idea, and no right to pry either."

Still curious, she wanted to ask more questions but she didn't want to anger Drake.

"What else do you wish to know?"

Had he read her mind? "When did she... your wife, die?"

"Three years ago, in June past," he said without any emotion Jennifer could detect, but that's when she had lost Dirk, too. Could there be a connection? Her heart told her there must be because everything about him was heart wrenchingly dear and familiar. His tender expression, the gentle way he touched her, his smile, his piney scent, that tiny mole under his right eye.

Had the real Drake and his wife died at the same time, and had Dirk somehow taken over Drake's life?

Unable to hide her excitement at the possibility, Jennifer closed her eyes. If Dirk had taken over Drake's life, he must have lost his memories, but not the limp he acquired after he'd been thrown by a horse and trampled.

Did reincarnation work forward and backward?

Jennifer swallowed. How could she think up such convoluted questions? Was she losing it? Or had she stumbled on some very real possibilities?

"Are you all right, Jennifer?"

"Yes, I'm fine." She opened her eyes. "I suppose she—your wife was beautiful."

"Like Helen of Troy, she had a face pretty enough to launch a thousand ships."

Envy and jealousy converged. Common sense deserted Jennifer. "Did you love her?"

"Love has nothing to do with marriage."

Jennifer touched the lump on her temple, and changed subjects again. "Does Prudence like Miranda?"

"Why do you ask?"

Jennifer shrugged. "Because I had the impression Miranda doesn't care much for Prudence."

"Where did you get that impression?"

"From my vision."

"The vision with the wizard?"

Jennifer nodded.

Instead of pursuing that, Drake asked, "How did you get in the tree? I do not believe you capable of climbing to the top in slippers and a voluminous gown."

"I wondered when you'd figure that out." Fascinated by his mustache, and the deep blue of his wondrous eyes, she added, "Sevil whirled me through the sky, and dropped me in the tree."

Drake frowned. "People do not whirl through the sky."

"Sometimes they do if a wizard's involved."

"Rubbish."

"It isn't rubbish." Jennifer shook her head, disagreeing. "Sevil did whirl me in a noxious fog, and I suspect he put me in that tree to prove something."

Drake folded his arms, his gaze narrowed in a scowl. "What?"

"I'll be demmed if I know."

"I will not have you using that kind of language."

"Why not? You do."

"What is appropriate for a man is not appropriate for a young lady!"

"Do you think I give a rip?"

"Jennifer," he enunciated each syllable slowly, "do not try my patience too far."

She gave him her most angelic smile and he cleared his throat.

"You are fortunate you suffered no broken bones when you fell. However, it may take considerable time for those bumps and bruises to heal."

Jennifer resisted the urge to squirm. "How many people saw me without clothes?"

"No one, except me."

"What about the doctor?"

"I explained you had no broken bones, merely bumps, scratches and bruises, and he advised me how to care for you."

Heat crawled up Jennifer's neck. To avoid Drake's probing gaze she looked around the shadowed cottage, wishing she had a way to record everything they said, as well as what she saw. It would be great material for her novel when she got back to her own time. Only now, she wasn't nearly as anxious to return as she had been this morning.

Deciding to change subjects, she asked, "How long did I sleep?"

"All afternoon."

"I'm glad the snakes and bugs weren't real." Thinking about them robbed her appetite and she set her utensils down before she switched subjects again.

"I know this may sound presumptuous, but I'd like to see Kacy, the Countess, as soon as possible. I lost my backpa—money, but if you'd help me arrange to travel to Surrey, I'm sure Kacy would repay you."

"The Countess is out of the country."

Jennifer's heart dropped to her stomach. "For how long?"

"Another week. Perhaps more."

"Do you know where she is?"

"In Europe. With her husband."

~ * ~

Drake knew his friend, Clay, and his wife planned to return in time for the wedding, but he saw no reason to mention that. He didn't believe Jennifer knew the Countess, and he wouldn't embarrass anyone by pretending she did.

"As I mentioned," Jennifer fidgeted under his regard, "I lost my money and can't pay for lodging, or anything else. Maybe I could go to Havenhurst and wait for their return."

"You are in no condition to travel." To calm the alarm in her eyes, he added, "Don't worry. I shall take care of you."

"I can't stay with you."

"Why the devil not?"

"Because I have no way to repay you. Besides, it wouldn't be proper."

"The harm has already been done. You have spent two days and a night alone with me," he reminded, irritated with the near panic surging through him at the thought of her staying elsewhere. "And I am indebted for your help with the foaling. Therefore, you are under no obligation to repay me for what little food you eat."

"You're very kind," she said quietly. "I'll sleep on the sofa so you can have your bed back."

Sofa? Did she mean the settee?

Bemused, he sipped his wine while his betrothed sipped the scotch he doled out half an inch at a time. A fortnight suddenly seemed like a very long time. Could he keep his hands off her till then?

"It feels really strange to be here."

Really strange? What odd expressions she used. "Why?"

With a dreamy, faraway look, she said, "Because I've never been in a small cottage in England's woods before."

"It doesn't feel strange to have you here. At the moment I cannot imagine you anywhere else."

Silently he cursed himself for that admission. It would not do to let her know how enamored he had become.

"I'm glad your eyebrows don't grow together," she said.

"Might I ask why?"

"Absolutely." Her dimples deepened as impish lights danced in her eyes. "My aunt cautioned me never to trust a man whose eyebrows grow together. Sevil's grow together. I'd better not trust him."

Drake chuckled. She'd concocted a wizard, a cousin, and now an aunt. "I am pleased you trust me."

"I have no choice." She smiled impishly. "After all, you're my gallant, white shining knight, and I seriously doubt I could have invented a better one."

Drake attributed her praise to strong drink, but it pleased him nonetheless. She looked relaxed, and less aware of her pain. He felt relaxed for the first time in days.

"Why do you think you invented me?"

"Because everybody knows if anybody really fell from the sky they'd be dead. Right? Right," she answered her own question. "Besides, you have blonde, pearl-white hair."

She raised her hand and touched the short lock that had fallen over his forehead. "And nobody has hair as pure blonde as yours, except fairies and angels. But I'm certain they don't smell as good as you do."

She lowered her hand and slid the candle, now burned to a short stub, aside. Then she moved her plate as well and rested her arms on the table.

"Pray forgive my bad manners." She laid her head on her arms. "I'd love to stay awake and gaze at your handsome face forever. My brain is ever so willing, but my flesh, I fear, is weak. Good night, Rake—*Drake.*"

The next sound that issued from her was a gentle sigh, followed by deep, even breathing.

Drake gazed at her with unashamed delight. Wisps of long cinnamon hair covered her cheek. He slid the strands aside and noted her manicured nails. Neither too short nor too long, yet shiny as though she had access to a kind of clear nail varnish. Her lips looked rosy. And kissable.

Lord, why did so many things about her please him now? Half the time he forgot she was Miranda, and that he didn't trust ladies. But since her fall the enchanting minx was completely without guile or pretentiousness. Perhaps it wouldn't be as difficult to be wed to her as he had previously imagined.

Without her assistance this morning, the colt might have died. Mordora as well. He decided to reward Jennifer by giving her the mare. Perhaps at Christmas.

In addition to her help in the stable, this evening she had made him laugh, and kept him entertained. What would it be like to have her as a loving, cherished wife?

That thought sobered him. Once he had wanted a wife he might love. But Helen had turned him into a jaded, embittered cynic. The miserable state of his marriage had driven him to a disagreeable affair. The two combined to sour him so much, he had vowed never again to become emotionally involved with another lady.

But for some odd reason he couldn't shake the feeling he had experienced during the foaling—that he had known and loved Jennifer in a previous lifetime. Why did it persist? He had never fancied himself in love, even as a youth. Why then, did he long for a happy, agreeable marriage now?

While he studied his betrothed, he convinced himself a happy marriage was out of the question. As soon as her memories returned, he would never see this side of her again.

If her memories failed to return prior to the wedding, he would introduce her to the Countess of Havenhurst, as promised, and expose her as a liar.

His conclusions should have pleased him. They fouled his good mood instead.

Eight

Wind Storm

Drake carried Jennifer, fast asleep, to the settee and covered her. Then he emptied the copper tub, banked the fire, and went out to the stable. After he checked on Mordora and the colt, Olvan asked, "The lass, how be she?"

"At the moment she's sleeping again."

Olvan rubbed the stubble on his weathered jaw. "A brave lass she be to help wit' the foaling."

"True," Drake said, as puzzled by her insistence that she help and her claim to have seen women and animals give birth, as he was by the way she now affected him.

Olvan raised a craggy brow. "Ye be pleased to have her here at the lodge with ye?"

The Scot was more than Drake's groom. He had been his first adult friend, his oldest confidante, and he acted more like a father than the duke who had sired Drake. Because of that, he got away with more than he should have.

"Do you have a point you wish to make, Olvan?"

"Why ye wedding the lass if ye dinna desire to?"

"Because I lost the wager."

As soon as he became the duke, Miranda had started to pester him to make her his duchess. Drake thought she did it to gall Prudence, who had recently married, and he sent Miranda away to Miss Treacher's Finishing Academy. But every week Miranda wrote, pleading with him to let her leave the academy and to marry her. He continued to refuse and insisted she remain in school for two full years. He could not, in good conscience, force her to stay longer.

During her coming out, he had expected offers for her hand, but she refused to see every young man who called. The *ton* labeled her a hoyden. Drake wondered if Prudence was behind that label.

When Miranda's pleadings to be his duchess increased, he dealt with them by allowing her to take the Grand Tour, a trip generally reserved for young men.

Upon her return she challenged him to a horse race and promised never to bring marriage up again if she lost. He accepted the challenge, expecting to put the matter to rest, once and for all. No horse in the kingdom galloped faster than Quicksilver. Miranda chose to race a mare provided by a friend. To his utter astonishment she won the race.

Although he suspected trickery might have been involved, he couldn't prove it. At first, he regretted being forced to honor the wager. However, Miranda had been easier to manage when he did, and he concluded that a second marriage might not be the disaster his first had been.

"Mayhap the lass willna revert to her former ways."

"I wouldn't count on that," Drake said, resigned to his fate.

Olvan eyed the whiskey in the bottle Jennifer had brought out for Mordora. "Mayhap we needs a wee dram."

"Perhaps we do." Drake sat down, and had a wee dram, then a few more. By the time he left the stable, he no longer regretted his agreement to wed Jennifer. Maybe she wouldn't regain her memories, as Olvan suggested, and they would enjoy a pleasant union as they had enjoyed these past two days together.

In the lodge Drake removed his boots and climbed beneath the bedcovers fully clothed. The hours dragged. His intended didn't make a sound, yet knowing she slept in the same room kept him wide awake. And aroused.

He rolled onto his side. She had called him her white knight. In the morning he must disabuse her of that silly notion, and tell her she was neither an American nor Jennifer Quinlane. She was Jennifer Miranda Allsop, English born and bred; also his betrothed, and they were to wed in a fortnight. Somehow he must also discover where she had left the betrothal ring.

Not pleased with the prospect of exposing her lies, or having to deal with the loss of her memories if she had indeed lost them, he punched his pillow in an attempt to get more comfortable.

"Drake, are you all right?"

With the exception of his grandmother, no lady, not even his mother, had ever expressed concern for him. That shouldn't have bothered him, yet it did. "Of course," he answered gruffly.

"Are you sure?" Her quiet tone contrasted with his loud one.

"Absolutely."

"Good night then. And thanks for everything, Drake."

"You are welcome, Jennifer."

Disquieting thoughts kept him awake. Sometime before dawn he concluded he must distance himself. Otherwise, he might succumb to the overpowering urge to make her his wife in every sense of the word, and he might not wait until their wedding night. When morning arrived, he would speak only when necessary, and discourage conversation. And he would take her home to Stonemeade where servants could pamper her while she convalesced. No sense spending more time alone with her and getting his hopes up that they might share more than the dukedom after they wed. In all likelihood she would be content with what his wealth could provide, and he would maintain his distance in order to avoid future disappointments.

~ * ~

Jennifer awakened to the smell of coffee perking in a new pot hanging over the fireplace. Everything else in the cottage looked about a hundred years old. Used to so many twenty-first century conveniences, she could barely comprehend what life had been like fifty years before her own birth. A hundred and thirty-odd boggled her mind. The Victorian era had been touted as refined and elegant. She thought primitive a more apt description. Still, she knew Tyler would envy her if he could visit Drake's cottage in England's beautiful woods.

A shaft of homesickness twisted through her. Would she ever see Tyler, Aunt Rachel or Uncle Mac again? Of course, she would. They were her family, and Sevil would take her home, probably soon.

Jennifer also missed her roommate, Catharine, who had switched places with Kacy about fourteen months ago. Jennifer missed her old cat, Mordora, too. Catharine had promised to take good care of Mordora until Jennifer returned. Hopefully she'd see Kacy soon, then go back to her own time, obtain Kacy's journal and keep her reservation on the flight home next week so she could return to college. She only had one year left. Then she'd write her novel.

Generally optimistic, Jennifer told herself the future would take care of itself. Miranda would return. She wouldn't miss her own wedding. After she visited Catharine, she'd likely insist upon returning, and Sevil would bring her back, just as he would return Jennifer to the twenty-first century.

In the meantime she might as well enjoy her adventure here, and whatever time she had with Drake, or Dirk.

"It's wonderful to be here," she said quietly.

Drake turned, his expression unreadable. In his hand he held a brown pottery mug. "You're happy to be in the woods?"

"Yes." When his gaze darkened, the nervous urge to wring her hands, or do something else equally dumb, seized her. She turned her attention to getting up. Although moving didn't hurt as much today, she felt stiff and sore, and her ankles were still swollen.

As the blanket dropped to her lap, cool air kissed her bare back. Somebody had unbuttoned her gown all the way to her waist. Who? Drake? Embarrassed, she pressed her back against the worn fabric of the dull brown sofa. Could she refasten the dress without his help? Not likely with him watching every move she made.

To her relief, he turned his intent stare from her to fill his mug. "Do you want coffee?" It sounded like a cool, polite question, not at all like the friendly tone he had spoken with yesterday.

"Yes. Please."

He filled another mug, a mustard colored one. His mouth was stretched in a straight seam, and he looked grim when he extended her coffee. Had something happened while she slept?

"Are Awesome and Mordora all right?" she blurted.

"Yes." His gaze shuttered, he strode to the table where he arranged bread, jam, and chunks of cheese and dark shriveled apple slices on a thick porcelain plate. Without uttering another word he walked to the sofa and set it on her lap.

She took a bite of bread and chewed. It stuck in her dry throat. Hurriedly, she swallowed a gulp of hot black coffee... and scalded her tongue. Hating to reveal her stupidity, she tried not to gasp.

With his feet braced apart, Drake loomed above her, his brown coffee mug in hand while he stared down at her. "If you require assistance, I'll button your gown."

Her breath caught in her throat. Would he do more than button the gown? Touch her intimately? Kiss her? The mere thoughts made her skin tingle.

As though he guessed her thoughts, he said, "If you are worried about my conduct, allow me to assure you I don't force my attentions on injured ladies. I suggest you leave the corset off today. Your injuries will heal more quickly, and make your journey more bearable."

Journey? Where were they going? "Have you changed your mind?"

"Must you ask half-questions?"

"I'm sorry. Are you taking me to Havenhurst?"

"No."

"Is that all the answer I'm going to get?"

"I've decided you are right. You cannot stay here."

Jennifer's heart thudded in disappointment.

"Where are you sending me?"

"Home."

Her heart plummeted. "All the way to America?"

"Don't be absurd."

Confused, she swallowed. Where did he think she lived? Not in London. She'd admitted she was an American.

"You need bed rest to recover from your fall, and servants to pamper you." He gestured at a short blue cape, lined with matching satin that hung on a peg by the door. "I brought that for you."

With a rush of gratitude, she said, "I'm afraid I don't know how to properly thank you, Drake."

"Gratitude is unnecessary," he said, his voice gruff.

Yesterday he'd been warm, kind, friendly, but today he seemed remote and cold. What had happened? And where did he intend to take her?

"Please don't feel you must accompany me if you have other things you need to do. I can take care of myself."

"You are in no condition to be left to your own devices." He stared at her plate. "Surely you intend to eat more than that."

With a scalded tongue, nothing had much taste, and she'd lost what little appetite she'd had. "I'm not hungry."

Drake set his mug down. "I must speak with Olvan, and I expect you to finish eating before I return."

He grabbed his brown jacket and left as though a demon pursued him. The instant he closed the door Jennifer struggled to button the back of her gown. She managed it, but just barely. And she ate the cheese, to give her body some protein.

When Drake returned, she'd put Miranda's shoes on, surprised at how well they and the gown fit. She had also brushed her hair. Tiny shivers darted up her spine as she met Drake's hooded gaze. Did he know how he affected her?

"Are you ready, my lady?"

"Yes." She stood and anchored the crutches under her arms, still wondering where they were going.

Drake plucked the blue cape off the peg and draped it across her shoulders.

At the door, supported by the crutches, Jennifer paused to take a last look around the cottage. Was her adventure to the past about to end? Her gaze settled on Drake, standing directly behind her, watching her like a hawk.

Flustered, she asked, "Do you think it will rain?"

He gave a noncommittal shrug. "Do you?"

"I don't know." He offered his umbrella.

"Thanks." She hung the curved handle on her wrist to keep her hands free to maneuver the crutches.

"In America, a rather strong opinion has formed regarding England's weather."

She decided Drake didn't appreciate her attempt at conversation until he said, "Are you going to share the American's opinion of our weather?"

She smiled. She couldn't help it. He looked like his mood had improved. "They say if you don't like Britain's weather, wait about twenty minutes and it will change."

The beginning of a grin touched his mouth.

"Is that all they say?"

"No. They also say England is a great place to experience summer, winter, spring and fall, all in the same day."

His grin spread to his eyes. "Anything else?"

"Yes. That without the weather as a conversation starter, people in Great Britain might have nothing to talk about."

"We seem to have no trouble conversing."

The warmth in his eyes lured her to forget he was engaged to Miranda, and that she didn't belong in his time. If he touched her, she'd throw herself into his arms. She knew she would. Just as she knew, suddenly without doubt, that he was Dirk. From way down deep inside, the truth gushed forth. That's why she was here! Her heart pounded joyously. What could she say to help him remember her?

"Shall we go?" he asked.

With a mental shake, she turned away, thinking she didn't have the right to remind him she was his wife. "Excuse me, please. I need to go out back. I'll meet you in the stable. I'd like to say goodbye to Mordora and Awesome, if I may."

"You may."

~ * ~

Drake followed her outside and closed the door, then watched her make her way behind the lodge with the aid of crutches, his umbrella swaying from her wrist and the skirt of her pale blue gown swishing as she went.

He hadn't realized how small she was until he helped her don the cape. Her head didn't even reach his shoulder.

Then he recalled the active part she'd taken in his kisses. Lord, he wanted to kiss her again. He also wanted to fondle every inch of her. Actually, he wanted more than that. For one of the few times in his life he wanted to pursue until he conquered.

What in the devil had happened to him? Men of his ilk did not become victims of their base desires.

Gloomily he wondered if desire was all he felt. When last he saw his best friend, Clay, and his wife, Kacy, Drake realized they weren't merely well suited; they were very much in love. He told himself he didn't envy them. He didn't want love, or the complications that emotion evoked. Why then, did something niggle his mind, and accuse him of being a coward for not giving it more thought?

While he waited, those strange words filtered through his mind again. *Lay your head upon my pillow*—Why did the melodic strain haunt him? Why did he think they had something to do with Jennifer, but nothing at all to do with this time in the history of the world?

Startled out of his preoccupation by a dark cloud that twisted down to the ground, he raced to the back of the lodge. He must protect Jennifer.

A fierce wind blew dust in his eyes. He raised his arm to shield them. Debris attacked his back. He ran faster. And saw the privy door banging on its hinges. Jennifer was nowhere in sight.

Lightning flashed as he dashed to the stable.

Thunder sounded while he mounted Quicksilver.

Outside the wind whirled broken branches and fire kindling through the air, making it difficult to see beyond his nose.

She couldn't have gone far on crutches, he reasoned.

Moments later the wild windstorm died down.

He found the crutches on the ground. Beyond them lay his black umbrella and the blue cape. But he saw no sign of Jennifer. Where had she gone? Why had she left? And how had she managed to go anywhere without the crutches?

Had she faked her inability to walk without them?

She couldn't, he realized, fake swollen ankles or the bumps and bruises he'd seen when he undressed her two days past.

Nine

The Crossing

Stunned by the strong wind and Sevil's sudden appearance, Jennifer couldn't even groan when he grabbed her arm and took a gigantic leap to the top of a tree. The borrowed blue cape flew off her shoulders and she lost the crutches in mid-air, along with her breath.

Sevil jumped again to another tree. Terror clogged her throat. They were a long way off the ground.

Gripping her arm tighter in his clawed fist, Sevil took several more leaps. He paused on the rooftop of a huge mansion surrounded by dense woods. Up close his slick, white, oilskin jumpsuit looked like slimy fish scales. Thank goodness it didn't smell fishy. She already tasted bile.

"Why are you dressed like an alien?"

The wizard laughed. The hollow sound gurgled inside the clear bubble that enclosed his head. "I am the Saucerman," he hissed. "I am. I am. Forget me not, for I am also a wizard and I can fulfill your deepest desires."

Puzzled by his riddle, Jennifer was caught off guard when he leapt again. Her stomach jumped up to her throat. Bile followed. She almost upchucked on the clean, blue, wrinkled gown.

Instead of landing in a tree or on the ground, Sevil scaled a black wrought iron wall that surrounded the huge mansion. Jennifer felt as though they were flying. *But without wings?*

Sevil paused once more, in another tree.

Afraid to move, Jennifer sucked in a deep, slow breath. "Are you taking me back to the future?"

Instead of answering, Sevil jumped again, in a series of long, high jumps that no human could possibly make. Each jump jarred her achy body, robbed her breath anew, and made her heart pound with raw, stark terror.

Finally he stopped on top of a cliff that towered above the sea. Marveling that they had landed on the rocky cliff without bashing in her skull, Jennifer glanced at the wide expanse of gray water beneath the cloudy sky. Heart pounding and pulse racing, she inhaled the fresh sea air, hoping that might help calm her nerves and queasy stomach.

"Where are we?"

Behind the clear, round bubble, a smirk gleamed in Sevil's black eyes. "I thought you might recognize the White Cliffs of Dover."

Jennifer didn't. They weren't nearly as white as she had expected. "Why did you bring me here?"

"Because I thought you had enough time with Drake."

"Is he Dirk? Is that why you brought me to this time?"

Sevil's snort hissed from the bubble and echoed eerily through the chilly, misty breeze. "He is Miranda's intended."

Annoyed, Jennifer said, "I know that. Where is she?"

"In the future. With Catharine."

"Catharine, my roommate in Denver?"

Sevil nodded. "They were classmates at Miss Treacher's Finishing Academy for Young Ladies, and they kept up a lively correspondence until Catharine left this century."

"How long will Miranda be there?"

"That depends."

"On what?"

"I shall reveal that in due time."

"How long will I be here?"

"That also depends."

Irritated with his non-answers, and unwilling to be baited, Jennifer turned to limp away. But without crutches she hobbled, and every step hurt like unholy heck.

"Where do you think you're going?" he asked behind her.

Her spirits sank. The nearest town or village was probably miles away. Besides, she had no money, and every step created excruciating pain. She might as well face it. He had her at his mercy. She turned back to face him and shivered in the cool ocean breeze. Did he want her to catch cold and suffer through that, along with her other injuries?

"You said you knew I wanted to see Kacy. Why did you bring me here when she's in Europe?"

"In Paris," he clarified.

"Why don't you take me there?"

"I shall do just that, if you ask me."

Jennifer blinked. "All I have to do is ask?"

"You shall never know unless you do."

"Please take me to see her."

One of his claw-like hands grabbed her arm.

"Prepare for a long jump, Miss Quinlane. The English Channel is rather wide."

Jennifer lost her breath again as he leapt off the cliff. Would she survive the crossing? It couldn't be worse than traveling through time, but jumping over water scared her. She closed her eyes to escape the fear of falling and drowning.

But as he lifted her higher and higher, curiosity got the best of her. She opened her eyes. They were already half way across the twenty-two mile Channel.

After that amazing feat, the rest of the journey was uneventful, but far from boring. In Paris, Sevil shaped-shifted to resemble the tall, skinny man she had first seen in her vision, also the cab driver. He snapped his bony fingers and conjured a coach, complete with groom and footman.

They rode through the city like normal humans, but Jennifer doubted she'd ever feel normal again. Her swollen ankles and battered body hadn't healed from her fall after the flight through time. Without the cape she shivered inside the cold coach. It was still August and shouldn't be this cold.

The carriage stopped in front of a hotel.

"This is where your friend and her husband are lodged," Sevil said.

He snapped his fingers four times. An old-fashioned black purse, or reticule, and a pile of money appeared on Jennifer's lap. At her feet lay a valise packed with clothes, and a black fur-trimmed cloak covered her shivering shoulders.

The footman opened the door. Sevil climbed out, then turned to help Jennifer.

When she winced, he asked, "Are you suffering some discomfort, Miss Quinlane?"

She nodded.

"Forgive me." He pointed one finger at her and snapped his fingers again. To her surprise, her headache and all her other aches and pain disappeared, including her bruises and swollen ankles.

He carried her valise inside, arranged for a room, then led her there. "How do you feel now?"

"Better. Thanks."

His weird smile resembled a sneer.

Her hand went to her throat, seeking the comfort of her talisman. It wasn't there. "If you took Dirk's opal, please give it back."

Sevil rubbed his pointed chin, as though deep in thought. "It must have been the stone."

"What?"

He stared, unfocused, beyond her. "I cast a spell for you to land in Paris, not England." He looked at her, his dark eyes refocused and probing. "Tell me, what power does the opal have?"

"I don't really know." Dirk had always believed it would guide her to him. Silently she prayed Sevil couldn't read her mind.

He pursed his lips and furrowed his brow before he changed subjects. "The rooms here are unnumbered. Your friend and her husband are lodged behind the second door on your right as you approach the stairs. Enjoy your visit." With a snap of his fingers, Sevil vanished.

Anxious to see Kacy, Jennifer glanced in a mirror on the dull green wall and discovered she didn't look as bad as she expected. Had Sevil taken care of her appearance, along with her bumps and achy joints? This magic business was something else. Even the blue gown that she'd slept in last night was no longer wrinkled. She shrugged the cape off, clutched the reticule, now stuffed with money, and found Kacy's door.

A middle-aged woman answered her knock.

"Is the Countess in?" Jennifer asked. "If she is, I'm her friend, and I'd like very much to see her."

Before the woman could reply, Kacy rushed forward.

"Jennifer!" Kacy pulled her inside and threw her arms around her. "I'm so glad to see you." She drew away to look at her. "How in the world did you get here?"

"It's a long story." Jennifer smiled at Kacy, then at the man she assumed must be her husband, who watched them with undisguised curiosity. "Maybe we should go to my room, so we can talk in private," she whispered.

"This is a large suite, and we have plenty of privacy," Kacy said. "But first, let me introduce you to our nanny and Clay. I'm sure he'll enjoy hearing everything."

Kacy's husband was as tall, dark, and handsome as she had described. From the look in his kind, green eyes, Jennifer knew Kacy had told him all about her.

After the introductions, Kacy showed off her twins.

"How old are they?" Jennifer asked.

"Six months."

"They smile and gurgle," Jennifer observed.

"And they can sit up by themselves," Kacy boasted.

"Do they crawl?"

"Not yet."

After the nanny took over, Kacy led Jennifer to a different room. Jennifer explained how she had come to be in this time, and answered all Kacy's questions about those she loved in the future. Then Kacy caught her up on what had happened after she returned to this time, fourteen months ago.

"Can you tell me about Drake?" Jennifer finally asked.

"What do you want to know?"

"Everything."

"I don't know him very well, but Clay does. I'm sure he'll be happy to tell you anything you want to hear."

"I think he's Dirk," Jennifer said.

Kacy smiled. "I've wondered about that myself. Do you want to ask Clay what he thinks?"

"Not yet. I might not see Drake again."

"Tell me if you change your mind."

Jennifer smiled. "I will."

~ * ~

The hours sped by.

As did the days.

In addition to exploring Paris, Kacy and Jennifer had time for girl talk. One day as she bounced the twin baby girl on her knee, Jennifer confided to Kacy. "Every night I dream, or have a vision of Miranda and Catharine in the twenty-first century. It's like watching them on TV. I hear their conversations, see where they go, and know what they do. And everybody, except Catharine, thinks Miranda is me. She's having the time of her life charging things to my credit cards, and enjoying all the modern conveniences Catharine was at first too shy to try."

"Are you worried about her spending too much of your money?"

"Yes. Wouldn't you be?"

Kacy nodded.

"I wish I could stop her, but I don't know how."

"Maybe you'll be lucky, and Catharine will slow her down. She knows there's only so much money available each month, doesn't she?"

Jennifer nodded. "I hope she can slow her down. Unlike timid Catharine, Miranda is neither shy nor afraid. She appears to be in her element. Eager to experience as much as she can, as fast as she can. Catharine likes quiet evenings at home, but Miranda dashes around trying to pack a lifetime into each day and every night."

"You mean like we've been doing?" Kacy grinned.

"Yes." Jennifer laughed. "Like us." Then she said, "I've missed you so much, Kacy, and I cherish these conversations."

"Me, too. And I hope each one won't be our last."

When the nanny came in to take charge of the twins and put them down for their naps, Kacy announced, "Clay's taking us to tea."

"I don't need to go out with you every time you go somewhere," Jennifer objected.

"Nonsense," Kacy said. "Clay and I want you to join us for every outing, adventure, meal and tea. This might be our only chance to see each other in this lifetime."

The reminder that she could be hurtled back to her own time any minute sobered Jennifer. "I'd like to spend more time with the twins."

Kacy smiled. "I'm delighted you feel that way."

Jennifer smiled too. "I've fallen in love with them, and I want to hold them every chance I get. They're so responsive, and it's such fun when they smile and coo back at me."

"I know," Kacy said. "Clay and I marvel at every new thing they do."

"I'm so glad you're happy."

Kacy smiled. "Me, too."

Jennifer's thoughts drifted to Drake. Did he miss her as much as she missed him? "I'm ready to talk to Clay about Drake."

"Come on then." Kacy drew her to the other room, where Clay waited to take them to tea.

After they were settled at a small table in the cafe downstairs, Jennifer asked, "How long have you known Drake?"

"We met at Oxford, about ten years ago."

"How well do you know him?"

"Well enough to tell you that he changed about three years ago, and yes, I think he could be the man you loved in the future."

Jennifer's heart pounded. Not in her wildest imaginings had she expected Clay to agree with her. "H-o-w did he change?"

"He used to be somber, serious, unapproachable. Now he's far more approachable, and he deals with Miranda and Prudence differently. He always gave them anything they wanted just because he didn't want to be bothered. Now he considers their requests, and gives only what he thinks they need or deserve. Personally, I don't think they deserve his benevolence. They've both taken advantage of his wealth. I can't imagine why Drake agreed to wed Miranda."

"I think the wizard, Sevil, who switched places with Miranda and I, tricked him," Jennifer said.

Clay nodded, his blue eyes troubled. "If the wizard doesn't switch you again soon, you may have to marry Drake."

Jennifer's heart pounded and her pulse raced like mad. "If he's Dirk, I'm already his wife."

~ * ~

Drake had just finished eating supper at the dower house with his grandmother when the butler stepped into the room. "Pardon the intrusion, Your Grace."

"What is it, Higgins?" Drake's grandmother asked.

The butler spoke to Drake. "Your man, Olvan, is here and requests an immediate audience, Your Grace."

"Show him into the lounge," Drake directed, wondering what had brought Olvan here at this late hour. His grandmother would be disappointed if she didn't see Olvan, so Drake said, "We'll join him there."

After the butler bowed out, Drake assisted his plump little grandmother from her chair and offered his arm.

As they strolled to the lounge, Lucilla asked, "How are things between you and Miranda?"

"At the moment I don't know where she is."

"I thought she went to London for the final fittings on her wedding finery, and to charge her heart's desires at London's finest shops."

"I thought that as well, however she isn't at my town house in Chelsea, nor is she with Prudence, and she dismissed her governess over a week ago."

"I wouldn't expect her to be with her sister. Prudence harbors a tremendous dislike for Miranda, and I must say I'm relieved she won't be attending the wedding."

Drake didn't comment. He had always believed Prudence was at the root of people misjudging Miranda, but Prudence had lost her husband a few years ago and he had tried to be sympathetic, so he never accused her of such vicious behavior.

In the lounge Lucilla sat in her favorite gold velvet chair. "You won't cancel the wedding, will you, Drake?"

He sat across from her, on the gold settee.

"No. Miranda fancies being a duchess. Like a number of women I can name, she covets the title."

"If she displeases you so, you needn't marry her."

"One lady is as good as another, Grandmother."

"That's not true." A gentle smile crinkled the laugh lines at the edges of her blue eyes. "Your marriage to Helen was a grave mistake. I don't wish to see you make another. If you don't think Miranda can make you happy, perhaps you shouldn't wed her."

They had been over this before. It was the only bone of contention between them. "As you know, I didn't intend to marry again," he repeated as he always did.

"You have both a duty and an obligation to produce an heir," she reminded as she always did. "Our call on Boyden last week didn't look promising. He may never walk again. And you do yourself an injustice by presuming you cannot love Miranda. I'm certain she'll do her best to please you. She truly is a sweet gel."

Recalling the days at his lodge last week, Drake silently agreed. Without her memories, Jennifer Miranda delighted him, and he didn't doubt she could please him.

When he said nothing, his grandmother added, "I think the reason I'm still alive may be to see my great-grandchild."

Drake expected her health to deteriorate anytime, and disliked disagreeing with her, which is why he had gone along with her suggestion for a huge wedding. He suspected Miranda had finagled her into taking on the preparations, but he hadn't discouraged her because his grandmother acted pleased to be in charge.

Lucilla lowered her eyes and folded her hands as a quiet tap on the door announced Olvan's arrival.

Higgins opened the door, then stepped aside.

Olvan entered, his battered cap in his hands.

"Is there a problem at the lodge?" Drake asked.

"Ah dinna think it be a problem, but ah thought mayhap ye oughta know the lass be back."

Something akin to excitement pulsed through Drake.

"When did she arrive?"

"Affer dark. She looked tired, but the bruises 'pear to be gone. I put her to bed a'fore I left."

His grandmother gave Drake a smile filled with love. "Could this mysterious lass be our missing Miranda?"

Drake nodded, unwilling to upset his grandmother by explaining Miranda had climbed a tree in the woods, been struck by lightning, fallen and apparently lost her memories.

"Excuse me for cutting the evening short, Grandmother. I must go see Miranda."

"Of course you must."

Anxious to discover whether she had regained her memories, he kissed his grandmother's wrinkled cheek and said quietly, "Pleasant dreams, my dear."

"I shall dream of holding and spoiling my great-grandchild."

When he frowned, his grandmother's smile grew. Because he didn't want to say something that might upset her, he left without speaking again.

From the dower house he rushed to Stonemeade's stable.

Where the devil had Miranda been for the last six days? Not in London at his town home. After he visited Boyden, Drake had spent three days in London. If Miranda returned, his staff had strict orders to notify him.

In the stable, he ordered a lad to saddle Quicksilver. The stallion would have him at the lodge in fifteen minutes, more or less.

Ten

Denial and Regret

Still surprised Sevil had whisked her back to England, Jennifer lay in Drake's bed in the dark cottage. The wizard had led her to believe he intended to return her to her own time. Instead he had dropped her near Drake's cottage. At least she wouldn't be totally dependent on him now, because she had money. The reticule and valise Sevil had provided, landed with her.

Beneath the thin wool blankets, she shivered when somebody opened the door and let a cold breeze in. Expecting Drake, she rolled over, unafraid. Footsteps approached the bed.

Drake struck a match and lit a candle. The golden flame burned between them.

"Hello, young lady."

"Hello yourself." Swamped by relief, she stared at the familiar mole under his left eye.

"I should be upset with you," he said. "You've been gone six days."

"I didn't have much choice. Sevil took me away."

Drake hiked a brow. "Did he bring you back as well?"

"Yes. Well, sort of. He dropped me nearby."

Drake's brows hiked higher. "Dropped you?"

"Yes. You know, from the sky, like last time."

"I see." But he didn't look like he saw at all. He looked perplexed.

Olvan had persuaded her to lie down, but now Jennifer felt awkward. "I guess I shouldn't be in your bed."

"A man who finds a lovely lady in his bed would be a fool to complain."

Jennifer laughed. "I don't feel lovely. I feel ballistic."

Drake's brows dipped in puzzlement. "Ballistic?"

Why had she said that? Puzzled her mind scrambled for an explanation.

"That's a new science that deals with motion and impact." She held her breath, hoping that would satisfy him.

It must have because he asked, "Where have you been?"

"With Kacy and Clay. In Paris."

Drake sat on the edge of the narrow bed. Jennifer's pulse, already racing, shifted to a much faster rhythm. "In Paris?" he repeated, his eyes boring into hers in the candlelight.

"Yes," she said, her heart racing.

"Presumably you know I'll ask Clay to verify your claim."

She nodded. "He—the Earl, is a wonderful man."

"Yes, he is," Drake agreed.

For a few seconds all they did was stare. Jennifer wished Drake would touch her. Kiss her. Then she wished for more—that he remembered her. She cleared her throat. "I guess I should find someplace else to stay."

"It's too late to travel tonight. You may stay here."

"I'm no longer economically disadvantaged. I have..."

"What?"

"Money. I have money now."

"Where did you get it?"

"From Sevil."

Drake raised his hand and smoothed his mustache. "Why did he give you money?"

"Because I don't have any, and Miranda's spending mine."

"What?" Drake's shout reverberated through the cottage.

Jennifer licked her lips. "I need to explain. We, Miranda and I, apparently switched places. Sevil did it, without bothering to ask me. Miranda's in America with my roommate. That's why I'm here. And my name really is Jennifer Quinlane."

"Preposterous." Drake stood and shook his head, as though to negate her words. "*You* are Miranda." He stomped away, then turned. "You must be overly tired."

"I am tired," Jennifer admitted, releasing a sigh. He didn't believe her, but she didn't know how to convince him. "I'm cold, too."

"Shall I build a fire?"

"I'd appreciate one."

~ * ~

Drake bent and busied himself with the task. He had a number of questions he wanted answered. Foremost was why she claimed she had switched places with herself—or rather some fictitious American. And what had she meant by economically disadvantaged? And ballistic? How did she come up with such odd phrases and words?

When fire flamed from the logs, he turned. She had sat up, the bed covers drawn all the way to her neck. He wondered what she wore beneath them.

He forced his mind off that, then frowned. How did she know Clay and Kacy were in Paris? Had Josian shown her the letter Clay posted before they went on holiday? It wouldn't be the first time his secretary did something Drake didn't approve. But Josian was Prudence's friend, and he rarely spoke to Miranda so why would he share that information with her?

To humor her, Drake asked, "How long were you with Clay and Kacy?"

"Six days."

"You could not possibly spend six in Paris. It takes considerable time to travel there and back."

"Sevil travels in minutes, not hours or days."

Unable to believe that unlikely tale, Drake asked, "What did you discuss with Clay and Kacy?"

Jennifer shrugged. "Girl talk mostly."

The bed covers slid off her shoulders. Drake didn't know whether to be thankful or disappointed to see her fully clothed in a fashionable gown of deep rose that he hadn't seen before.

"Could we continue this interrogation later?" she asked. "I really am tired. I didn't get much sleep in Paris and being whirled through the air drained me."

"We must talk now."

She gave him a weary, wary look, and he found himself softening.

"What do we need to discuss?"

"You."

"Why?"

He knew he shouldn't put off reminding her they were to wed in little more than a week. But from somewhere deep inside, he recalled reading or hearing that if a person had amnesia, the best way to deal with it was to let them remember on their own. He must act with care and treat her gently.

"I worried about you," he said softly. "And I do not wish you to disappear again."

"Do you think I had a choice?"

"I don't know what to think, except that you are my responsibility and I must take care of you."

"I'm not your responsibility," she disagreed.

"Every young lady is the responsibility of her guardian, and I assumed that role in your life a number of years ago."

Jennifer laughed.

"What do you find amusing?"

"Me," she said. "And you too, Drake. Do you assume responsibility for every unchaperoned girl you meet?"

He stiffened. Why did he allow her to rattle him? "Only those in need. You are in need, aren't you, my lady?"

"You know I am," she said, her humor gone. "And please forgive me if I offended you. This is an unnerving experience."

"Being with me unnerves you?"

It did, but she didn't want to admit that. "Being jumped through the air and whirled through the sky, and not knowing when the horrifying experience might happen again."

"You cannot expect me to believe some wizard whirled you through the sky."

"I know it sounds farfetched, but that's how Sevil transported me here last week, and from Paris today."

For a few seconds, Drake remained quiet, his arms folded. Finally he said, "I should engage a chaperon for you."

"No," she protested. If Miranda didn't return, Jennifer didn't want to be stuck with somebody who might boss her around and tell her what she could and couldn't do. "That isn't necessary. Sevil gave me money. And I can take care of myself. Honest. I've been doing it—"

"For how long?" Drake asked, his stare full of disbelief.

"More than three years." That's when she graduated from high school, and her trust fund had become available. *The trust fund Miranda was now spending as though it belonged to her, although Catharine was trying to slow her down and had explained there was only so much money available each month.* Nightly visions continued to give Jennifer glimpses of them. Miranda loved being in the future. She also loved her freedom. But her quarrel with Sevil hadn't been resolved. What had they quarreled about? Is that why Sevil hadn't taken Jennifer back?

Drake jarred her thoughts when he asked, "How old are you?"

"It isn't polite to ask a lady's age, but I'll answer anyway. I'm almost twenty-one. How old are you?"

"Beyond the age of chatting like a simpleton to the young lady to whom I am betrothed."

"I'm not your betrothed," Jennifer gasped. "Miranda is. But I envy her."

"You envy her?" Drake looked startled. "Why?"

Tempted to admit the real reason—that he was Dirk, Jennifer said, "Because I think you might be a fun husband."

"Fun?" Drake scoffed. "To expect a husband to be fun is not merely foolish, it's an insult."

"No, it's a compliment," Jennifer disagreed and yawned. She couldn't help it. She hadn't recovered from all the hours of sleep she'd missed while in Paris. When she'd first come back here to Drake's cottage, she'd been too much on edge to relax, let alone sleep. But now, for some reason, she felt totally relaxed and very drowsy.

"Would you mind if I crash now, Drake?"

Again he looked startled. "Crash?"

"Sleep."

"No. Lie down." It sounded like an order... an angry one.

"I'll move to the couch—sofa."

"Stay where you are."

"Then where will you sleep?"

"On the settee."

"It's too small for you." She wrapped a blanket around her shoulders, tiptoed barefooted across the cold floor and plopped on the sofa. With Drake now home, she felt safe and secure. She closed her eyes. In a matter of seconds she was oblivious to all conscious thought.

~ * ~

Drake couldn't summon enough gumption to move. He couldn't even walk to the bed. His body rebelled against enforced celibacy, and made its needs urgently known. While he stood like a clod-pated fool, Jennifer kicked the blanket off. Her bare shapely legs trebled his desire. Maybe he should have kissed her when he sat beside her. That might have doused his lust. But the memory of their previous kisses denied any possibility of disappointment.

It took every ounce of willpower he possessed to cover her and walk away.

He knew spending another night alone with her in his hunting lodge would be improper. But she looked so peaceful he didn't have the heart to disturb her for the short journey to his ancestral mansion. In any event, he didn't want her out of his sight. She might disappear again.

The bed smelled like her. Sweet. Womanly. Sexy. The dark hours stretched ahead of him. He couldn't imagine why she claimed to be someone else. He shouldn't have put off telling her she had apparently lost her memories and they were to wed next week. In the morning he would take her home, or to his grandmother's where she could be chaperoned around the clock.

Those decisions made, he closed his eyes.

But he didn't get much sleep.

~ * ~

Daylight filtered through the two uncurtained windows and Jennifer idly wondered if Drake thought his cottage so isolated that curtains were unnecessary. She'd like to make some to cheer the austere cabin, but Miranda would likely perform that wifely chore.

Disappointment sloshed through Jennifer when she discovered Drake wasn't in bed. Where had he slept?

She slid off the sofa, grabbed her cloak, and headed out the door, combing her fingers through her long, tangled hair.

In the stable she didn't see Drake, but Olvan gave her a toothy grin. "Gud mornin', lass."

"Good morning." Jennifer smiled as he turned from Awesome, who pranced around as though on display.

"How ye feel today, lass?"

"Much better, thank you." Jennifer nuzzled the underside of Mordora's jaw. A wave of pleasure rolled through her when the mare sniffed and trustingly leaned her head against her cheek.

"Have you seen Drake this morning, Mr. McDougal?"

"Aye," the Scot said.

"I'm here," Drake announced behind her.

Jennifer turned her head, and lost her breath. Dressed in tan trousers and a tweed jacket with a brown shirt, his light blond hair and mustache contrasted with his suntanned skin. He was so handsome! And he was Dirk. How she wished he remembered her, and that she hadn't lost the opal.

"Did you sleep in the stable?" she asked.

He shook his head, then nodded at Olvan, apparently a cue for the Scot to leave, because he did.

"I slept inside with you," Drake said when they were alone. "I trust you slept well."

"Like a baby," she said. "How about you?"

He reached out to fasten the blue cape beneath her chin. "I've had better nights."

"I hope I didn't disturb you."

Amusement glittered in his eyes. "As my betrothed, in a matter of days you may disturb me as often as you wish in the night."

Jennifer blinked and stopped muzzling the underside of Mordora's jaw. *A matter of days? How many? And when would Miranda return?*

The mare snorted. Drake cast an annoying glare her way before he said, "Am I to assume you do not wish to marry me?"

Jennifer rubbed her stiff neck, trying to decide what to say. "I told you last night that I think it would be fun to marry you, but I'm not Miranda."

"Yes you are."

"I don't have any of her memories."

Drake reached for her arm. "I'll take you home. When you see your own things and familiar surroundings, perhaps your memories will return." He glanced at a saddle hanging on the wall. "Are you fit to ride?"

Jennifer shook her head. She hadn't ridden for a long time, and was way out of practice. "I'd prefer to walk."

"That will take twice as long."

"Feel free to ride if you wish," she said sweetly.

He scowled and led her outside, leaving the already saddled white stallion behind in the stable. "Lead the way," he said when they reached the narrow footpath that accommodated single file only.

"I'd rather you led," Jennifer said. "I don't know where we're going."

He dropped her arm and stomped ahead.

As she followed him through the woods, her thoughts wandered. She wanted to tell Drake they had been married in the future, and in her heart they still were husband and wife. They had eloped as soon as she graduated from high school, but she'd lost him six tension-filled days later. They had consummated their marriage, but that was about all before her cousin Tyler pounded on their hotel door and announced, "Dad had a stroke. We have to fly home."

Jennifer's throat clogged. She'd spent hours at the hospital with Aunt Rachel and Tyler, waiting for Uncle Mac's condition to improve. The day it finally did, she called Dirk, and he'd offered to come pick her up. But he never did. Somebody broad-sided his car, on the driver's side. The air bag inflated, but ambulance workers had to pry his mangled body from the wreck.

Remembering how terrible life had been after Dirk's funeral, Jennifer swallowed. For a whole year she'd wished she were dead, too.

She sucked in some deep breaths, trying to calm herself. Now she was here with Dirk, but didn't know how to convince him they'd known each other in previous lives. He obviously didn't remember her or any other lives. And since she didn't expect to stay here much longer, maybe she should let him believe she was Miranda.

Tired of unproductive thoughts and curious about their destination, she asked, "Does Miranda have her own room in your home?"

"Of course." Drake paused until Jennifer caught up. An odd look tormented his eyes.

Without warning he hauled her into his arms, and lowered his head. Delightful shivers trembled through her as his lips claimed hers. Stunned at first, she didn't respond. Then she responded with such enthusiasm, it should have embarrassed her.

The richness of his mouth awakened passions she had thought dead. She reveled in the hard strength of his chest pressing ever closer to hers. For a few dazzling seconds he deepened the kiss. For the next answering seconds, she gave herself completely to the wonder of him. She twined her arms around his neck, urging him closer, trying to show him how she felt by answering his passion.

He ended the kiss abruptly, before she'd had her fill. Too startled to unwrap her arms, she moaned a protest when he shoved her away. Bewildered, she touched her tingling lips with her fingertips.

"You shouldn't have done that," she said quietly.

"That is precisely what I should have done, and a good deal sooner. Where in the devil did you learn to kiss like that?"

"Where did you?"

Standing tall, proud and arrogant, he blustered, "That is not a proper question for a lady to ask a man."

"What's good for the goose is good for the gander," she disagreed with an airy flick of her head.

He seized her shoulders and shook her. "I will hear your answer, Jennifer Miranda, and I want the truth. Who taught you to kiss?"

"You."

"I did not." Drake gave her a dark frown before he turned and trounced down the footpath, once again leaving her to follow.

She glared at his back, so caught up with mutinous thoughts that Sevil caught her unaware. He hooked a slick white-sleeved arm around her waist and covered her mouth with his clawed paw.

"Oh, no!" she wailed, "Not again," just before he jumped her away.

~ * ~

Curious about the muffled wail, Drake turned. He didn't see her. Drat the girl... lady... woman.

Forgetting his decision to call her Jennifer, he shouted, "Miranda, where are you?"

A gust of wind blew dirt in his face. He sheltered his eyes with his arm and tore through the woods, calling, "Miranda, where the devil are you? Answer me!"

She didn't reply.

After a fruitless search in every direction, concern replaced his anger.

He returned to the lodge, harboring a small hope that she might be there.

"Jennifer Miranda is gone," he told Olvan. "Did she return here?"

The Scot's solemn expression confirmed what Drake's lonely heart already knew. "No, she dinna, but a strange lookin' creature left this message fer ye."

"What did he look like?" Drake seized the message in Olvan's gnarled fist.

"Like nothing I ever saw bafore. His body, it be covered by a stark-white one piece suit that outlined the shape of his skeletal torso, and his head, it be completely encased by a clear bubble, fastened to the collar of a slick, white tunic, and his hands, they be paws with claws."

Unable to imagine such a creature, even though Jennifer had already described him, Drake asked, "Did he speak the Queen's English?"

"He didna speak a'tall."

Drake ripped the seal off the message and read, "You may rescue your betrothed at the Shaverly's masquerade on Wednesday next."

Tomorrow night. The masquerade ball Miranda had pestered him to attend with her. The ball he had refused to attend.

Prior to Helen and Albert's deaths, Drake had rarely missed a soiree or a ball. Now he shunned socials. But how could he not go? The wedding was Thursday, following the next.

Eleven

The Masquerade

Drake leaned a negligent shoulder against a white pillar, watching costumed couples whirl around the gaily decorated ballroom. Masked ladies in colorful wide-hooped gowns, made of satins and silks and trimmed with laces, flirted with masked men garbed in elaborate wigs, garish pantaloons and waistcoats. A group of men boasting white knee-high stockings and black pointed shoes nibbled on succulent aperitifs. Other guests sipped drinks from leaded crystal goblets. Many ladies tapped their feet to the music. A few spoke too loudly, to be heard over the din and laughter.

If not for the message, Drake wouldn't be here. On the rare occasions he attended a social, he never danced. Although his broken leg had healed ages ago and he walked without a limp, he would not risk embarrassment by a possible stumble on the dance floor.

So far he hadn't seen a soul who remotely resembled his betrothed. Waiting for the unmasking at midnight held no appeal. But he couldn't leave. The wedding was a mere eight days away, and he might not have a bride. When he found her, he wouldn't allow her out of his sight again, even if he had to chain her to his side.

He had been tempted to call the wedding off. With Parliament about to reconvene, however, he needed to speak in the House of Lords. Britain and Afghanistan had joined against Persia in the Treaty of Peshawar, and he intended to add his verbal support. A broken betrothal would, once again, embroil him in the heart of a scandal. And Jennifer Miranda, would presumably, raise an enormous fuss and make the scandal worse when her memories returned.

In his current frame of mind, Drake didn't wish to socialize. To avoid being drawn into a conversation, he readjusted his white half-mask, and strolled to the far end of the ballroom where he stopped by another pillar, away from the music and noise. The dim corridor suited his dour mood.

He should have married Jennifer Miranda off as soon as she left the finishing academy. But the thought of another man possessing, even so much as touching her, spawned quick stabs of jealousy. She belonged to him. *Dash it, where had that thought come from?*

He slid his hand into his white trouser pocket and withdrew the opal he had removed from her neck after she fell from the tree. In his palm, the opal changed colors, and an illusive memory of a young girl with speckled green eyes surfaced. Where had Jennifer gotten the stone? And why did he feel as though it belonged to him? Riddled with guilt for taking it and not telling her, he slid the stone back in his pocket. He must return it when he found her, although for the life of him, he couldn't understand why she'd worn the stone around her throat, rather than one of the expensive necklaces she'd conned him into buying.

Sometimes when he thought about her, he could almost smell the flowery fragrance of her skin. Lord, he could smell her even now. Knowing that at any moment the sweet aroma would disappear, along with her illusive image that now wandered in and out of his dreams on a nightly basis, he inhaled deeply. The flowery scent wafted closer.

He turned his head. And damn near choked. Jennifer stood behind him... And her two-piece skimpy red costume covered practically nothing!

"How did you get here?" he asked, stunned. And, although they stood in a sparsely lit corridor away from the rowdy crowd, he shifted his body to shield her from other prying eyes. His own were plastered on her costume, what little there was of it, and he found himself fully aroused.

She unclenched her fists and passed one hand wearily over her masked eyes. "Sevil brought me."

Drake glanced beyond her. A man scurried away, his voluminous black cape flapping behind him. Drake's hackles raised as jealous images converged. "Is that man Sevil?"

She nodded and swayed. Drake reached out to steady her.

The red costume consisted of shimmering layers of gossamer fabric, so sheer in some places he could see through them. Her midriff—the space between her slender waist and voluptuous breasts—was bare.

Lord, even her navel was exposed! The low slung waistband of her pantaloons clung to her slender hips and billowed around her legs like a soft cloud. Snug at her ankles, the multiple layers did nothing to conceal the outline of her shapely legs.

On her small feet were red sandals with lots of straps. The red half blouse with its low neckline barely contained her breasts and exposed the valley between them, while the long sleeves, made of a single layer of sheer fabric, exposed her arms.

Thank God nobody was nearby. He had never before seen such garb. It looked as though it belonged in a sultan's private harem, not in public, especially in London at an affair where prominent members of the *ton* could view it and label the wearer a loose woman.

Drake tore his gaze from the indecent costume. A bright red half-mask covered the upper half of Jennifer's face, but nothing could conceal her lovely speckled eyes.

"Where are we?" she asked, her eyes dazed, her luxuriant hair streaming down her back in wild disarray.

"At a masquerade."

Her costume left little to his imagination, and he hated the thought of any other man seeing her in it.

As though she read his mind, she said, "Can you get me out of here before anybody else sees me in this... get-up?"

"Yes."

She swayed again. Drake scooped her up and whispered, "Gather your hair in front of your shoulders and turn your face toward me while I carry you past the crowd."

As soon as she did, he whipped his white cape around her scantily clad body and strode swiftly outside, ignoring the stares that followed them.

Lighted torches attached to posts made it easy to summon his carriage. "Drive us home," he ordered Winslow, his driver, before he set Jennifer inside and climbed in after her.

She shivered when he sat beside her. "Are you cold?"

"Yes."

Realizing again how little her costume covered, also how frigid the interior of the carriage had grown, he unfastened his white cape and wrapped it around her.

"Thanks." She shivered again.

He took his mask off, then hers, before he lifted her onto his lap. His aroused body reacted to her feminine curves and the sweet enticing scent of her skin.

"Where did you get your costume?"

Snuggled against him, she said sleepily, "Sevil snapped his fingers and I found myself dressed in it."

Gazing down at her, Drake tucked a long lock of hair behind her ear. "Did he harm you?"

"No."

"Where have you been?"

"At Havenhurst."

"Were the Earl and Countess home?" Drake asked, wondering if he could believe her.

"No. Kacy and Clay are still in Paris, but their butler Montfort let me in and made me feel welcome."

She knew the butler's name. "Was the wizard Sevil with you?"

"Only long enough to jump and dump me there last night. Then he showed up a few minutes ago and whirled me here." She reached up and touched Drake's cheek, tenderly. "I'm sorry if I embarrassed you. I didn't want to make a spectacle of myself, but I didn't have a choice."

"I believe you," he said, surprised that he did.

"Thanks." Then she asked, "Where're we going?"

"Home."

"That sounds nice." She spread his white cape to cover him too and curled her hand around his neck to hold the cape in place. "I don't want you to catch a chill."

A mental picture of her whirling through the air flashed. He shook the image away. Concern took its place. "Are you all right?"

"Yes. But Sevil's mode of travel zaps my strength."

Zaps? Mode of travel? Drake didn't know what 'zaps' meant, but he decided it must mean she had no energy. "Then rest, my dear."

"Drake?"

"Yes."

"Thanks for rescuing me."

"You're welcome."

A few moments later her limp weight confirmed she had fallen asleep. Accustomed to the near dark, Drake gazed at her, nestled in his arms. Yesterday he had noted that the nasty lump on her temple was gone, as were the bruises on her chin, and arms and hands. Still amazed she had survived the fall last week, he wondered if she had, in truth, fallen again yesterday and spent last night at Havenhurst.

The man who had brought her to the masquerade didn't resemble the creature Olvan had described. Did she need protection from two men? Or a man and a wizard? Drake recalled she'd said Sevil changed shapes... another story too difficult to fathom.

When her arm that held his cape slipped from his neck and slid down his chest, lusty thoughts took over. Her round derriere pressed against his groin, while her fragrant scent filled his senses. In the near dark he stared at her face. Why had he failed to notice her long, spiky lashes and delicate features before? He half regretted covering her with his cape. Garbed in the sexy costume, she had truly been a sight to behold.

He didn't doubt she would please him. Whenever he touched her, she made him feel alive. And he hadn't felt alive for a long time. So long, in fact, he couldn't remember when he last had before Jennifer fell from the tree.

As they rode through London's dark streets, another refrain from that strange song echoed through his mind. *Lay your warm and tender body next to mine.* He'd never thought about that song until she fell from the tree. Why did he think about it now? Where had it come from?

His thoughts turned to how to protect her from Sevil, and the creature that had abducted her yesterday, whether they were one or two men. He must keep her close, at least until the formal ceremony, or he might not have a bride. A plan began to form. It could create a scandal, unless they kept it a secret. The plan would protect her, also satisfy him. And if he didn't find satisfaction soon, he would go mad.

Winslow stopped the carriage and climbed down from the driver's perch. When he opened the door, Drake glanced at his Chelsea town home. He had given scant thought to gossip when he carried Jennifer from the masquerade. His concentration had been fully occupied with wayward, erotic fantasies, and a compelling desire to have her all to himself.

He made a swift decision to put his plan in action.

"Drive us around to the stable, Winslow."

His driver looked surprised by the order, but all he said was, "Yes, Your Grace," before he turned to obey.

A few minutes later when Winslow opened the carriage door again, Drake said, "Have a carriage without the ducal crest put to, instruct Teeny to pack some gowns for her mistress, and have Bevins pack a bag for me. Also tell Lenore to bring pillows and blankets to the stable."

Winslow eyed Jennifer, still asleep on Drake's lap.

"Make haste, Winslow. We have miles to travel tonight. I intend to head north."

"Of course, Your Grace." Winslow turned and walked briskly away, barking orders as he went.

As Drake prepared to move to the other carriage, his stout London housekeeper, Lenore, rushed into the stable and dashed to the open ducal carriage. Her gaze went from Drake to the unconscious bundle in his arms.

"Did something dreadful happen to Miss Miranda?"

"No. She's merely exhausted. Apparently she traveled a great distance in a short time."

He didn't intend to explain more than that. His loyal, anxious housekeeper, however, never missed an opportunity to speak her mind.

"Deary me. I know she tries your patience at times, Your Grace, but your betrothed truly is a sweet gel."

Drake knew his London servants adored her, but only during the week past had he discovered they disliked Prudence because she often belittled Jennifer Miranda in front of them.

Lenore clucked her tongue. "Mayhap you should bring the Miss inside and allow the lot of us to pamper her."

"No," Drake grumbled. "I intend to take her where she can rest. In quiet and solitude."

"May I ask why she cannot rest here?"

"No, Lenore, you may not." His impatient tone brooked no argument. "Where are the pillows and blankets?"

"They shall be here momentarily, along with her gowns." Lenore folded her arms across her ample bosom. Her expression indicated she didn't approve, but she had the good sense not to voice her opinion out loud.

To Drake's relief, Jennifer slept through the move to the smaller carriage. Lenore, ever helpful, climbed in and arranged the pillows to her satisfaction.

"There now, lay her here," she instructed.

Drake wanted to throttle his efficient housekeeper. He had intended to hold Jennifer. But he had to admit that foolish notion would likely numb his legs and arms before an hour passed.

By the time Lenore climbed out of the carriage, Drake's valet, Bevins, had entered the stable. Half a dozen curious servants were lined up beside him. Did the entire household intend to join him before he left?

"Did Miss Miranda suffer an accident?" a plump scullery maid asked.

"No. She's merely exhausted," he repeated.

Teeny, her maid, then asked, "Do ya needs me ta go wiff ya, Yer Grace?"

"No. Go back inside, and seek your beds. I do not intend to dally half the night in the stable."

"Do you wish me to remain in London?" Bevins asked, as the subdued servants turned to do as bidden.

"Yes. Tell Josian I wish him to join me at Stonemeade when he completes the business at hand."

Bevins raised heavyset brows. "Do you plan to travel to Stonemeade tonight, Your Grace?"

"No."

"May I ask where you are going, milord?"

"I'm in no mood to be questioned," Drake snapped, then barked at Winslow. "Let us be off."

As the carriage pulled away, Drake scowled. Good Lord, what had prompted him to snap at Bevins? He glanced out the window at his valet. When their eyes met, Bevins grinned. Drake heaved a sigh of relief. If he had offended him overmuch, Bevins would be wearing a frown instead of that smarmy grin.

When the carriage turned a corner, the motion threatened to land Jennifer on the floor. Giving in to the urge to be nearer, Drake moved across the aisle, raised the pillow under her head, and slid beneath it. Decency required that he keep his hands to himself, but he ached to touch her. Once he did, his body throbbed with the most urgent need. He forced his hands away from her face and concentrated on holding them absolutely still. The effort made him stiff, in all the wrong places. His body couldn't endure much more torture without relief.

After they left London Proper, Jennifer stirred and opened her eyes. "I feel safe when you hold my hand, Drake." She groped around until his hand closed over hers. "Nobody will ever believe I fell from the sky three times and found my own white knight every single time."

"I wear no shiny armor," he said quietly.

"Doesn't matter. You're dressed all in white; you ride a spectacular white horse. Besides, you're gallant, and you smell divine."

Drake smiled as his heart reacted to her praise.

"I'm sorry to be so tired, but I can't seem to help it." She closed her eyes and slept again.

Drake found it impossible to relax. His plan had been set in motion. All that remained was to convince his intended to go along with the plans. He didn't expect her to disagree. With or without her memories, she had nothing to lose, and everything to gain. Sooner or later, she would be his bride. It might as well be sooner.

Twelve

The Plan

At the inn Drake put Jennifer to bed and stretched out beside her, on top of the bed covers. He slept fitfully and woke up when she kicked the covers off.

He climbed off the bed and lit a candle. With the sheer red fabric twisted and bunched around her arms and legs, she looked uncomfortable. Convinced he was doing her a favor, he took the liberty of unfastening the flimsy half-blouse. His hands shook while he parted it and his breath caught in the back of his throat when he exposed her breasts.

He moved the candle closer. Angry red welts, created by the scratchy fabric, marred her smooth skin. Concerned, he removed the bottom of the costume, too. Surprise whipped through him when he discovered she wore no undergarments of any kind.

While he stared at her in the altogether, his blood heated and his body burgeoned out of control. Unable to resist the desire to touch her, he caressed the scratches on her back, then felt like a wretch for taking advantage of her while she slept.

With great difficulty, he mastered the urge to fondle her more fully and went to search for a bed gown. But all Teeny had packed were day and evening gowns.

He hated to cover Jennifer's loveliness, but knew if he didn't, he might lose his battle to act honorably. His body throbbed with repressed need, and it required great fortitude to take his shirt off and ease it onto her slender body without fondling or waking her. As soon as he finished, he walked away. Being near her was like being too near a fire.

To regain his control he sat in a chair and reminded himself she might not be as innocent as she looked. She kissed like an experienced maid. Why that bothered him was as much a mystery as her memory lapse and his fascination. He wouldn't have missed a moment of the recent time they had shared. She'd kept him entertained, and although he damned himself for it, he was delighted she hadn't regained her memories.

As he watched her face in slumber, an odd thought struck him. Could he be falling in love with the little minx? Had he already fallen? If so, he must proceed with caution. It would never do for her to know he was smitten, that he wanted to cherish her for the rest of their lives.

Smiling, he added logs to the fire, then blew out the candle and went to lie beside his betrothed. He closed his eyes and enjoyed the awakening of new and wondrous emotions.

For the first time in a week, he allowed himself to wonder if she might truly be an American and not Miranda. The thought should have troubled him, yet it didn't. Whoever she was, she belonged to him, and he intended to wed her as soon as possible.

~ * ~

Jennifer had an itch. It started below her left shoulder blade and worked its way to the middle of her back. She rolled over and wiggled against the straw-filled mattress. That made the bed squeak, but didn't help the itch. In fact, it spread. In all directions.

"Is something wrong?" Drake's whisper sounded close.

"I have an itch I can't reach."

He rolled close. Only then did she realize he lay beside her. "Would you like me to scratch it?

Her pulse raced. She sucked in a quick breath. "That would be helpful."

"Where is it?"

Not trusting her voice, she whispered, "In the middle of my back."

He reached out. His fingers grazed her breast. She gasped, and he jerked away, as though burned. She doubted his hand felt hotter than her face.

"I'll roll over," she said, grateful for the near dark. A fire burned in the grate and she could make out the shape of most things. Nothing looked familiar, so she knew they weren't at his cottage.

"I'm ready now, Drake."

He touched her arm, then slid his hand slowly, almost cautiously, she thought, across her back, between her shoulder blades. "Here?"

"Yes."

He started to scratch. His touch felt like one long caress. A flood of yearning spiraled through her.

"Harder," she said, hoping that might take her mind off the erotic sensations his stroking fingers evoked.

His other hand joined the first. Intensely aware of the heat of his body so close to hers, she inhaled slowly, filling her lungs with his wonderful, unique scent. Dirk's scent. Her husband's scent.

"Does it still itch?" Drake asked.

"Yes." It seemed worse than ever now, and his touch created a different kind of itch, one deep inside her.

"The costume scratched your skin," he said. "That's why I took it off. I have a salve that might help your itch and the welts. I'll fetch it." He rolled off the bed.

She couldn't see his face clearly in the dim light, but she saw his bare shoulders and chest, and realized he didn't have a shirt on because she was wearing it. She knew by the feel and smell. He had undressed her again.

"This is becoming a habit," she said with droll humor.

"What?"

"Wearing practically nothing when I'm in your bed."

"I wouldn't mind if it continued."

A few charged moments passed while an image of him running his hands all over her surfaced. The itch on her back paled in comparison to the hunger inside her.

"I'm fine now," she fibbed when he returned.

He must not have believed her because he sat on the double bed and reached for her.

"Be still," he ordered when she scooted away.

She bumped into the wall and had no choice.

He raised the back of the shirt and rubbed salve on her welts. She tried to relax. He was right. The salve did help. In addition, his hands did marvelous things, and not just to her itch and the welts. His sensual strokes made it hard to breathe, and the passion she'd lived without for more than three years flared to life.

He finished applying salve, but continued to caress her skin. "Are you satisfied yet?"

"If that's what you are attempting to do, you're failing." As soon as the words left her mouth, Jennifer realized how wanton and flirtatious she sounded.

Drake chuckled as he moved his hands to her shoulders and turned her to face him. He was still chuckling when he kissed her.

Not knowing whether to be insulted or overjoyed, she kissed him back. Heady sensations stormed her senses, creating a burning sensation that vibrated deep inside.

Desire swiftly changed to churning need. She'd almost forgotten there could be so much feeling, so much wanting, so much yearning. She strained against him, giving more in that kiss than she had thought it possible to give.

A sudden vision interrupted her pleasure.

She saw Drake at his wedding, watching his bride walk down the aisle in a room filled with people.

Jennifer's eyes stung as tears threatened. She pushed against his chest and tore her mouth from his.

"What's wrong?" he demanded.

She didn't answer.

The vision continued. Standing beside a man who Jennifer instinctively knew was a vicar, Drake waited for his bride to reach him. Her gorgeous white gown had a long train, and although the bride looked a lot like her, a voluminous veil hid her face. Jennifer assumed she was Miranda. Drake smiled down at her, then placed his arm around her waist before they repeated their vows. Jennifer could almost feel his touch bolstering his bride's flagging courage. The vicar pronounced them man and wife. Drake raised his bride's veil. They kissed... and the vision ended.

Jennifer started to slide away. But once again, Drake came after her.

"What is it?" he asked, his voice quiet and husky, his warm breath fanning her cheek.

"I had a vision."

"Of what?"

"You and your wedding."

"And you were my bride." His husky voice seduced her senses. He found her chin with his hand and turned her mouth back up to his. "You have such sweet lips."

Jennifer's pulse raced. Her lips still tingled from the aborted kiss, her body from the feel of his hands on her.

"And you smell as good as you taste," he added, caressing her cheek, his lips inching close to hers again.

Her traitorous body went still. She knew in her heart she should resist him. It unnerved her that she couldn't.

When his mouth reclaimed hers, she coiled her arms back around his neck and melted against him. To do otherwise was beyond her. This kiss too turned out to be more than she bargained for, also more than she expected. Glorious sensations poured through her, melting her bones, turning them to liquid. She whimpered. To her own ears it sounded like a joyous submission.

Drake's hand skimmed over her breasts. Her nipples, covered only by his shirt, sprung to rigid attention. Tantalized by his wonderful scent, passion sizzled through her. The heady pleasure made her dizzy. With all the love she had stored up inside her, she responded, loving the feel of his bare flesh beneath her fingers.

When he laid down and pulled her with him, she didn't resist. But when he started to unbutton the shirt that covered her, she finally came to her senses. Another moment more and she'd let him do anything he pleased. For that matter, she'd encourage him, and enjoy every minute if it. This might be their only chance to be intimate.

But her heart knew one night would never be enough. And even though she believed she was his wife and had the right to sleep with him, she thought it would be unfair to Miranda to make love to her intended.

"We have to stop."

Drake pulled away. She still smelled his piney scent with every breath she drew. It could have been due to wearing his shirt, but she didn't think so. Every inch of her trembled with need. She wanted him so badly she nearly threw herself back into his arms and begged him to make love to her. It felt so right to be with him, and she knew if she didn't move away soon, she'd give in to the passion vibrating so strongly between them.

She started to sit up, intending to climb off the foot of the bed because she was on the side by the wall.

But he caught her, and brought her back to the middle of the mattress. When she tried to get away again, his hands captured her head and held it still while he placed tiny kisses all over her face. Moving his mouth to her ear, he whispered, "I want you."

Tendrils of pleasure enveloped her as he lifted strands of her hair and let them sift through his fingers before he scattered more seductive kisses across her cheeks and slowly worked his way toward her lips.

She could hardly breathe, let alone speak, but she forced herself to resist. *He was engaged to Miranda, and she could return any minute.*

"No—o."

"What's wrong?"

Jennifer dragged air into her lungs. "We can't do this. One of us must be sensible."

Drake shifted away and stared at the wall behind her. "Should I apologize?" His voice sounded strained.

"No." Her voice quivered and she shivered.

Although he didn't move for a timeless moment, he finally reached for her hands.

Curious, she let him hold them, ready to bolt at the least provocation.

"With or without your memories, I intend to wed you. Soon."

In the near dark she barely made out his features.

"But I'm not Miranda."

"It matters not. Whoever you are, I want you."

"Why?"

"If you would like another demonstration, I'd be delighted to accommodate you, my dear."

Her face heated again. "Is—passion the only reason?"

"No. Months ago I agreed to wed Miranda if I lost the horse race she suggested. And I did lose. Plans for the wedding have been six months in the making. Invitations were sent out more than a month ago. If the wedding is canceled, a scandal will ensue. I lived through one when my wife and my brother died; I do not wish to endure another. Whether you are Miranda or not, I have compromised your reputation and am honor-bound to marry you."

Speechless, Jennifer watched Drake dig something out of his pocket. Then he moved to sit beside her, so close his white trouser covered leg touched her bare thigh.

"You were wearing this the day you fell from the tree."

He dangled the opal by its chain. The stone caught the firelight and reflected all the colors of a rainbow. Jennifer resisted the urge to reach out and touch it.

"Although I knew I had no right to take it, I also felt compelled, as though it belonged to me. Every day I have examined it and tried to understand why. I still don't know."

Jennifer swiped at the sudden tears trickling down her cheeks. "I thought I'd lost it."

"It is important to you, then?"

"Yes. Very."

"Why?"

"Because I think it guided me to you."

He took her hand and placed the opal in her palm.

It felt warm and glowed in spite of the near dark. She had planned to return it to Dirk on the ninth day of their marriage as a sort of anniversary, to commemorate the day they'd met when she was nine years old. But they'd only been married five days, and she'd spent most of those at the hospital with Aunt Rachel and Tyler, waiting for Uncle Mac's condition to stabilize.

"Jennifer?"

She looked up from the opal.

"Are you all right?" Drake asked, still tenderly holding her hand.

She nodded and swallowed in an attempt to get her emotions under control.

"I wish to protect you, and I believe that if I keep you close, I may foil any attempt that might be made to take you away again. With that in mind, I suggest we elope to Gretna Green. Sevil and the creature who abducted you yesterday may look for you in London or Kent, but unless they are mind readers, I do not think they will look to the North."

"Sevil and the creature are one and the same. He shape-shifts. I told you, remember?"

"Be that as it may, I think we should elope."

Jennifer sighed and wished she knew what to do. Drake didn't believe Sevil shape-shifted. He didn't believe she had switched places with Miranda, either. Maybe if she waited till morning, Miranda would be back, and she wouldn't need to make a decision.

"Could I have some time to think about it?"

"You may." Drake stood and walked to the fireplace.

All Jennifer could see was his silhouette as she slipped the chain with the opal over her head and tucked it under his shirt. The stone warmed her chest as it always did, and a large piece of her heart, too. Dismayed by the thought that she might leave Drake, she punched a dent in the thick pillow and lay down.

As Drake sat in a chair, Jennifer's thoughts drifted to Dirk. Were they destined to find each other continually, but never fulfill their love?

Her only consolation when he had died so suddenly was the belief that she would see him again, if not in this life, then in another. Now she'd found him—in a different century. But he didn't recognize her. He didn't know he was Dirk or that he had lived in the twenty-first century. But her heart knew and ached because he didn't remember her.

Would Drake think she was crazy if she tried to explain? Or would he believe her? Afraid he wouldn't, she fingered the opal. Sevil indicated it had led her to Drake. But how long would she be allowed to stay with him? That was the million-dollar question. And except for Sevil, Jennifer didn't know who could answer it.

Too bad she didn't have a guardian angel. Kacy did. He might help her understand, but Jennifer didn't have the vaguest idea how to summon otherworldly beings.

She closed her eyes. If she were still here in the morning, she'd have to make a decision. Should she pray for Miranda's quick return? Or for fate to allow her to stay?

In the end Jennifer prayed that whatever happened, Drake wouldn't be hurt, and she wouldn't be heartbroken again.

Thirteen

Decisions

Jennifer awakened at daybreak and saw Drake slumped in the chair where he'd spent the remainder of the night. The blanket had fallen to his waist. She couldn't tear her eyes from his bare chest. Smooth, flat, and covered with a smattering of blond curls, the blatant display of masculinity sent blood rushing to her face. To top that off he appeared totally unaware of how his semi-nudity affected her.

"If you don't mind, I would like an early start on the road." His voice sounded formal, a stark contrast to the intimate feeling engendered by the dim room and their mutual state of undress.

"Where are we?"

"At an inn."

"I figured that out. How far are we from London?"

"Quite far."

Not happy with his short, clipped answers, Jennifer sat up and swung her bare legs off the bed, trying to keep them covered with the blanket. Suddenly Drake's bare chest stared her in the face. Dressed in nothing more than the white trousers he had worn at the masquerade and a pair of white stockings, his sensuality threatened more than ever.

Shaken by his nearness and the way it affected her, she said, "I don't have anything decent to wear."

"Teeny packed a valise," Drake said. "Unfortunately she didn't include a bed gown. That's why you're in my shirt."

"Teeny?"

"Your maid—Miranda's maid."

Unable to ignore his nude chest, Jennifer asked, "Where is she?"

"In London. She will join us when we return."

Remembering the clothes and money Sevil had provided, Jennifer asked, "What happened to my valise and reticule?"

"They're at my lodge, where you left them."

"Are we on our way there?"

"No."

When he didn't seem inclined to say more, she asked, "Would you mind stepping outside while I dress?"

"Do you expect me to go out in public without my shirt?"

"No." She ducked under the blanket to take it off. It still smelled of him. Masculine. Piney. Sexy. She hated to part with it. She hated the idea of losing him again even more.

Inhaling slowly, she fumbled with the buttons, and heard Drake drag his shoes across the rough plank floor before he grumbled, "It seems unnecessary to preserve your modesty given that I have twice undressed you. And when we wed, I'll own the right to watch you dress or undress any time I please."

Now naked beneath the blanket, Jennifer blushed. Although she'd married Dirk, he'd only seen her without clothes for a short time on their wedding day, and she hadn't overcome the modesty Aunt Rachel had drummed into her head for so many years.

When Jennifer peeked out, Drake had his white shoes and jacket on. In his hand he held an unfamiliar valise.

"Yours gowns are in here." He plunked the valise on the foot of the bed. "Wear a chemise, petticoat and gown. Don't bother with the corset. We'll travel all day, and there's no need for you to be uncomfortable."

Jennifer grinned. She hated corsets.

"Here." She offered the rumpled shirt, grateful she and Miranda were the same size and her clothes fit so well.

Without taking the shirt, Drake stomped to the door. After he closed it behind him, Jennifer shrugged the blanket off and dressed fast. The fire had burned out during the night and the room was cold.

When Drake re-entered, the first thing he said was, "Have you had ample time to consider an elopement?"

Not eager to spoil Miranda's plans, Jennifer said, "I get the feeling I don't have much choice."

"You don't. We have lain together. I've seen you in the altogether, and compromised you. Honor dictates that I make you my wife. And in order to avoid the wizard Sevil, we must go to Gretna Green."

The thought of eloping appealed to her. It bothered her, too. Before she could stop herself, she blurted, "My vision of your wedding didn't look like an elopement. Your bride wore a beautiful white wedding gown, and there were tons of people to witness the ceremony."

"A formal ceremony is planned for Thursday next. Travel to Scotland takes three days. We have time to elope to Gretna Green, and return in time for the ceremony in Kent. And, as I said before, the best way to protect you from the wizard Sevil is to keep you at my side day and night. As my betrothed, that would be scandalous. As my wife, however, it will be quite proper."

"What name will I use—if I marry you?"

"What name do you think you should use?"

"Jennifer Miranda's," she said half-heartedly, and thought Drake looked relieved.

"Good. 'Tis settled then."

Feeling far from settled, Jennifer busied herself brushing her hair. She didn't intend to watch Drake while he changed his clothes. But curiosity drew her eyes to him. She wondered where he had gotten the small scars that crisscrossed the middle of his back, and concluded he must have been very brave to endure such pain.

She also worried about Sevil. How much longer would he allow her to be in this time before he took her back to her own?

~ * ~

In spite of her worries, Jennifer neither saw nor envisioned Sevil as they traveled, and she relaxed. Except for the fear that Miranda would return and she would be thrust back to the twenty-first century, Jennifer enjoyed the trip.

She sat across from Drake, her back to the front of the carriage. Whenever they touched accidentally, sparks of awareness glittered between them. Every time he helped her in or out of the carriage, he looked like he didn't want to let her go. To her disappointment, he always did. And he never kissed or fondled her.

Each night he slept in a chair, rather than the bed at the inns where they stayed.

Near noon of the third day, he said, "There's the sign."

Eager for a glimpse of the village she'd read about, but never seen, Jennifer leaned forward. "Gretna Green," she read out loud. *Where couples eloped to avoid long waits, or to appease angry fathers.*

The carriage wheels hit another bump. Both she and Drake were leaning forward and their shoulders brushed. Self-conscious, she pulled back, her heart pounding. Soon she would be Mrs. Drake Edward. And Drake would no longer spend the night in a chair. He would sleep with her unless Miranda came back.

The carriage stopped in front of a small dwelling that looked like a shed.

"Is this our destination?" Jennifer asked, uncertain.

"It is." Drake climbed out, then turned to help her.

Her pulse drummed as she glanced from his handsome face to the shed-like structure. "It doesn't look like anybody's here."

But just then a man with wild brown hair, and a shaggy beard and mustache stepped through the open doorway.

"Be ye wantin' ta git hitched?"

"Yes," Drake said.

"If ye be needin' witnesses, it'll cost ye more."

"My driver will act as one witness, however, we'll need another."

"Me wife, she kin act as t'other."

Drake lifted Jennifer from the carriage to the damp ground. As cold seeped through Miranda's borrowed slippers, Jennifer remembered the old cliché; 'the bride got cold feet'. Thinking it rather apt, she grinned, then bit her bottom lip. Was she making a mistake? One that would harm Drake if Sevil took her away?

Drake seized her arm as though he too feared Sevil might appear and whisk her off. They followed the wild-haired man inside the weathered shed, which Jennifer decided must be a stable when she saw stacks of hay or straw. She knew hay was green and straw yellow, but in the dim light she couldn't tell what color the odd shaped stacks were. Funny that's what filled her thoughts when she was about to take a monumental step, and elope for the second time in her life—in a century in which she didn't belong.

Looking up she found Drake's warm gaze on her. Her pulse rocked crazily. With all her heart she wished Miranda would stay in the future, so she could stay in this time. She'd miss Aunt Rachel, Uncle Mac, and Tyler, but Jennifer had loved Drake all her life, as well as in prior lives, and she'd give just about anything to stay with him and be his wife for as long as they lived.

~ * ~

What Drake saw in Jennifer's lovely eyes humbled him. Could it be love? Throughout their journey, she had been a great sport. Never a complaint... nor did she nag. He couldn't have asked for a better companion. Would she change once they were married? He sincerely hoped not.

Silently he thanked his Maker they had finally reached their destination. He couldn't endure much more of her presence without losing control. Her appeal threatened as no other lady ever had. Drake uttered another silent 'thank you' that the wizard Sevil hadn't made an appearance. Perhaps, as he hoped, the wizard hadn't expected them to head north. But would Jennifer be in danger when they returned to Kent? If so, could he outfox the wizard by keeping her always at his side? How long would that be necessary?

The blacksmith cleared his throat. "Be ye ready?"

Forcing his gaze from Jennifer, Drake noted the man had summoned his wife, a plump, squat lady with ruddy cheeks and bright green eyes. He glanced at his driver, Winslow.

"This ceremony is not to be discussed with anyone. Do you understand?"

Winslow nodded.

Drake turned his attention to the Scottish blacksmith. "You may begin."

With Jennifer's hand on his arm, they faced the man who had united couples in matrimony for years, often with a shotgun pointed at the reluctant groom who had compromised some man's daughter.

Drake's voice was strong and steady as he pledged his troth and promised to honor and cherish Jennifer Miranda for as long as they both lived. Her voice trembled when she spoke her vows, and he wondered if she regretted her agreement to elope, or if she was just nervous.

Regretting he had no ring for her, Drake removed the ruby from his small finger and placed it on her fourth. She smiled, and their eyes held. On their way home, they would stop in London, and he would collect the wedding ring he had ordered from his jeweler. Perhaps he would also discover what had become of her betrothal ring. Had she lost it? Or taken it off and forgotten where she left it?

To his surprise, Jennifer pulled the chain with the opal attached over her head, and eased it over his. Why did it feel as though it belonged where it now lay, just above his heart that pounded with the thought of living with her for the rest of his life?

Jennifer surprised him again by whispering, "With this opal, I thee wed, for time, eternity, forever."

A distant memory stirred. Although he tried to recall the incident in its entirety, it didn't come. Yet his mind told him he had heard those words before, but he couldn't recall where or when. *But from whom? When? And where?*

He shoved the questions to the back of his mind while he paid the blacksmith, thanked the plump wife for being a witness and led his own bride outside.

"What now?" she asked as they approached the carriage.

Drake would have liked nothing more than to find an inn and spend the rest of the day in bed, consummating their vows. But he told himself he should wait until nightfall, and they should put as many miles behind them as possible with what remained of the day.

"Would you object if we start home? 'Tis a long journey and I wish to stop in London before we travel to Kent."

"I'm happy to do whatever you want."

Drake's heart thudded and he almost changed his mind and ordered Winslow to find the nearest inn. Instead he instructed him to start back to England.

As they traveled, Jennifer said, "I thought your last name was Edward, but the man who married us called you Drake Edward Castlebury."

"Now you know all my secrets," Drake said.

She blinked her bewilderment. "Why didn't you tell me your last name?"

"Because I thought you knew and were pretending you lost your memories."

Jennifer smiled. And Drake spent most of the afternoon in a state of agony. He wanted to touch her, explore her, possess her. Every time their eyes met, she smiled again and he wondered if she could guess his unholy thoughts.

At dusk, Winslow found a proper inn. The well-appointed rooms pleased Drake. He didn't relish spending their wedding night in shabby surroundings. He wanted all their shared memories from this moment on to be good ones.

After they ate, he led Jennifer up the stairs.

As soon as he closed the door, he did what he had wanted to do for three long, tormenting days—lowered his mouth to hers.

Her response delighted him. She kissed him with such ardor his heartbeat sped up and his desire trebled.

Mine, he thought. *She's mine. And even if the wizard Sevil takes her away and she misses the ceremony next week, I can announce we eloped, and she's already my wife.*

A feeling of contentment stole through him. He raised his head and smiled down at her.

"We're married," she said, smiling, too.

"Yes, we are."

She pressed her body against his and slid her arms around his neck. He kissed her forehead, her cheek, then captured her lips again. The kiss was gentle and rough, all at the same time. Drake fought to keep it from getting out of control. But what he had intended to be slow and sweet had already turned hot.

Her enticing fragrance mingled with the scent of burning candles, and he knew he would treasure the memory of this night forever.

She unlocked her hands and laid one against the back of his head.

Coherent thought deserted him. Need and passion burned hotly inside him. He kissed her senseless. And still he kissed her. Time ceased to exist. Nothing mattered except the two of them, bound together by a compelling force.

Love. It must be love. His startled brain could not move beyond those words.

~ * ~

Never wanting this night to end, Jennifer uttered a small groan of protest when Drake dragged his mouth from hers. When he buried his face in her hair and held her close, she felt his heart thumping against hers. Delighted that she apparently affected him the same way he affected her, she moved her head to look up at him. He loosened his hold, but kept her in his arms. Close. While they stared, he lifted strands of her hair and let them slide through his fingers.

"Promise me you will never cut your hair."

"You have my promise," she said, resisting the temptation to say she had already given him that promise long ago, when she was only nine years old.

"You have too many clothes on," he murmured.

"As do you," she said, torn between guilt for marrying him with Miranda's name, and the opposing belief that he belonged to her because he was Dirk.

Eager to make love, she ignored the guilt.

They disposed of his coat, then came together as though they were made for each other, and couldn't bear to be apart.

Jennifer lost all sense of modesty. Between hot kisses, and seductive caresses they discarded their clothes, slowly, piece by piece. She couldn't wait to see him, all of him again. It had been so long; a lifetime it seemed.

Finally they lay on the bed, naked. Trembling, she looked him up and down. Candlelight added romance she had never before experienced. Not even in other lifetimes. But then, they hadn't consummated their love before. That's why they had eloped when she finished high school.

"Do you like what you see?" Drake asked, a sexy smile in his tender blue eyes.

Jennifer nodded, too happy to be embarrassed by her blatant inspection. "I think you're built like Michelangelo's David."

"And you're more beautiful than a sea goddess."

His familiar, fresh piney scent filled her senses. Impatient to get on with their loving, she invited, "Kiss me."

"With pleasure." He kissed her face, her cheeks, her lips, then gazed at her breasts before he tongued each aroused peak.

Jennifer couldn't believe all the sensations pouring through her—the aching, the longing, the wanting.

He moved his mouth to her throat and kissed the sensitive spot behind her ear. His hands caressed her breasts, her nipples, and she felt paradise within her grasp.

With a ragged moan, she reached for his penis, rigid and erect. He shifted to accommodate her, and groaned when she began to stroke.

"I'm losing control," he mumbled, his voice low and husky.

"Me, too."

She wanted to excite him. And knew she did. His mouth found hers, while his hands explored the contours of her body. He caressed and stroked, forging a path to her slick, ready flesh. With each erotic stroke, need churned inside her.

She thrashed beneath his tender assault, aching for fulfillment, and pleaded, "Love me. Please, love me."

He moved atop her.

She pressed her lips against his shoulder.

"Hurry," she urged in a desperate whisper. "Please hurry, Drake."

He poised above her moist, eager entrance and probed gently. Her hands glided down to his buttocks, pressing him closer. He probed a little deeper, then retreated.

"Now. Please. Don't tease."

Drake kissed her, silencing her words, and thrust inside.

Matching his thrusts, her body rocked in sweet unison with his. He murmured sweet endearments. She murmured in return.

Rapture rippled though her in waves of pure pleasure. They were one, in thought and need. Each thrust seemed a journey all its own. An intoxicating journey Jennifer wanted to take over and over again.

Her climax started as a slow, deceptively quiet wave, rolling through her with ever-increasing force until it escalated like a tidal wave of unimaginable force. Her heartbeat ceased. Her chest tightened. Drake held her high on a swell for a few breathless seconds. Then he plunged her headlong into the deep noisy ocean. Pleasure crashed over her and her flesh convulsed in a series of tumultuous sensations.

She held him tight, wanting him to share the intense, intimate emotions, wondering if they would ever achieve anything as wonderful again, greedily hoping this wouldn't be their last time to make love.

Jennifer hated for the sensations to end. But they did. Slowly though, not quickly. Fulfillment followed, washing through her, creating a contentment she had never known. Marveling at the intensity of what they had just shared, she rolled with him when he moved, onto her side, her head nestled beneath his chin.

No other man could possibly be as tender or gentle. He belongs to me. And always will. No matter what happens.

Loving him with all her heart, she wished she could stay with him forever. The fear of Miranda's return threatened to spoil Jennifer's happy elation. She forced the fear aside. Tonight she and Drake were together. At the moment, nothing else mattered.

~ * ~

Drake stirred until Jennifer looked up at him. Then he stared into her dazed eyes. He felt a little dazed himself, as though he had just made love for the very first time. No woman had ever pleased him as she did. No other woman could make him want to hold her and never let go.

Holding her lovingly close, he realized she could make him forget himself. She pleased him in bed, and out of bed as well. In addition, she could quite possibly give him both an heir and a spare, and some daughters as well. She would be a good wife and mother, too. He sensed that as though he had always known he would find love.

What was love? Contentment? Satisfaction? Peace? All those things and more. The desire to protect her, keep her near, and never let he stray far away.

While he marveled at the emotions melding inside him, a deep-seated possessiveness filled him. He wouldn't let her go. If the wizard Sevil attempted to take her away again, Drake would strangle him with his bare hands.

And then, as he inhaled her sweet intoxicating scent, a near strangling thought tormented him. His little bride had known exactly what to do, and what to expect. *She hadn't been a virgin. She'd already lain with a man. Or men. Who? Where? When? Why?*

Fourteen

The Journey Home

After breakfast the next morning, they continued their journey. Worried that Drake might ask why she wasn't a virgin, Jennifer stared out the carriage window, waiting for his question, worrying and stewing that he wouldn't believe anything she said.

"With whom did you lose your virginity?"

She turned her gaze to his, unwilling to lie or pretend. "On my wedding day, more than three years ago."

He frowned. "What?"

"His name was Dirk. And he was very much like you. In fact, I think he was you. No, I don't think that. I'm sure of it."

She reached across the aisle and touched the outline of the opal beneath his shirt before she continued. "You gave this to me when I was nine to seal our agreement to marry. And you promised it would guide me to you if I ever needed it to."

Drake looked incredulous. His voice sounded the same. "Are you making up a tale because you do not remember?"

"No." She shook her head to add emphasis. "I'm telling you what I believe in my heart and soul—that you're Dirk. We knew each other in the future, where I came from, also in other lives. We're soul mates, and you're the only man I've ever been intimate with."

~ * ~

Other lives? Soul mates? Drake searched her eyes, and some of his doubt and anger fled. "You obviously believe that."

"Yes, I do. If you had your memories, you'd believe it, too."

He told himself it would be foolish to resent a man she didn't remember. He should be pleased she believed he was the only man she had lain with. Still, he resented her prior experience. Could he forgive not being her first? In truth, he didn't know. But he loved her. He didn't doubt that.

Unwilling to deny himself the pleasure she offered, he moved to sit beside her. "You're mine, now. Only mine. And you will have eyes for no one else."

"I never have had," she murmured, as he lowered his head and spread tiny kisses all over her face. "And you're mine, whether I call you Dirk or Drake."

~ * ~

They traveled back to London in bliss. Jennifer had never been happier. Every day they enjoyed each other more. Each night in bed Drake was tender, exciting, inventive, wonderful. He didn't mention her virginity again, and Jennifer thanked her lucky stars.

Whenever they stopped, he purchased things for her. She couldn't convince him she didn't need anything. In addition to a bed gown she wore no more than a few minutes, he bought new day gowns and a beautiful gray wool cloak, trimmed with gray fur. Although the sun warmed her each day, at night the cloak was most welcome.

"It gives me pleasure to see you in something of my choosing," he said when she objected to the expense of yet another gown.

The next time they stopped, he took her to a jewelry shop and bought a gold locket.

"Now we both have something to wear near our hearts."

Dazzled by his thoughtfulness, Jennifer swallowed a lump of emotion, and turned so he could fasten the locket around her neck.

"Next time you get your hair cut, will you save a lock for me to put inside?" she asked.

"If that would please you."

"It would."

He smiled. "Then I will save a lock with pleasure."

~ * ~

On Tuesday they reached London. When Winslow brought the carriage to a halt in front of a well-appointed house in a nice neighborhood, Jennifer asked, half in fear, "Who lives here?"

"I do," Drake startled her. "And you will as well when we are in town."

It had occurred to her that the clothes he wore were tailor-made, also that having a driver and comfortable carriage at his disposal indicated his means might be more than she had expected after seeing his humble cottage in Kent. But it hadn't occurred to her that he might be wealthy until he kept buying things.

A feeling of uneasiness crept through her as Winslow opened the carriage door.

"We are home, Your Grace."

"So we are." Drake stepped out and turned to help Jennifer, but she was too stunned to move.

Your Grace? Jennifer's uneasiness grew. Dukes and royalty were called 'your grace'. If Drake had a title, why hadn't Kacy or Clay mentioned it?

Jennifer waited until Winslow busied himself unloading their valises and purchases before she asked, "Are you a duke or a prince, or what?"

"A duke," Drake said.

"Then I—I can't be your wife."

"Nonsense. You already are."

"But I don't know anything about being a duke's wife."

He gave her a wolfish grin. "You know how to please me."

She blushed.

"Whatever else you need to know, you will learn."

He plucked her off the seat and set her on her feet outside the carriage.

"The servants will be pleased to see you."

"How many—" she stammered, "do you have?"

"Here? Or in Kent?"

Jennifer's heart pounded. "Olvan isn't the only person who works for you in Kent?"

Drake shook his head. "Olvan has been with me since I was a lad. He's more friend than servant, and often accompanies me to the hunting lodge. None of my other servants do, although they deliver food at meal times."

Jennifer almost gulped. "You should have prepared me," she mumbled as he tucked her hand in the crook of his elbow.

He cupped her chin and tilted it until she looked him in the eye. "I think I was wise not to tell you a thing."

Perplexed, she asked, "Why?"

"You might have fretted and stewed, and I am a selfish man, Duchess. I preferred you the way you were, with no one to think about except me."

"I rather liked the way you were, too." She blushed again, recalling how eager she'd been to please him every time they so much as touched. "Will things change now? Will you have to concentrate on other people, and have less time for me?"

He bent his head, kissed her cheek. "Nothing need change."

As he led her toward the front door, Jennifer hoped with all her heart that was true, just as she hoped Miranda wouldn't return. But even if Miranda didn't love Drake, she must want to come back to be his duchess. Dismayed, Jennifer frowned, wondering what to expect.

The door opened and a stout woman walked toward them.

"Who is she?" Jennifer whispered.

"My housekeeper, Lenore." Drake lowered his voice. "Once she gets a notion in her head, it's not easy to dissuade her. If you find her difficult, tell me and I'll deal with her."

Lenore, nearly upon them, paused. "Welcome home, Your Grace. Will you be in London long?"

"Just for the night."

"Welcome home, Miss Miranda. How are you, my dear?"

"Fine, thank you," Jennifer said, uncomfortable with the deception, but feeling she had no other choice.

Drake smiled down at her, and she wondered how he'd handle their sleeping arrangements if he didn't explain they had eloped. She hated the idea of sleeping apart, even for one night. Every hour brought her closer to the time when they might be parted.

"Let us go inside where we may speak in private."

Drake led them to a room Jennifer knew was called a lounge in the future. She didn't know what it was called now, but it held two burgundy settees, arranged across from each other with Louie XIV chairs facing each other on each side, along with small end tables, and a tea table in the middle of the square furniture arrangement. Tapestries, tasteful paintings and gold candle sconces decorated the walls. Velvet burgundy curtains covered the two long windows. She thought about the bare windows at Drake's cottage—or rather his hunting lodge. Would he think she was silly if she offered to make curtains when he had scads of servants and probably tons of money?

Drake sat beside Jennifer on a settee, across from Lenore before he spoke.

"What I am about to tell you is in strict confidence."

"I understand," the housekeeper said, her expression grave.

"We were married three days ago, however, we plan to proceed with the wedding plans on Thursday next at Stonemeade."

Lenore clapped her hands to her cheeks. "I be honored ye shared yer wonderful secret with me, Your Grace. May I share it with the servants?"

"You may. However, I do not wish the news to travel beyond the walls of my home."

Lenore clucked her tongue. "I will ensure it does not."

As soon as she left, Drake turned his attention back to Jennifer. He wanted to believe her recent disappearances weren't of her own volition. Even though he loved her, he still had doubts.

"I have errands to attend to. Will you stay inside whilst I am gone and promise not to venture out?"

She nodded. "I'm sure I'll be all right. Sevil has only shown up when I've been outdoors."

Deciding he'd have to be satisfied with that, Drake led her to the hall where the maid, Teeny, waited.

"Show my lady to her new room; the gold one beside my chamber, and see that she is made comfortable. I shall return in time for tea."

He planted a kiss on Jennifer's palm, then hurried away to talk with Lenore again.

"Kindly inform the servants that Miss Miranda fell from a great height less than a fortnight ago. She may not remember their names. However, I expect them to help her adjust without making her feel ill at ease."

"Yes, Your Grace," Lenore said. "You know she holds a special place in me heart and theirs."

Drake nodded, concerned about Prudence. How would she deal with their elopement? And Miranda's memory loss? He decided not to tell her yet.

"If her sister calls whilst I'm out, don't admit her. Nor when I return either."

"Miss Prudence, I mean Mrs. Bennet called this morning, Your Grace. She calls most every day to express concern about Miss Miranda's whereabouts. I do not believe her concern genuine, and I be confident she will not call again until tomorrow at midday."

Drake winked. "And we shall be gone by then."

"Good plan, Your Grace, if I may say so."

"Take care that my Duchess is not disturbed by anyone."

"I shall," Lenore promised.

~ * ~

Drake completed his errands in record time and rushed home. At the front door, he gave his gloves and top hat to the butler, his recent purchase concealed in his coat pocket.

"Where's my bride?"

"She be up in the Gold Room, Your Grace. She refused Teeny's services, and hurt the poor gel's feelings. Mayhap you can convince her that she must have a lady's maid."

"I'll talk to her."

Drake dashed up the stairs, tapped on the Gold Room door, then walked in as Jennifer called, "Please come in."

She sat in a chair, smiling and waiting for him. *As he wished she always would be.*

He smiled back. Although he preferred to have her in the master suite, he knew if he installed her there, the servants might gossip. They might gossip in any event, with them closeted in her new bedroom in the middle of the day, but he didn't care. His servants knew he abhorred scandal, and would be careful what they said and to whom.

Jennifer had changed from her traveling clothes, and brushed her long hair, apparently unhindered by the lack of a lady's maid. Everything about her, including the effect she had on him, was different—odd.

When she sat on the bed and bounced, he fought the urge to make love to her in broad daylight.

"It doesn't feel like a straw mattress," she said cheerfully.

"It's goose down ticking."

His gaze took in the new pink gown, one he had purchased during their trip. It fit her to perfection. In spite of that he wanted her without clothes. Telling himself not to expect to make love every time he had the desire, he looked away.

A few candles had been lit and the room felt warm and cozy with the curtains drawn. Another glance at the bed revealed the covers had been folded back, as though his wife intended to rest.

"Are you tired?" he asked, recalling how little sleep they'd had during the last three nights.

"A little. Are you?"

"No, but I would be happy to hold you while you rest."

"I'd like that."

She eased her slippers off, and unfastened the top buttons at the back of her gown. Then she lay down and opened her arms to him. He removed his coat, joined her on the bed, and gathered her close. As he caught a whiff of her flowery feminine scent, it put him through the riggers of the damned. He drew in a sharp breath. Holding her might prove more difficult than leaving her alone.

"Jennifer?"

"What?"

He waited until her eyes met his. "I want you."

"I want you too, Drake. I hoped I wouldn't after I realized you're a duke, but I do. Is that wrong?"

"Absolutely not."

He lowered his mouth and claimed hers.

And they spent a long, delightful time soaring toward heaven.

~ * ~

Later, while they dressed, Drake watched her. Lord, would he ever tire of watching her? Is this how love felt? For every certainty, he had a hundred doubts.

"Do I disturb you?" he asked, when she finished dressing, and saw him staring.

"Sometimes." She blushed becomingly, and shoved her long hair behind her shoulders.

Drake grinned. "You're lovely when you're flustered."

"I'm not flustered, and I know how I look. I have freckles, and they're about as appealing as a spotted snake when my face turns red."

He reached out and gently cupped her cheek. She tried to brush his hand away. Drake didn't let her. "Your freckles are far more appealing to me than flawless, ivory skin."

"Ha," Jennifer snorted inelegantly. "If you expect me to believe that, you're more dim-witted than I feared."

"You fear me, do you? What an intriguing admission."

"I—I don't fear you," Jennifer stammered.

"Don't you?" he asked, and she wondered if he was teasing. Or flirting.

"You're lovely... And you're mine. He stepped closer. "Tell me why I cannot get enough of you."

"I don't know, but I hope it never ends," Jennifer said, exhilarated by his admission, and his arms closing around her.

"It must or I may never get anything done."

"I wouldn't call making love not getting anything done. For all we know," she quipped, "we might have already created a baby."

"An heir." Drake snuggled her against his solid chest. "This is where I want you—for the rest of my life."

He looked startled by his admission, but he kept her close. Jennifer liked that... a lot. At the moment nothing felt more important.

"I'd like to spend the rest of my life in your arms."

Drake frowned. She hadn't seen him frown for quite some time, and wondered what caused it. "What's wrong?"

"I think I am besotted."

"Me, too." She stiffened and frowned at the sudden vision of Sevil.

Unable to ignore it, she couldn't even reply when Drake asked, "What is it, Jennifer?"

A brilliant orange-red glowed where the whites of Sevil's eyes should have been and his black pupils were hugely dilated. He wore black as he had at the masquerade, and his cape flapped as he rasped, "I can fulfill all your heart's desires, Jennifer. I can make this man worship you. I can provide you with riches, servants and a life of luxury beyond your wildest dreams. I am all-powerful and I can give you anything you want. But heed this warning. You must do as I say." His grin looked cunning, frightening, and sinister.

The vision ended as quickly as it came, and Jennifer shuddered. The ardor in Drake's eyes cooled to concern.

"Are you cold?"

She shook her head. There wasn't a doubt in her mind that Sevil meant what he said. But what did he want?"

"What is it?" Drake pressed when fear made her tremble again. "What happened to you just now?"

When she didn't reply, he said, "You were in a trance."

Unable to hold back, she blurted, "I'm not Miranda. I'm truly not." Jennifer pressed her hand against her throat and found it feverish. "I'm not even from this time."

"What?"

"My name really is Jennifer Quinlane. Miranda and I switched places. She's in the future. That's where I came from."

Drake's eyes bored into hers. "That is impossible."

"No. It isn't. It happened, and somehow we have to deal with it."

Drake's eyes were still filled with disbelief.

"I'm sorry," Jennifer apologized. "I should have made you believe me sooner, but I thought Sevil would bring Miranda back by now, and return me to my own time."

Drake stared, his blue eyes ablaze with disbelief, but he said nothing.

"I told you before, but you wouldn't believe me."

"I still think it's a preposterous tale."

"But it's true. My name is Jennifer Quinlane. I was born in the 1980's, and I traveled here from the twenty-first century. Sevil took Miranda there to—"

"That's absurd." Drake backed away and started to pace.

"I know it sounds absurd to you. It probably would to me too, if it hadn't happened to me. But it is true."

"I don't wish to discuss this any further," Drake said, continuing to pace.

Unwilling to give up, Jennifer said, "Tell me what made you think I was in a trance."

He paused to stare. "Your eyes."

"I had a vision."

Drake rammed a hand through his hair. "Did you?"

"Yes. And it scared me."

"Why?"

"Because Sevil said he's all powerful, and he can fulfill my heart's desires, and give me wealth and a life of luxury beyond my wildest dreams, but I must do as he says."

"And what did he say?" Drake asked.

"Nothing. He just disappeared. So I have no idea what he wants."

"Are you sure?"

She nodded. Morbidly afraid Sevil had some ulterior motive in mind, she blurted, "I don't want to hurt you, Drake."

"Are you planning to?"

"No, but I'm afraid of..."

"Of what?"

"Sevil."

"I won't allow him to harm you."

"I'm not afraid he'll harm me. I'm afraid he might hurt you."

Drake's expression turned from concern to indignant. "I'm not a weak man who cannot take care of himself."

"I know you're not, but…"

"But what?"

"What if I'm taken away and don't return?"

"I'll take my chances on keeping you here, and you should know I am as relentless as the North Sea."

A quiver tugged at her lips when she tried not to smile.

He reached for her shoulders. "I adore your smiles, Jennifer. They're like sunshine. They warm those they touch."

She rewarded him with a brilliant one. "That's one of the nicest compliments I've ever had, Drake."

"And this will be one of the nicest kisses," he promised, capturing her mouth with his.

The kiss was gentle and sweet. Everything a kiss ought to be, just as Drake was everything a man ought to be. Fate had surely smiled on her when she landed in the tree near his lodge.

Drake kissed her long and leisurely, and Jennifer enjoyed his tender onslaught, with no thought of going back to bed. At the moment all she wanted was to kiss, and taste the texture of his lips and mouth and tongue. He, too, seemed content to kiss, and she marveled that she felt so in tune with him now, when moments ago they had been engaged in a heated disagreement.

When the soul-stealing kisses finally ended, Jennifer stood transfixed. Drake too looked dazed. *I love you,* she wanted to say, but didn't. She'd startled him enough for one day.

~ * ~

Drake had an uneasy feeling as a nagging thought arose within him. Would his wife leave him as Kacy had once left Clay? If she did, would he be accused of murdering her? No. He would go after her before the accusation could be made, even if that meant he must travel across the ocean and bring her back.

Back from where?

Why did he suddenly picture Jennifer in America, in a far distant time dressed in clothes that were scandalous in this century, but quite appropriate in that other time?

She couldn't have come from the future. Time travel was impossible; too ludicrous to consider.

He shook his head to clear the disturbing images. He must not allow his imagination, or those strange dreams that surfaced when he least expected them, to become important. Or real.

The fall had robbed her memories. She had invented new ones to make up for the loss. And to keep the peace he would go along with some of her pretense. He would continue to call her Jennifer, but he wouldn't dwell on the inconceivable. To do so would be not only be absurd, it would be downright foolish.

As they left her room to go downstairs for tea, Drake considered having her installed in his chamber. Although titled men shared their chambers with their wives only when they wished to be intimate, Drake wanted to share as much as possible with his. In the back of his mind, he admitted he wanted more than to share time with her. He wanted to hear her say she loved him, and he didn't give a fig whether she recovered her memories or not.

Fifteen

Autumn Wedding

Thursday arrived with a clear, sunny sky. Having slept alone in the master chamber because his grandmother insisted that Jennifer stay with her, Drake went to the dower house as soon as he dressed. Unaccustomed to knocking, he walked in and started up the stairs.

His grandmother appeared at the top. "What are you doing here, Drake? People say 'tis bad luck to see the bride before the ceremony."

"She's already my wife," he reminded, because they had confided in her when they arrived at Stonemeade yesterday.

"Nevertheless, you cannot see her until this afternoon."

"I came to see if she is all right."

"She's fine. Teeny is about to wash her hair and the wedding gown must be altered."

Drake decided to settle for hearing Jennifer's voice. He had awakened from a vivid dream that she had gone off again, and left him to face the vicar and multitude of guests alone.

Stalking up the stairs, he brushed past his grandmother, tapped on a door, and called, "Jennifer, are you all right?"

He heard a scuffle, then her voice. "Yes. Are you?"

"Yes," he said, unhappy with their separation.

"I'll see you in a few hours," she called.

"Right." He glared at his grandmother, then stomped down the stairs, feeling like a foolish youth.

Back at the mansion he closeted himself in his study to answer correspondence that had piled on his desk.

By late afternoon the sky clouded over, as it had in his dream—not a good omen. He took the opal off to bathe, shave and dress in new formal attire, and forgot to put it back on.

Downstairs he greeted the vicar.

As time for the ceremony approached, three hundred guests took their seats in the ballroom. Drake stood before the vicar, awaiting the bride who was already his wife. The wife who pleased him in ways he could not have imagined a mere week ago.

When they made love, she elevated him to a place of extraordinary beauty. The thought of reaching that plane again made him throb with anticipation. Instead of diminishing, his desire escalated. Did all men in love feel like this? Possessive? Afraid they might lose their beloved?

The tempo of music from the twelve-piece orchestra changed.

Drake turned his attention to the door and heaved a sigh of relief.

Jennifer stood there, but not in the ivory wedding gown she had ordered and gloated over to Prudence. Instead Jennifer wore a gown of pure white satin, trimmed with pearls, ribbons and frilly lace. A voluminous gossamer veil covered her face, head, and shoulders. She looked lovely, but the dream lingered, and he couldn't relax.

Outside a streak of lightning flashed. Blinding brilliance catapulted through the row of tall windows. Musicians' fingers fumbled. Instruments squealed. Thunder sounded. Guests twitched in their seats. Many gasped in startled fright when lightning flashed again.

Halfway up the aisle, Jennifer's steps faltered. When she teetered, Drake almost rushed forward to steady her. But she steadied herself and continued, slowly, gracefully, toward him.

Through the veil, he met her beautiful speckled eyes, and his body gave an involuntary jerk. He had missed her last night, and was eager to have her in his arms again. Eager to be alone with her, and have her all to himself. Too eager, he thought, admiring the wedding gown that showed off her slim figure and entrancing, feminine curves.

Intricate beadwork adorned the bodice and hooped skirt of the gown that flowed behind her in a long, formal train. Pearls had been sewn into the frothy, gossamer veil, and beneath the white veil her long cinnamon hair flared down to her hips, the way he liked.

Drake had no idea what alerted him that the man-wizard who had delivered her to the masquerade was there, but he slipped his arm around Jennifer's waist in a possessive, protective gesture as soon as she reached his side. Then he looked around and saw the black-eyed wizard watching.

The vicar cleared his throat.

Tightening his arm around Jennifer, Drake ignored the wizard and nodded at the vicar to begin.

"Dearly beloved..."

Although highly unusual, Drake kept his arm around Jennifer as he repeated his vows. She belonged to him, and he would protect her at all costs. With his life, if necessary, for she might already be with child. His? Doubt slithered through him. Or another man's? She hadn't been a virgin. *Who else had she lain with? And when?*

Disliking the jealous feelings conjured by his doubt, he gave himself a mental shake. At the moment she believed she had lain only with him. He must accept that or go mad.

When his bride spoke, her words were slow and careful.

"I, Jennifer Miranda..." Drake gave her waist a gentle squeeze to add moral support, and she leaned slightly closer as she repeated after the vicar, "do solemnly swear to take Drake Edward Castlebury..." She looked up as she said his name and all the worry of the past hours dissolved. The dream was only a dream after all.

When they finished pledging their troth, the vicar said, "You may now kiss your wife."

Jennifer's eyes turned to limpid pools when Drake lifted her frothy veil. She spread her arms, presumably to protect her bridal bouquet, and tilted her head up. He angled his down.

Their lips met hesitantly, almost shyly. And then, as though their separation had been days rather than hours, the kiss consumed, threatening Drake's control. But he couldn't embarrass himself or Jennifer by behaving improperly. Flooded with love and tender emotions, he kept the kiss from getting out of hand. His Duchess deserved respect... his, as well as the three hundred guests who watched.

~ * ~

In a daze, Jennifer wondered how a single kiss could bestow such pleasure. Breathless when it ended, she realized that Drake, too, looked deeply affected. While they stared, the faint smell of orchids drifted up from her beautiful bouquet. Nothing had been left to chance. Everything was perfect. Her gown, Drake's new black three-piece suit, the flowers, musicians, and guests.

Drake's grandmother rushed forward and playfully tapped him on the shoulder with her fan before she smiled at Jennifer.

"Welcome to the family, my dear. I believe you and I shall continue to be great friends."

Lucilla had the sort of eyes a person could never tire of looking at, and Jennifer smiled. "I'd like that."

"No more than I, my dear. And it gives me great pleasure to be the first to offer congratulations."

To Jennifer's delight, Lucilla embraced her. She smelled pleasant, like lilac water and rose powder combined. "Thank you," Jennifer whispered over the sudden lurch in her stomach when she saw Sevil at the back of the room near the double doors.

He winked. She blinked. And Drake seized her wrist in a firm grip. After that everything happened in a rush.

"A toast to the bride and groom," one man said.

"Here, here," another added.

Silver trays with long stemmed champagne crystals appeared as though by magic. Somebody shoved a glass into her hand. As she lifted the bubbly liquid to her lips, she studied Drake's face over the rim of her glass.

You're mine, his eyes seemed to say, and she felt as if she'd just won the million-dollar lottery.

"Here's to the Duke and his Duchess," one man said.

"The Duke and Duchess of Stonemeade," another chimed.

Sevil pushed his way through the crowd. Frightened, Jennifer clutched Drake's arm.

"What is it?" he whispered.

"Sevil's here," she gasped.

"I won't allow him to take you." Drake curled his arm around her waist again. "Hang on to me, as well."

She turned to wrap her arms around him, wondering what kind of impression that would make on the guests.

Sevil, dressed all in black except for his white shirt, clapped his hands. Lightning flashed outside, then to Jennifer's horror everyone in the spacious ballroom froze—everyone except her and Sevil. Even Drake. Although he still held her, his body felt as stiff and cold as a marble statue.

"What have you done?" she asked Sevil.

"Cast a spell to render them immobile."

"Why?"

"Because I wish to speak to you."

Jennifer's heart thumped wildly. Frightened, she leaned closer to Drake, and pressed her chest against his solid, frozen side. Did Sevil plan to take her away now?

"What do you want to discuss?"

"Catharine and Miranda."

"What about them?" Jennifer croaked.

"They had a joyous reunion, and your relatives believe Miranda is you. Although they don't see her often, she enjoys America and the newfangled inventions there."

He must not know about her nightly visions, Jennifer thought, then asked, "Can Drake hear us?"

"No."

"Does Miranda plan to return to England?" she asked then.

"No. It seems the switch is to her liking. I presume it is to yours, as well." Sevil smiled that funny sneer.

Creepy chills crawled up Jennifer's spine.

"My wedding gift," he continued, "is to allow you to remain here with the man you have known and loved in other lives, and to keep Miranda in the future with Catharine."

"I thought Miranda wanted to marry Drake."

"She prefers the freedom she has in America, and you prefer to be here with the man you love. Is that not true?"

"Yes," Jennifer admitted, afraid Sevil might use that against her when he finally got around to telling her what he wanted.

"You were wise to pretend to be Miranda. The duke would not have married you otherwise."

Jennifer stifled a groan. "Will he ever remember me?"

"He may, if you give me what I want."

"What do you want?"

"You need not concern yourself with that tonight. You shall know eventually. Until then, I'm sure you'll enjoy being a duchess."

"I won't," she said. "I don't want to be a duchess."

"Of course you do, just as you wish to be the Duke's wife."

"I wish to be Drake's wife. I'd wish that if he were a pauper and lived in his cottage in the woods."

"Fortunately for you, he doesn't." With a cunning grin, Sevil added, "Your life will be much easier if you continue to impersonate Miranda."

"I'm not going to..."

Sevil clapped his hands.

The spell ended and everybody came back to animated life as Sevil wove his way back through the crowd.

Drake squeezed her waist, a question in his eyes, as guests pushed close to shower felicitations. As though nothing out of the ordinary had occurred, he introduced her to every person. Not by any stretch of the imagination did she expect to remember their names, but she smiled until her facial muscles ached.

Wondering where Kacy and Clay were, Jennifer glanced around the lavishly decorated ballroom. Gigantic vases of flowers decorated every corner, nook, cranny and table. People seemed to be everywhere flowers weren't. When she spotted Kacy and Clay advancing toward them, her forced smile turned genuine.

"I was beginning to think you weren't here," she said after Kacy gave her an enthusiastic hug.

"We had a mishap with the carriage," Clay explained.

"But we arrived in time to see you walk down the aisle," Kacy added. "You're a beautiful bride, Jennifer."

"Yes, she is," Drake agreed, and Jennifer saw surprise in his eyes. Why? Because he didn't believe she knew Kacy?

"Am I allowed to kiss your bride?" Clay asked.

"On the cheek, where I kissed yours," Drake said.

Clay leaned forward and gently kissed each of Jennifer's cheeks, as he had in Paris, the French custom. Then he shook hands with Drake. "If you're half as happy as a married man as I am, you'll live a contented life."

Drake grinned. "We are content, are we not, Duchess?"

Jennifer nodded and blushed, eager to tell Kacy they had eloped, and anxious to ask if she could summon her guardian angel to answer some questions.

~ * ~

Although Drake focused most of his attention on their guests, he kept Jennifer close to his side. Each time she lifted her gaze, he turned a smile to her. Knowing looks passed between the guests, and he resisted the urge to chuckle. If they knew he and his little bride had already consummated their vows many times, they might be shocked.

When Drake saw the wizard Sevil lurking near a window, anger throbbed through him. Why was he here? He hadn't been invited. And why had he frozen everyone, except Jennifer? Did anyone else know a spell had been cast that froze them for that brief time? Drake had been unable to hear or move, but he had felt Jennifer's heart pound against his stiff side, and he'd seen her lips move, though he didn't know everything she and Sevil had said.

Lucilla drew them across the room to talk to the Earl of Buckingham. While Jennifer conversed, Drake studied her. Poised and charming, she looked as though she had been born to be a duchess. His anger calmed, replaced by pride. What magic made her different from any other woman in the kingdom? Made him want her with a ferocity that a fortnight earlier would have amazed and appalled him?

She actually seemed to be from a different society, and the difference wasn't merely because she spoke like an American and claimed to come from there. She used words he couldn't begin to comprehend. *Where had she learned them? Could she be from the future, as she claimed?*

Despite his cynicism where women were concerned, Jennifer delighted him. Part of him wanted to believe they were soul mates, as she said. Lord knew, no other had ever pleased him as she did. But the cynical, jaded part of him believed she was Miranda and her memories would eventually return. If they did, would he tire of her as he had tired of other women? Did men who loved fall out of love after the newness wore off?

He waited for a lull in her conversation with the Earl before he squeezed her hand. She looked up at him, her colorful eyes full of concern. "Is something wrong, Drake?"

"I would speak in private." Taking her elbow, he excused them and guided her to a corner, near a huge vase of fresh flowers.

"What's bothering you?" she asked.

"What did the wizard say to you while the rest of us were paralyzed?"

Without taking her eyes from his, Jennifer said, "He—congratulated me on our marriage."

Drake's hold on her elbow firmed, his thoughts turned grim. He suspected she hid things from him. Important things he had a right to know. Things he needed to know to protect her.

Before he could press her Olvan joined them. His face in a broad grin, the Scot bowed politely. When Jennifer offered her hand, he kissed it on both sides.

Moment's later Lucilla approached with Clay and Kacy.

"Your friend has been entertaining me with stories of you when you were girls."

"We had some marvelous times," Jennifer said.

"Yes," Kacy agreed, smiling.

Lucilla flicked her gaze from one to the other before she asked, "Did the Countess teach you to speak with an American accent?"

Jennifer shrugged. She had married Drake as Miranda, so she'd better not rock the boat. "She might have. I never thought much about it."

"How long have you known each other?"

"We met when we were very young," Kacy said. "And we've been friends all our lives."

Approval shone in Lucilla's blue eyes before she said, "You must have kept up a lively correspondence."

"We did." Jennifer nodded, thinking about all the phone calls they'd shared and the emails they'd sent as they'd grown older and computers became commonplace.

"Do you know Prudence as well?" Lucilla asked Kacy.

"No. I've never met her."

Jennifer breathed in relief when the housekeeper signaled, and Lucilla said, "Dinner is waiting to be served."

"Then let us dine." Drake hiked a brow at Olvan. "Will you accompany Grandmother?"

"I canna'," Olvan declined the honor.

"Of course you can," Lucilla insisted. "You're an old and dear friend, and I shall be hurt if you refuse."

Olvan smiled and offered his arm. Lucilla smiled as she took it.

Drake led Jennifer from the ballroom, flanked by the people who meant the most to him—his grandmother, Olvan, Clay and Kacy. Forced to admit Jennifer hadn't lied about knowing the Countess, Drake watched them. Even a cynic like him couldn't doubt they knew each other very well. They must have met before he married Helen, before he knew Jennifer Miranda and Prudence. But if so, how could she remember Kacy and nothing about her recent life? Had Jennifer forgotten everything unpleasant, and remembered only the good?

Once again he wondered if she might not be Miranda. *Could her claims be true? Could she be from the future?*

If so, was Kacy from there as well? There was one way to find out. Ask Clay.

Sixteen

Second Wedding Night

Jennifer had never eaten in such grandeur. The dining room rivaled the interior of the opulent Brighton Pavilion. A long dining table covered with a white tablecloth dominated the center of the room. Set to perfection with colorful Royal Crown Derby china, gold silverware, and stiff new napkins, or serviettes as the Brits called them, the table looked fit for royalty. Scattered around the room were more tables, set to accommodate all three hundred guests.

Drake guided Jennifer to one end of the center table and seated her in a gold brocade chair. Then he sat beside her at the head of the table. Olvan and his grandmother sat at his left, Clay and Kacy at his right, beside Jennifer.

She was so glad to be by them, instead of at the opposite end by a bunch of strangers, she leaned close and whispered, "Thanks for seating me near you."

Drake whispered as well. "The wizard is here. I dared not seat you anywhere else."

Jennifer smiled. "I'm glad."

He smiled fondly, his eyes warm with promise.

Although the lavish meal was a feast, Jennifer was too keyed up to eat very much. In addition to being nervous that she might say or do something to embarrass Drake, her first glimpse of Stonemeade had taken her breath away, and she still hadn't quite recovered. Located on the crest of a hill, the palatial estate, with acres of well-tended gardens, extended to the nearby woods. Half surrounded by a lake that she assumed might have once been a moat, Jennifer recognized the mansion as the one Sevil had briefly landed on top of before he took her to Paris.

"Do you really live here, in all this splendor?" she had asked Drake after they entered the mansion yesterday.

"I do. You do as well."

"I expected to live in your cottage—hunting lodge."

His blue eyes had twinkled as he flirted. "The bed in my chamber here is far more suitable for making love than the cot in my lodge."

"But the lodge will always hold a special place in my heart."

"Then we must return."

"Could we make love there?" Jennifer had cheerfully asked.

The glint in his eyes was a wicked promise. "Certainly."

Drake interrupted her thoughts when he inclined his head and whispered. "You should eat. You may need strength for what I plan after the celebration."

His suggestive words made her cheeks burn. "I'll remember this time forever."

And she would. Too bad she didn't have a camcorder to record everything—the wedding, the banquet, the people. Perhaps later, with paper and pen, or parchment and quill, she could describe their surroundings, and write about her feelings... and Drake's. If only she knew what they were.

After the feast, Lucilla withdrew the ladies. She led Kacy and Jennifer to a small powder room, and left them a short time later. Delighted to have a few private minutes alone with Kacy, Jennifer explained, "Drake and I eloped to Gretna Green last Saturday."

Kacy smiled. "Does he know you're not Miranda?"

"I told him, but he doesn't believe me. He didn't believe I knew you, either. I think we shocked him when we hugged each other."

"If I can do anything to help convince him, you'll let me know, won't you?"

"Yes. Of course, and I do have a favor to ask."

"Ask away."

"Could you summon your guardian angel, so I can ask him some questions?"

"I'll try," Kacy promised, "but I don't know if I can. Now that I'm happily married, I rarely see Rey."

When they rejoined their husbands, the chairs in the ballroom had been cleared. At a nod from Drake, the orchestra struck up a waltz. Without a word, he drew Jennifer into his arms.

She loved dancing with him, and wished it could continue for the rest of their lives. Remembering his limp, she asked, "Does dancing hurt your leg?"

"Not at the moment."

"You're a marvelous dancer."

"As are you."

"Dancing isn't all you do that's marvelous," she flirted with a teasing smile.

His blue eyes sparkled with amusement... and desire. "Be careful, Duchess, or I may end the celebration straightaway and my conduct thereafter will be most improper."

"I love your idle threats."

He cocked his brow. "My threats are never idle, my dear."

"I hope not," she laughed, thrilled to be called *his dear.*

When the first waltz ended, Kacy and Clay joined them on the dance floor. Tickled to see Lucilla flirting with Olvan, Jennifer mentioned it during the next waltz. She expected Drake to smile. He didn't.

"They are fond of one another, however, Olvan will never allow their affection to develop beyond friendship."

"Because your grandmother is the dowager?"

Drake nodded, and Jennifer realized how much she had to learn about this time, its customs, and being a duchess. She didn't want to embarrass Drake or herself. Hopefully Kacy and Lucilla would teach her everything she needed to know.

Jennifer danced continually, with Olvan, Clay, and Drake's friends, before she danced with him again. Finally the white candles in the overhead chandeliers burned low and the celebration dwindled to an end.

As their guests departed, Jennifer realized she was tired. She hadn't slept much last night. Discovering Drake was a duke still boggled her mind; seeing his ancestral mansion amazed her, meeting so many people at once overwhelmed her, and Sevil's announcement that she could stay in this time both thrilled and worried her.

Finally only Kacy, Clay, Lucilla and Olvan remained. Kacy and Clay would spend the night in a guestroom.

Lucilla fanned herself as she said, "Your marriage has made me very happy." She smiled and stopped fanning. "I shan't delay you. I know you're tired, Jennifer. However," she added with a suggestive gleam in her blue eyes, "I do hope you're not too tired to satisfy the Duke."

"Don't be vulgar, Grandmother," Drake chided, but he spoke kindly, his expression tender.

"Good night, Your Grace," Jennifer said.

"You must call me Lucilla."

"I'll consider that a privilege."

"Stuff and nonsense," Lucilla said, her eyes sparkling.

"Good night, Grandmother." Drake placed a gentle kiss on her wrinkled cheek before Olvan led her away.

"Be sure to look at yourself in the mirror before you undress," Kacy said then.

"Yes do," Clay said. "You truly are a beautiful bride, Jennifer, and it's a pleasure to see you again."

"Thank you." Jennifer blushed as Drake took her hand.

They bid Kacy and Clay good night, then Drake led Jennifer away. At the grand winding staircase he swept his arm beneath her knees and lifted her, cradling her against his chest.

Delighted, she draped her arms around his shoulders, admiring his handsome face while he climbed the grand staircase.

Upstairs, inside the master chamber, he set her on her feet while he closed the door.

"Do you mind if I take this off?"

His eyes widened in surprise as his gaze traveled over her like an all-consuming flame.

"The veil," she explained, heat crawling up her throat. "It's lovely, but it's heavy, and I feel as though I've had it on for hours."

"You have." Drake's husky tone matched his potent stare. "However, first you must see yourself in the mirror as the Countess suggested."

"You won't think me vain if I do?"

He shook his head. A lock of wavy hair fell over his forehead. She resisted the urge to put it back in place as he drew her to the full-length mirror beside his bulky bureau.

Under his close scrutiny, she stared at their reflection, first his, then her own. Beadwork adorned the frothy veil, as well as the bodice and skirt of the gown. The pearls shimmered in the candlelight, and Jennifer felt as though she was staring at a dream.

When she'd married Dirk, she had worn a simple white dress and he had worn a blue suit that complimented his blue eyes. In Gretna Green she and Drake hadn't changed from their traveling clothes. Now, in formal attire, they looked like something straight out of a fairy tale. For a few seconds she stood in a trance of disbelief. Not in her wildest imagination had she considered she might be the bride in her vision of his wedding. Gratitude swelled inside her.

"Clay's right," Drake said, his gaze holding hers in the mirror. "You are a beautiful bride, Jennifer."

Basking under his compliment, she raised her hand to push his wayward lock of hair back in place. "You look rather grand, yourself."

"Where did you get the gown?"

"It's your grandmother's. She had a new ivory one that Miranda purchased, but she said she married your grandfather in this one, so I chose to wear it."

"It fits you very well," Drake said quietly, his expression unreadable.

"Your grandmother had it altered." Flustered, Jennifer fumbled with the pearl-studded hairgrips that anchored her veil. Drake came to her aid, freed the grips, then slipped the veil off her head.

He didn't move when he finished, nor did he set the veil down. He continued to stare at their reflection in the mirror, his mouth parted ever so slightly.

Her heart fluttered, then started to race. She forgot everything except her husband who stood so close and smelled so wonderful. *When would he kiss her?*

Drake blinked and looked away. A frown marred his brow as he turned to set her veil on the back of an overstuffed chair.

Hoping he would confide in her if something were bothering him, Jennifer glanced around his chamber. Yesterday Lucilla had whisked her off to the dower house so quickly she hadn't seen much of the mansion.

Furniture built of rich mahogany graced Drake's spacious bedroom. Decorated in shades of blue with splashes of gold and white, Jennifer felt as though she had fallen into the lap of luxury. A small fire glowed in the grate of the marble fireplace. The flames of a half dozen gold candles added romantic ambience. Jennifer thought the room exquisite. Perfect for a wedding night.

"I can hardly believe this is your home and that I'm your wife."

"Duchess of Stonemeade," he said, his eyes still unreadable.

But as they stared, awareness radiated between them.

"I don't feel like a wife at the moment," she said in an attempt to relieve the budding tension.

Without changing his expression, he asked, "Why did you marry me, Jennifer?"

"Because I already considered you my husband," she said, looking him square in the eye. "And because I wish to be with you forever."

He hiked dubious brows. "Forever is a very long time. No doubt you will tire of me after the novelty of being wed wears off."

Dismayed by his attitude, her heart dived. "I'll never tire of you, Drake. I promise. Not even if I'm taken away and never see you again."

He raised his hand to smooth his mustache. "While you were in the powder room, I asked Clay if Kacy came from the future."

Understanding the significance of his admission, Jennifer's thumping heart swam back up to her chest.

"What did you think of his answer?"

"It confirmed what I already wished to believe."

"Oh, Drake, thank you."

Instead of taking her in his arms as she hoped, Drake stuck his hands in his black trouser pockets. "Now I find myself in somewhat of a quandary."

"Why?"

"Because I'm married to the wrong lady. I married Miranda. However, I wish to be married to you. I have compromised you, Jennifer. Doesn't that bother you?"

"Not at all," she cheerfully said.

"Why?"

"Because I'm your wife no matter what name I used, and if Miranda doesn't return, nobody needs to know I'm not her."

"If she returns, I could not possibly claim her as my wife."

"I know how you feel," Jennifer said. "I couldn't live with any other man either."

Drake pulled her into his arms finally and murmured against her temple, "The wizard, or man you call Sevil, said more than congratulations while the rest of us were frozen and unable to hear. What more did he say?"

"He said Miranda likes the future and wants to stay there, and that I can stay here as long as I do what he wants."

"What does he want?" Drake pulled slightly away to gain eye contact.

"I haven't a clue. He said I'll know, eventually."

To her surprise and delight, Drake kissed her. And he didn't maintain control as he had earlier. He kissed her long and passionately. Jennifer thrilled to his seeking, probing tongue, and his wandering hands that fondled, explored and caressed.

The sweet, tormenting kiss ended too soon. "You must not go out and about without my approval," Drake said. "I cannot protect you unless I know where you are at all times. Will you abide by my request?"

"Yes, of course." Jennifer reached up to smooth the creases on his forehead. "I'll try to do what you think best always, Drake. And a wedding night should be a happy event, not a frustrating one."

He smiled. "I agree." He started to loosen his cravat. His Adam's apple bobbed. Fascinated, Jennifer simply watched him.

A discreet knock sounded on the door.

Teeny, the small maid, stood in the hall when Drake opened the door. "The Countess, she bade me give this bed gown ta the Duchess, Yer Grace."

Drake took the nightgown and started to shut the door.

"Will the Duchess need me assistance ta prepare fer bed?"

"I shall assist her. Inform the staff we do not wish to be disturbed."

A rush of gratitude for Kacy's thoughtfulness raced through Jennifer as Drake set the bed gown on the bed.

"Turn around," he said. "I'll unfasten your gown."

She turned, catching another glimpse of her reflection in the mirror. The beautiful gown snugged her waist. Petticoats and a hooped crinoline swelled the skirt into a swaying bell shape, and a white ribbon attached the long train to her wrist. Would she ever wear anything as elegant again?

Tiny thrills traced up her neck and down her arms as Drake unbuttoned the small, satin-covered buttons all the way past her waist. Having him perform the personal task brought back lusty memories. Every time he had helped her out of her clothes while they traveled, they had made love. The memories made her tremble.

Drake paused in his task. "Are you cold?"

"No."

Gently, yet firmly, he turned her chin until their eyes met. They stood so close their breath mingled and she smelled the wine he had consumed with dinner. How could she love him so darn much when he didn't remember her?

"Why did you tremble?"

"Your nearness does that to me sometimes."

Grinning, Drake resumed his task at the back of her gown. When he finished, he pushed the pearl-studded gown off her shoulders, down her arms and waist, then shoved the camisole aside and busied himself loosening her rigid corset stays.

"Your slenderness needs no corset," he said crisply.

Breathing became a chore. Even with the restrictive corset loosened, his hands were still on her and she felt their warmth through the underclothes. Deep inside yearnings burned and she wished he would kiss her, take her in his arms.

When he backed away and started to remove his suit coat, she felt awkward, almost shy. But he'd seen her naked a number of times. She slipped the wedding gown over her hips, stepped out of it, and worked on the undergarments, struggling with the corset even though Drake had loosened the stays. Finally naked, she slid the new, sexy white nightgown over her head.

Ready for bed, she set her undergarments on an overstuffed chair and laid the petticoats and gown over the back. Not knowing where to put the crinoline hoop, she dragged it to a corner. "I feel as though I've shed ten pounds." She nodded at the hoop.

Drake laughed. "You've shed more than that."

She blushed and glanced at the bed again. It was too high to get in without assistance unless she hoisted herself up, which would be unladylike and awkward.

"I don't see a stool. Will you help me get in bed?"

"With pleasure," Drake said, a gleam in his eyes.

She smiled when he extinguished all but two candles before he picked her up and set her on the edge of the bed.

For a few seconds Jennifer didn't know what to do or say. Then she remembered what she had saved to say on this special night. Even if he rejected her words, she had to say them. This might be her only chance.

"I love you, Drake. I think I'd love you even if I hadn't loved you many times before."

He sat beside her and gently took both her hands in his. "I love you, too, Jennifer."

A hundred thousand thrills wiggled through her. "You do?"

Drake nodded.

On the verge of tears, she cried, "Oh Drake, what are we going to do? I don't want to leave you. I want to be with you forever!"

He drew her close. "Don't cry, darling. This should be one of happiest nights of our lives."

"I can't help it," she sniffed. "I'm so happy, and so afraid."

He bent his head and kissed her.

Her tears vanished as she kissed him back with all the love she had stored up for more lifetimes than she could remember.

When he trailed kisses from her jaw to her throat, she started to unbutton his ruffled white shirt.

Drake lifted his head. "Downstairs you looked tired. Are you sure you have the energy for this?" His hands were already fondling her breasts.

She splayed her hands on his bare chest and felt his thudding heart. "I'll always have energy for this."

"I should have known you wouldn't disappoint me."

"And I, you," she murmured. A few seconds later, she added, "Being in your arms feels like coming home after a long, tiresome journey."

"I know." He kissed her again, breathing her name in a voice that sounded choked with hunger. "Jennifer..."

She trembled. "Yes, Drake?"

"Why can't I get enough of you?"

"Beats me."

He delighted her by pulling her down on top of him. All the emotions assaulting her weren't new. She'd felt them before, in the future as well as in prior lives.

While he kissed, fondled, and explored, her desire grew to unparalleled heights. When he fumbled with the new bed gown, she didn't think he could get it off fast enough. Or his own clothes, even though she helped him.

Finally he wore nothing; not even the opal. She wondered where it was. All she had on were the pearl earrings she'd worn the day she fell from the tree, the locket Drake had purchased during their return from Scotland, the ruby ring he had given her after the first ceremony, and the new betrothal and wedding rings he'd given her today.

"I like you wearing nothing more than jewels."

"I like you without clothes, too."

She sighed with pleasure as he brought her lips down on his again, and her body pulsed with need when he pressed her pelvis against his erection.

Inflamed, she groaned and clasped him tighter, kissing him, running her hands over his face and shoulders, through his hair, down his neck, around to his chest and below, murmuring soft phrases against his mouth while her body trembled against his.

At last she rolled off him and grasped his arousal, stroking him while he caressed and explored her.

A long time later she moaned, "I can't wait any longer, Drake. Love me now. Please."

He kissed her deeply, preparing to bury himself inside her.

"I'm delighted you open every part of yourself to me," he murmured, his voice thick with need.

"And I'm delighted that you want me as much as I want you," she breathed.

He sank into her moist flesh.

"I love you," she moaned. "I love you so darn much."

"I love you, too."

Then conscious thought deserted her. Their bodies rocked in unison and they spun into the wild inferno that consumed her every time they made love.

~ * ~

Afterwards Drake held her close. Jennifer could barely breathe. Once again he had taken her to that glorious place that made her feel like an immortal with her eternal mate. Pleased that he still held her, she caressed his chest and shoulders, then let her hands wander over his back, and lower. Feeling the uneven bumps, she remembered the scars.

"How did you get these?" she asked, gently rubbing them.

Not proud of his disfiguration, Drake had tried to keep her from seeing them, although he knew she must have felt them when they made love.

"From a fire."

"They must have hurt for a long time."

"They did." As much as the scandal and Helen's infidelity with his brother, but he didn't want to think about that tonight.

Jennifer startled him when she pulled free from his embrace and said, "Turn around."

"Why?"

"Turn, and I'll show you."

He didn't want to, but he did, grateful for the near dark so she couldn't see his scarred back clearly. When she started to scatter kisses all across his back, he tensed.

"What are you doing?"

"Kissing your scars so you'll never be ashamed of them again."

"I'm not ashamed."

"Good, then you won't try to hide them from me in the future."

She startled him again by sprinkling more kisses on his back, until he was sure she had kissed and caressed every inch, even the flesh where he had no scars.

After she urged him to turn back around, she touched his chest. "I love this part of you, Drake." She touched his arms. "I love these too, and I love your mouth and eyes. I love everything about you, but..." she wrapped her arms around him and ran her fingers lightly over his scars again, "I think I might love these a little bit more than some of you."

Too choked up to say much, he grunted, "Why?"

She snuggled between his arms before she answered. "Because they're proof of how brave you are."

Love flowed through Drake. He kissed her because he didn't know what to say.

Sometime later, she asked, "What did you do with the opal?"

"I took it off when I bathed. I'll put it back on in the morning," he promised.

But he wouldn't think about the opal or his scars anymore tonight. Not on their formal wedding night. All he would think about was pleasuring Jennifer, pleasing himself.

And that's all he did, tumbling more deeply in love with each tender caress.

Seventeen

Autumn Bliss and Winter Gloom

Seated at the small table in Drake's chamber, Jennifer wrote on a new page in her journal, *September and October passed in a blissful daze.* Then she leaned back, relaxed and content. When she told Drake she wanted to keep a journal, he had taken her to Canterbury where they purchased a bound blank volume, as well as ink and pens for her use.

Pen still in hand, she wrote; *With the help of Drake's grandmother and Kacy, I have learned the differences between the titled gentry and the proper way to treat his peers. Stonemeade is often crowded with guests, and I play hostess, helping Drake entertain, as we did again tonight.*

Leaving the journal open so the ink would dry without smearing, Jennifer climbed in bed, using the stool Drake had also bought for her. A single candle still burned, an invitation for him to awaken her when he came up. They usually retired together, but tonight they had entertained some of his peers from London, and she had left the men to their discussion hours ago.

She had barely closed her eyes when she heard Drake enter the room. Opening her eyes, she smiled. "Are your guests gone?"

"All save two. The butler Jacob, showed them to guestrooms."

Jennifer's stomach growled. "I'm hungry. How about you?"

Drake grinned. "Should we go see if Cook left any tasty morsels in the pantry?"

"I'm game if you are." She scooted out of bed and reached for her robe. Drake snagged it from her fingers and slung it behind his back. His hungry gaze feasted on the white bed gown Kacy had provided on their wedding night nine weeks before.

"You truly are a sight to behold, Duchess."

She smiled. "So are you, Duke."

"Tis a shame to cover your loveliness."

"I'm glad you think so."

His eyes on her breasts, barely concealed beneath the flimsy fabric, he bent his head and placed a gentle kiss on the valley between them. Then he held her robe open for her to put on, and kissed the tender spot below her ear, making her quiver with sweet anticipation before she slid her arms through the sleeves.

Like conspirators, they crept hand in hand, quietly down the stairs. The small stump of a candle in Drake's hand lit their way.

"Chocolate cake." Jennifer licked her lips when she saw the treat on a pantry shelf. "Do you think Cook will be upset if we filch it?"

"No. I think she expects our midnight raids, and ensures there's something for us to filch."

Jennifer spied a tray on the worktable, along with two plates and forks, and a knife. "I think you're right."

Back up in Drake's chamber a few minutes later, he lit a new candle, then sat across from Jennifer at the small table. She closed her journal and moved it aside before she gave him the biggest slice of cake.

She took her first bite, savoring the delicious chocolatey flavor before she swallowed. "I love these midnight snacks."

"I do as well, along with our conversations."

Jennifer smiled agreement. "Have I convinced you that we've known each other in other lives yet?"

Drake nodded. "There's no other explanation for our quick attraction, nor for how in tune we are with each other."

"We're soul mates," Jennifer proclaimed before she forked another bite of cake.

Drake steepled a brow while he chewed. "I have never heard anyone except you use those words."

"They're popular in the future. There's an emerging theory that soul mates are kindred spirits, perfect mates, and they meet in several lifetimes. Sometimes things get messed up so people don't always meet the one person right for them. My memories tell me that you and I met in a number of different lives, but never had a chance to fulfill our love. In the last one, maybe I should say, in my current life in the future, you moved in next door to where I lived with my aunt, uncle and cousin, Tyler. We both had our prior memories even though we were children. That's why we eloped when we did. We were afraid if we waited, something might part us."

"And something did?"

Jennifer nodded. "We were married on a Saturday, and you were accidentally killed the next Thursday while driving to be with me."

"Was I driving a car?"

"Yes. An old red Jaguar." She had previously described cars, planes, trains, electricity, computers and everything else she could think of. "It was June. You had just returned from Harvard University, and I had just graduated from high school."

In previous conversations, she had explained the education system and told him she had been orphaned at the age of four.

Drake smiled. "Now we've had a chance to fulfill our love."

Jennifer smiled, too. "Yes. Finally."

But how long would it last? That question nagged her every day. The fear that Miranda might return and Sevil might take her away was never far from Jennifer's thoughts.

After they finished the cake, Drake disrobed and they went to bed. As usual, he gathered her close and kissed her. Jennifer responded with abandon.

To her continued delight, their passion knew no boundaries.

She fell asleep in his arms.

~ * ~

Each week Drake presented Jennifer with another gift. One of the nicest was Mordora. Jennifer learned to ride English style, in a sidesaddle. Often they took early morning rides in the woods; sometimes just the two of them, sometimes with their guests.

One morning they rode by themselves to his hunting lodge.

"Shall I build a fire?" Drake asked when they were inside.

Jennifer grinned. "Yes, please." She planned to seduce him when the lodge warmed.

Apparently he had the same plan in mind. "Come sit on the bed with me," he invited, a teasing glint in his blue eyes.

Happily Jennifer complied.

He gathered her close, and she arched up to kiss him.

To Jennifer's delight, they warmed each other, long before the lodge warmed.

Afterwards they moved, still naked, to the sofa. Cuddled together under a soft blanket, Jennifer glanced out of one uncurtained window.

"What do you think makes the sky so blue?" she asked.

"It looks blue because the sunlight is scattered by nitrogen and oxygen."

"Did you learn that in this life? Or a previous one?"

"I honestly don't know, " Drake said. "Sometimes I dream I'm someone named Dirk, and the dream often lingers for days. Last night I dreamed I attended a huge university. It wasn't Oxford. It wasn't even in England."

"Maybe it was more than a dream. Maybe it was a memory."

"Perhaps."

"Your family mourned your death as much as I did," Jennifer said. "It was terrible. I can't begin to explain how much I wanted to die too, so I could meet you in another life."

Drake folded her between his arms. "We mustn't dwell on that now."

"We need to discuss it," Jennifer disagreed as a vision flashed and she saw herself back in the future with Catharine, and without Drake. "In case Sevil parts us." Tears threatened, but she ignored them. "We have to have faith that we'll meet again, somehow, someday, somewhere."

"I believe." Drake said, before he started his tender assault all over again.

The beautiful days were all that her marriage to Dirk hadn't been, and Jennifer cherished every hour of every day.

~ * ~

A few days later they traveled to Sussex to visit Drake's paralyzed cousin, Boyden, and his devoted wife, Charlotte.

"We wanted a family," Charlotte said, her eyes sad as she looked from Drake to Jennifer.

Sitting across from Charlotte and Boyden in the lounge of their country home, Jennifer said, "I'm sure you'll have one."

"I wish I could believe that."

A vision flashed. Jennifer saw them with three daughters during the years to come.

"Don't fret, Charlotte. Have faith, and be patient. I'm sure you'll have children."

Charlotte smiled. "Thank you for being sympathetic. Most people are not." She turned her gaze to Drake. "I think you have chosen well this time, Your Grace."

He nodded, and Boyden gripped the arms of his wooden wheelchair.

"Whether I'm out of this contraption or not, Charlotte and I plan to take you up on your invitation to spend Christmas with you at Stonemeade."

"We look forward to your visit," Drake said.

"Yes, we do," Jennifer added, making a mental list of gifts they would need to buy.

~ * ~

They concluded their trip with a stopover at Havenhurst, to visit with Kacy and Clay in Surrey. After the initial greetings, the men repaired to Clay's study to discuss business.

Jennifer followed Kacy up to the nursery. The twins, now nine months old, were crawling, and Jennifer and Kacy enjoyed watching them play.

When the nanny left the room, Jennifer asked, "Have you seen your guardian angel yet?"

"No. But if I do, I'll be sure to ask him to visit you."

"Thanks. I'd appreciate it. Sevil wants something from me, but he hasn't said what, and I have a feeling I can't trust him."

"What did he say at your wedding when he froze all the rest of us?"

"You knew he froze everyone except me?" Jennifer asked, surprised Kacy hadn't mentioned it before.

"Yes. Clay knew, too."

Jennifer explained what Sevil had said, then added, "I'm so relieved Drake no longer thinks I'm Miranda. I understand he asked Clay if you were from the future."

"Yes," Kacy said. "Clay told me. We tell each other everything."

"You must be very close."

"We are, but it wasn't always like this," Kacy reminded.

"You told me when we were in Paris, but I want to read what you wrote in your journal about your return to this time."

"Does that mean you don't expect to stay here?" Kacy asked.

"I'd like to, but I'm afraid if I don't give Sevil what he wants, he'll take me back. I had a vision of myself back in the future with Catharine."

Kacy frowned. "If the wizard takes you back, and Miranda doesn't return to this time, Drake might be accused of murdering you, or her."

"I've thought about that and it worries me. Maybe I should ask Drake to have his solicitor prepare annulment or divorce documents so if I'm taken back, he can terminate our marriage, and say I've gone to live in America."

"That's a solution, but I don't like it because I don't want you to leave," Kacy said.

"But it might help Drake, if I'm taken against my will."

"It might." Kacy frowned, then smiled down at the twins as they crawled across the floral-patterned carpet, hindered by their long gowns.

"I've started a journal," Jennifer said, "but I'm afraid it might not have a happy ending."

"You have to believe it will."

"You're always so optimistic."

"So are you. That's why we're such good friends."

Jennifer smiled.

And Kacy asked, "Do you miss the future?"

"I miss Tyler, Aunt Rachel, Uncle Mac, and my cat."

"Is Mordora still alive?"

"Yes, but she's lost her appetite. Catharine takes good care of her, but I never dreamed I'd be gone more than a week."

"Do you still have visions of Catharine and Miranda every night?"

Jennifer nodded. "Sometimes I see Mordora too. She's the only one who apparently doesn't think Miranda is me. At first she wouldn't go near her, but now she seems to accept her."

Kacy's baby girl bumped against Jennifer's legs, and she leaned over to pick her up. "Do you miss the future, Kacy?"

"Sometimes. But this is where I want to be." She reached down and picked up her son after he put his chubby little hands on her legs and attempted to stand. "I love Clay with all my heart, and I love my babies, too."

"I know you do." Jennifer kissed Kacy's baby daughter on her soft cheek. "I love Drake with all my heart, too, and sometimes I'm so happy I think my bubble might burst. Oops," she laughed as she felt a warm spot soak through her gown and wet her thighs. "I think one of us needs to change a diaper."

"They're called nappies in England. And I'll change hers." Kacy winked. "Our nanny's so efficient, I don't usually get a chance."

Jennifer smiled. "If I'm somehow allowed to stay in the nineteenth century, maybe next year I'll be happily changing nappies, too."

"I'll pray for that." Kacy and Jennifer exchanged babies. As Kacy changed her daughter, she asked, "What do you miss about the future, Jen?"

"Conveniences, like the bathroom. And gadgets. If we had phones, we could talk to each other every day. Or if we had computers, we could email. I miss electricity, too. The ability to flip a light switch, make toast, microwave popcorn. How about you? What do you miss?"

Kacy grinned. "Music."

"But you play the piano."

"I miss modern music, and my boom box. Don't you?"

Jennifer laughed. "Yes. Movies too, and soft drinks. Pepsi. And riding in a car on a smooth road instead of in a buggy or a carriage on a bumpy lane."

Kacy's baby boy started to wiggle in Jennifer's arms. She raised him to her shoulder and patted him on the back.

"What don't you miss?"

"The rat race. Pollution, especially Denver's brown cloud. And most of the news on TV and in the newspaper. Why do you think reporters only report bad stuff?"

"Because," Kacy said, "they think that's what sells newspapers and glues people to the TV."

"In the twenty-first century everything is built bigger and better than ever before, but people are pressured, and they have short tempers, narrow viewpoints, prejudices, phobias, and less time to enjoy life."

"That about sums it up," Kacy agreed.

"Shall I tell you what I love about this century?"

Kacy nodded. "Please do."

"You and Clay and Drake are here, and I'm grateful for every minute I spend with each of you."

"I'm grateful as well."

"What are you grateful for?" Clay asked as he and Drake entered the nursery.

"Your hospitality." Jennifer smiled at Drake, conveying with her eyes, that she was also grateful for him.

"We'll have an opportunity to reciprocate," he said. "I've invited Clay and Kacy to spend Christmas with us at Stonemeade."

Jennifer beamed. "That's wonderful!"

~ * ~

The day after their return to Stonemeade, Jennifer got sick. Nauseated, tired, lethargic. Not wanting to worry Drake, she started to distance herself, hoping he wouldn't notice. He didn't seem to.

First he was busy with Olvan, planning which mares to breed with which stallions. Then they had more houseguests and Drake entertained the men late each night. He even stopped going to bed with Jennifer. She usually fell asleep before he came upstairs and he was gone before she awakened.

After their guests left he had to catch up on work that had piled on his desk. She had stopped spending each day with him in his study, and he often used Josian to communicate with her. She hated that, but didn't complain because she didn't want Drake to know that half the time she felt deathly ill.

The rest of November passed in a dismal, nauseating blur.

After three and a half months of marriage, that included two weeks of feeling sick and sorry for herself, Jennifer forced the doldrums aside, and got a new lease on life. She now felt healthy, vibrant, alive... Also pregnant. Thankfully the morning sickness, that had plagued her day and night, no longer bothered her.

But the fear that she might not be in this century when her baby was born, scared the heck out of her. She was even afraid she might not be here for Christmas.

Eighteen

December Doldrums

Early one December morning, bundled in her black cloak with a gray wool lap robe over her knees, Jennifer and Drake left for London. As the ducal carriage rumbled beyond the black iron-gated entrance, she looked wistfully back at the mansion. Every time they left Stonemeade, Jennifer got the jitters. So far her fears had proven groundless, but she still worried she might not return.

Was Sevil biding his time to lull her into a false sense of security before he told her what he wanted? Would he demand something she couldn't give? The same thing he had demanded from Miranda that she had refused?

Worried about that possibility, Jennifer said, "Most good experiences can never be repeated."

"That's true of bad experiences as well," Drake said, with cryptic, yet casual elegance.

"Nor are they ever forgotten," she said softly.

His mustache twitched. She thought he might be suppressing a smile. "Have you had more good experiences than bad, Jennifer?"

"Yes. Haven't you?"

"No."

In spite of his dour tone, Jennifer smiled as she stared at the crooked hedges that bordered Kent's twisty roads.

"What brought that smile to your face?"

Delighted to be alone with him after all the company they'd had, Jennifer said, "I was thinking about Teeny, and all the servants. I adore them."

"They adore you, too. All those at Stonemeade as well as those in London."

Jennifer blushed. "Did you know they call your secretary The Gaffer?"

"Josian?"

When she nodded, Drake said, "I suppose it suits him."

"He has a rather uppity air, as though he's better than..."

"Than who?" Drake demanded when she hesitated.

"The servants. And me."

"He treats you shabbily?"

Jennifer wished she hadn't mentioned Josian. She didn't want to create more friction. "I'm not complaining, Drake. I don't think Josian means anything by his attitude. It must just be his way."

"I'll talk to him."

"Please don't. That might make matters worse."

"Then I'll dismiss him."

"You don't have to do that." She reached for his hand and held it with both of hers. "I have something more exciting to discuss than Josian."

"What?"

"First, I want to apologize for neglecting you this past fortnight. I didn't do it because I wanted to, but I felt ill, and I didn't want to worry you."

He looked worried now... and concerned. "You should have told me. We could have postponed our journey to London."

"I don't feel ill anymore. Actually, I wasn't ill. I..."

"Are you sure you are not ill?"

"I'm sure. And I want you to know I love you with all my heart."

"Thank God." He lifted her onto his lap and wrapped his arms around her. "I love you, Jennifer. I don't know what I'd do if anything happened to you."

"Nothing's going to happen to me, except..."

"Except what?" he prompted, his tone full of concern.

Jennifer felt loved, special, protected, and she felt guilty for distancing herself. Although Drake had accepted her withdrawal without comment, he still held her hand whenever they went outdoors, as though afraid she might disappear if he let go. Even now, in the carriage, he held her close; ready to defend her should the need arise. They might have grown apart during the day, but whenever they went to bed together, they made passionate love.

She wiggled a little away so she could look him in the eye. She wanted to see his expression when she shared her news. "We're going to have a baby."

He looked so startled; a small breeze could have blown him over, if she hadn't been on his lap to anchor him. "A baby?"

"Yes. You do want one, don't you?"

"Yes. Certainly. But I don't wish you to suffer."

"I won't. Not anymore. The morning sickness is over."

"Is that why you stopped spending each day with me?"

"Yes."

"I feared you had tired of my company."

"Never," she vowed. "I'll always want to be near you."

Drake smiled. "For that I thank God... Again."

Then he kissed her, for a long, lingering time. The blood in her veins turned warm. So did her body.

A little later, Drake said, "You haven't asked why we're going to London."

"I assumed you have business to discuss with your solicitor, and your presence is desired in Parliament."

He nodded. "After we visit my solicitor I'll take you shopping for new gowns."

"You needn't buy me any more gowns, Drake. You've already given me too much. Besides, I might not be here long enough to enjoy them."

"We cannot dwell on the possibility that the wizard may take you away. We must dwell on happy thoughts, so that we have a happy, healthy child. And you'll need new gowns to accommodate the changes, now that you're increasing."

"We should shop for Christmas gifts, too. We'll need gifts for our guests, and all the servants, in both London and at Stonemeade."

Drake looked concerned. "I don't want you to overdo."

"Don't worry. I won't."

"Is that a promise?"

"If you need one."

"I do."

Delighted to be on his lap, and in his arms, she smiled. Even after all these weeks, he still had the capacity to make her heart throb and her pulse race with a mere look. She raised her hand to fluff her hair off her neck; surprised and delighted when Drake kissed her on that tender spot. She turned her head to kiss him on the cheek, remembering their first kiss when she was nine years old, as he touched her chin and held it while he kissed her chastely on the mouth.

After a while she asked, "Will we go out in the evenings while we're in London?"

He hiked a blond brow. "Would you like to go out?"

"Yes. To the theater. I love plays." It was the first time she had suggested an outing, and she wondered if she should have kept quiet.

"Would you like to attend a ball?"

"I'd love to, but don't we have to be invited?"

"We have a number of invitations from which to choose."

Her cheeks heated. Of course, he would be invited to all sorts of social affairs. He was probably very popular at soirees, balls, and masquerades. Would she be? Although they had entertained at Stonemeade, they hadn't gone out much, and she worried about how others would treat her away from the comfort of their home. She'd heard London society was quite different from the country, and she hadn't yet experienced the *ton*.

"How many people will know I'm a duchess?"

"Everyone who counts, as well as everyone who doesn't."

"If that doesn't sound ominous, I don't know what would."

"You'll dazzle them."

"I doubt it," she said, her dour tone drawing a grin from Drake.

"After you finish your business in London, I'd like to go to Havenhurst. I think Kacy might be able to help me get information about my relatives."

Drake frowned. "How can she get information from the future?"

"She can't, but maybe her guardian angel can."

The thought of Jennifer seeking assistance from someone else galled Drake. She was his responsibility and he wanted to see to all her needs. Did she miss her relatives and wish to return to them? He shoved his irritation aside and thought about their marriage. Time and time again, she satisfied him, and he knew he'd never tire of her.

There were times when he had a fleeting memory of knowing her previously. She had converted him to believe in reincarnation. He missed their late night conversations, just as he missed their midnight pantry raids. At times Jennifer made him feel young and invincible. Handsome and masterful, too.

A rush of pride surged through him as he thought about her condition. Their passion had created a child. The thought filled him with quiet joy.

~ * ~

As they traveled, Drake watched Jennifer, as he often did when she wasn't aware of it. He still wanted her with every breath he drew. When she distanced herself, he had suffered, but he'd had too much pride to ask why she no longer wished to be with him during the day.

Before they married he had scoffed at the tender side of marriage, and thought himself above that. But Jennifer reacted favorably to every single act of tenderness, and he found himself wanting to spend hours doing little things just to please her.

Knowing he had the right to bed her whenever he wished kept him in a state of near-constant arousal. Never before had he lusted after a woman, yet now he sometimes wanted Jennifer so badly he felt he might die of need.

There were days when he convinced himself they could share his bed each night without making love. He could sleep, too, once she did. But he knew those thoughts for the lies they were. No other lady's nearness had ever affected him so intensely. Their lovemaking drove him to the brink of insanity itself. With all his heart he hoped she stayed with him, and that Miranda never returned.

Feeling guilty for that last thought, he forced his concentration on the business matters he must see to in London. His solicitor should have the documents prepared for the sale of his interest in a small fleet of ships. Also, Christmas gifts must be purchased. His mind drifted to past years. Miranda had loved to shop... for herself, not others. She loved to spend his money. So did Prudence. To his knowledge, neither of them had ever given each other or the servants anything worthwhile. Their gifts were always so trivial he wondered why they bothered.

"Do you have any ideas in mind for gifts for the servants and our guests?" he asked.

Jennifer smiled up at him. "I had hoped you might have some suggestions, but I have a few myself. Is there a limit, or an amount you wish to spend on each servant?"

"I'm not a miser. Allow your ideas to blossom."

"Thanks." She smiled. "I will."

Her smile seemed an invitation and Drake struggled to maintain his calm facade. The desire to kiss and explore her, right there in broad daylight in the ducal carriage, attacked him. He wanted to muss her up and ravish her. The thought should have scandalized him. Instead it aroused him. And made him mighty uncomfortable throughout the remainder of the journey.

~ * ~

Seated in the reception hall while Drake talked to his solicitor, Jennifer made a mental Christmas list. All sorts of ideas popped into her head for their guests and the servants. But what could she get for

Drake? Something unique; something he wouldn't buy for himself. She couldn't think of anything special, but her mind kept searching.

From the solicitor's office, they went to Drake's home in Chelsea. When he handed her from the carriage, he asked, "Do you feel up to shopping today?"

"Yes. When do you wish to leave?"

"After we have tea to refresh ourselves from the journey. I must be in Parliament tomorrow."

They left an hour later. Drake took her to a shop where he announced, "The Duchess wishes to order an entire wardrobe."

"Drake," Jennifer protested. "I only need a few gowns."

His warm breath feathered the curls on her forehead when he stepped closer and quietly said, "Humor me in this, Jennifer. I wish to see you in gowns I select."

She forced herself to breathe, not an easy task with him standing so close she could smell his unique, wonderful breath.

"If a bribe is in order," he continued for her ears alone, "I'll take you to the theater tomorrow night, and as soon as a ball gown can be made, we shall attend a ball."

She smiled and raised a hand to his chest. "It's insane for you to bribe me to give me gifts."

He covered her hand with his. "I'm insane about you. Now tell me you'll order the gowns I wish you to have."

"All right, but only if you let me to do something for you."

"I'll be happy to oblige." A grinned tugged at his mouth, and she caught the expectant gleam in his eyes before he turned toward London's most popular seamstress.

He selected fabric for two dozen gowns. Then they looked at patterns. "Can the gowns be altered?" Drake asked.

The seamstress smiled. "Of course."

Jennifer blushed. She'd need them altered, let out to accommodate her pregnancy.

"We should go Christmas shopping," she said a few minutes later.

"First we must buy you some new shoes."

She'd been wearing Miranda's, but Drake apparently wanted her to have her own.

"As you wish."

He smiled, then said to the seamstress. "You may expect our return tomorrow afternoon."

Taking Jennifer's arm, he led her from the shop.

Dusk approached while they selected shoes, hats, under garments, nightgowns and other accessories.

"You look tired," he said when they walked outside and she saw how dark it had grown. "I'll summon the carriage."

"But we haven't done any Christmas shopping."

"You may shop tomorrow. I don't want to overtire you now. I have erotic plans for tonight."

She gave him a spunky grin. "I'll always have energy for that."

He kissed her cheek then settled her hand on his arm.

"You take such good care of me," she said.

Drake smiled. "Because I love you."

He waved his hand, and Jennifer marveled that Winslow waited not far away, and immediately started toward them.

While Winslow loaded packages, they climbed inside.

Soon they rode along London's crowded thoroughfares.

"Would you like to go out this evening?" Drake asked. "Or are you too tired?"

"I'm not too tired, but I'd prefer to stay home, if you don't mind. I need to make a list for my Christmas shopping in the morning."

Drake looked pleased. "Very well."

"Thank you for the new clothes and everything you've done for me, Drake."

"I don't want your gratitude," he said softly. "All I want is your love."

"You have that."

She opened her reticule, peered inside at the money Sevil had provided, then slanted it for Drake to see. "Do you think this will be enough to buy gifts for the servants?"

"Don't spend Sevil's money. I don't want you indebted to him. I'll instruct Josian to give you a new supply. If you find yourself short, charge whatever you wish. I have accounts at all of London's finest shops."

Jennifer studied Drake's grim expression. "Are you upset with me?"

"No. Should I be?"

"I hope not. But sometimes I get the impression you're not very happy."

"Life is not all made up of happiness, but I'm happier now than I've ever been."

Joy washed through Jennifer as she smiled at her husband.

Suddenly the carriage swerved and tilted on its side. Jennifer flew off the seat. But Drake reached out, snagged her, and pulled her onto his lap.

Struggling to breathe, she felt her heart pounding in her throat. She clasped her hands over her stomach. The baby could have been hurt!

Winslow righted the carriage and jerked the horses to a stop. Jennifer's heart still pounded when he opened the door.

"My apologies, Your Graces," he said. "Another carriage near ran me off the road. Be ye all right?"

"Yes," Drake said.

"And ye, Duchess?" Winslow asked, concerned.

"Yes, I'm fine. Thanks to the Duke's quick reflexes."

"Very good. I shall resume our journey."

It took a few minutes for Jennifer to calm her racing heart. Then it raced for another reason—being on Drake's lap with his arms wrapped around her. When she looked up, that awful premonition that she might not be here indefinitely, flashed. Worried, she wrapped her arms around him.

"Are you all right?" he asked.

Shaken, she said, "Yes, but I'm afraid."

"Of what?"

"Sevil. He might have made that other carriage swerve in our path."

"Not to worry, my dear. You're safe now." Drake cuddled her close and whispered sweet things in her ear, dissolving the worry that had twisted her insides into knots.

Nineteen

The Documents

With little Teeny, who often chatted non-stop, at her side, Jennifer spent the next morning and early part of the afternoon Christmas shopping. Grateful for Teeny's suggestions, Jennifer purchased dozens of gifts. Then, defying custom, she treated Teeny to lunch at the nicest restaurant she could find.

As the time she agreed on to meet Drake at the seamstress's shop approached, Jennifer sent Teeny home in a hansom cab, and told John, the groom Drake had assigned to her, to drive her to Oxford Street.

Inside the seamstress's shop, Jennifer stood by the window, waiting for Drake. A quarter of an hour passed before she said to the seamstress, "I'm ready to go over the patterns and select trims."

By the time they concluded their business, two full hours had passed. Drake still hadn't shown up. Worried, Jennifer bid the seamstress good day and left.

Three hours later she paced the floor in her room next to Drake's. He hadn't come home either. She didn't know whether to be concerned, worried, mad, or upset. He hadn't ever done anything like this before.

She went downstairs and asked Josian if he knew where Drake was. He gave her a loftier than thou look. "I believe he planned to visit your sister."

Prudence. Jennifer's heart dropped to her stomach.

Back in her room, she felt so wretched, she knew she couldn't eat. When Teeny came with a tea tray, Jennifer sent her away and continued to pace.

Drake finally arrived—long after dark. Relieved when she heard his voice, Jennifer dashed out into the hall to greet him.

His hair was tousled, his clothes rumpled, and even at a distance he smelled like he'd tried to drink some pub dry. His man, Bevins, had followed him up the stairs. They both paused when they saw her.

"Are you—all right, Drake?"

"I'm fine," he growled, strolling past her into his bedchamber. Baffled, Jennifer trailed after Bevins. Drake sprawled in a chair, then rubbed his neck, as though to relieve aching muscles before he drawled, "I need a brandy, Bevins."

"As you wish, Your Grace." Bevins hurried out the door.

"Haven't you had enough to drink?" Jennifer asked.

"No." Drake eyed her with the first distaste she'd ever seen in his eyes.

"I've been so worried. What detained you?"

"Not what. Who. Prudence."

Jennifer's heart thumped wildly. Was Prudence his mistress?

"I visit her every time I come to London."

"Do you drink with her, too?"

"Among other things."

The vision Jennifer had had of Miranda and Sevil, when he suggested Prudence might be Drake's mistress flashed, and Jennifer stifled a sob. How did wives handle such matters?

She decided she didn't care how other women handled their husband's mistresses. She didn't like it, and wouldn't pretend she did. "Is Prudence your mistress?"

"That question is not worthy of an answer."

Jennifer's voice squeaked when she asked, "Are you trying to make me jealous?"

"No."

Tears stung her eyes. To keep him from seeing them, she spun around and dashed from his chamber. In her own room, she threw herself on the bed, buried her face in pillows and cried great soul-wrenching sobs.

How could Drake go from her to Prudence? Didn't the beauty of their lovemaking mean as much to him as it meant to her? Could she ever be intimate with him again without wondering if he were comparing her to Prudence?

And how could she love him so much in spite of that?

~ * ~

Alone in his chamber, Drake raked his hand through his tousled hair. How many times had he done that today? While in Parliament that morning, he had listened with only half an ear to the honorable gentleman speaking for the Treaty of Peshawar, in favor of Britain's alliance with Afghanistan, and against Persia.

He couldn't get his mind off Jennifer. Prior to his arrival, he had stopped by his solicitor's office and discovered that Jennifer had written a letter and instructed the solicitor to prepare divorce documents.

Why? Because she wanted to leave him? Intended to leave?

She hadn't seen the wizard Sevil since their marriage, and Drake didn't believe he would return. If Jennifer left, it would be of her own volition. He might stop her, if he kept her chained to his side, or locked in her chamber—his chamber.

Drake had sworn his solicitor to secrecy, and ordered him not to proceed with the divorce documents.

After he left parliament, he went to visit Prudence. And he stayed far longer than planned. The pouting letters she had posted since his marriage were nothing compared to the tongue-lashing she gave him for neglecting her. It had taken hours to calm Prudence, and she was still upset when he left.

Bevins arrived with a silver tray that held a crystal decanter half-full of brandy and an empty snifter. After he poured a generous amount and handed it to Drake, he left, excused by Drake's curt nod.

Drake drank the brandy without pause. He'd been furious about the divorce documents. Still was. Didn't Jennifer love him anymore? Had last night's performance in bed been nothing more than an act?

Befuddled, he poured more brandy. Why did Jennifer want a divorce? And what about the child? If she thought she could walk off with his heir, she was in for a surprise of her own.

For a few moments Drake wished he could break the tie that bound him so tightly to her. But he truly had no desire to break it. He loved her, damn it!

Past experience had taught him women couldn't be trusted. What a fool he'd been to fall in love, to want to share his life with her to the exclusion of all else.

He touched the opal beneath his shirt—a constant reminder of her—and considered removing it. Would that anger her? Dash it. Why did she want a divorce? Didn't she want to be his wife? His duchess? Bear his children?

Drake stared at the fire. Plagued by guilt for not having sent a message that he would be delayed this afternoon, he rammed his hand through his hair again. He'd been so busy trying to placate Prudence, he hadn't had a chance to do anything except deal with her hysterics. When she poured him a brandy, he drank it only to pacify her. Then she poured another. When he said he didn't want any more to drink, she threw it at him, sobbing and accusing him of not caring about her, for neglecting her, for banning her from the wedding. Drake frowned at his empty glass. He'd had enough of Prudence to last a lifetime. Never again would he allow her antics to control him as she had this afternoon and evening.

He inhaled deeply. The dried brandy on his shirt and jacket had gone through to his skin. Disgusted with the sticky feeling and the way he smelled, he shook his jacket off and pulled the cord to summon Bevins.

Jennifer owed him an explanation for the letter she'd sent to his solicitor. And she deserved an apology. But she deserved it from a clean man.

When Bevins arrived, Drake said, "I'd like to bathe before dinner."

"Very good, Your Grace."

"Inform the Duchess we will not attend the theater this eve."

"As you wish." Bevins bowed out of the room.

~ * ~

Jennifer cried until she had no tears left. Then she decided she needed fresh air. She needed food, too. The last time she'd eaten was at lunch, eight or nine hours ago.

Using the clean water a servant had previously poured in a large porcelain bowl, she splashed her face, hoping nobody would notice how puffy and red her eyes looked. Then, grateful for the dimly lit room, she pulled the cord to summon Teeny.

While she waited, Jennifer opened the window for fresh air. Leaning out, she breathed deeply, filling her throat and lungs with cold, winter air.

She nearly fainted when Sevil jumped to the window ledge.

"What do you want?" she managed to ask.

He jumped inside, forcing her to move before he said, "You're very clever. You know nothing is given without payment."

When Jennifer didn't comment, he added, "You've been happy, and now you're with child."

She still didn't speak. She didn't know what to say. But dread filled her. She crossed her arms over her stomach as though that would protect her unborn child.

"What do you want?" she asked again.

"Your soul."

Jennifer gasped. "I can't give you that."

Anger glittered in Sevil's black eyes, and suddenly red glowed where the whites should have been. "You must."

"No."

He spread his arms. "It seems a little convincing is in order."

Just then Teeny opened the chamber door. She shrieked when she saw Sevil with his long black cape, lined with red, spread out by his outstretched arms.

"My lady. Who be this man?"

Before Jennifer could answer, Sevil said, "I am a wizard, a powerful one. Your mistress has displeased me, and I am about to teach her a lesson."

With that he grabbed Jennifer around the waist. She struggled against his hold and fought to get free, but he dragged her to the window... and jumped.

Behind them Jennifer heard Teeny's blood curdling screams. "No. No. Bring me mistress back!"

~ * ~

In his bath, Drake heard the screams. Water sloshed over the sides as he jumped out of the copper tub. He grabbed a towel and wrapped it haphazardly around his waist mere seconds before he jerked the door between his chamber and Jennifer's open.

The maid, Teeny, was leaning out the window, still screaming, "Bring me mistress back. Bring me mistress back!"

"What the devil is going on?" he barked.

"The Duchess. He took the Duchess."

"Who?"

"A man." Tears streamed down Teeny's face. "A wizard."

Lenore and half a dozen servants plowed into the room. All looked upset and frightened.

Teeny gulped, her eyes on Drake. "His cape matched his red an' black eyes. He said he wuz a powerful wizard, an' me mistress displeased him. He said he wuz gonna teach her a lesson."

"Did you see where they went?"

Teeny shook her head. "I couldna see. They disappeared in the dark." Sobs shook her head and shoulders.

Bevins stood amidst the servants and Drake ordered, "Have Quicksilver saddled."

"Aye, Milord."

Drake raced back to his chamber and dressed in his brandy-smelling clothes. Clean ones hadn't been set out. He had intended to wear only his robe when he went to talk to Jennifer.

Moment's later Drake rode up and down the streets, looking at rooftops because Jennifer said that's where Sevil jumped. But Drake saw no trace of her, or the wizard.

Finally he galloped home and sent for Scotland Yard.

When two uniformed men arrived, Teeny explained what she'd seen. They talked for a long time. The men didn't leave until after midnight.

Drake sat up half the night, then went to bed. But he didn't sleep well. Half a dozen times he reached for Jennifer and came wide-awake when he realized she wasn't there.

Fit to be committed to Bedlam by morning, he dressed, cursing himself for allowing her out of his sight, and duly praying she hadn't been harmed.

Downstairs he growled at Josian. "Go immediately and inquire about the best private investigators in London."

"Yes, Milord."

Being idle got on Drake's nerves and made the waiting worse. He intended to head first for Scotland Yard, then to ride through every street in London.

At the front door, Jacob, the butler, held Drake's hat while he donned a coat. When Jacob opened the front door, Drake heard the clomp of horses and the rattle of a carriage. Then one of Clay's pulled to a stop in front of the house.

~ * ~

Pain slashed through Jennifer's whole body. She twisted and turned, and heard herself scream. The pain ripped through her insides. Hot. Scalding. Searing. She screamed again.

"Don't take my baby," she cried. "Please no. Don't!" And then she whimpered, "Please, no, no, no!" and she rocked from side to side.

Until somebody shook her.

"Jennifer, it's me Kacy. You're having a nightmare."

Her body bathed in sweat, Jennifer frowned and forced her eyes open. Something was wrong. She felt it in her bones, and in her heart. "How did I get here?"

"I thought you might tell me. It stormed last night. Clay heard a loud noise by the front door. When he opened it, you were lying on the ground, cold and wet, and huddled in a ball."

"My baby. Is my baby okay?"

Kacy nodded. "As far as we know. Clay sent for the doctor. He examined you and couldn't find anything wrong. How do you feel?"

"Pretty good, I guess. I dreamed I lost the baby. It was terrible."

"I'm sure it was," Kacy soothed, sitting on the edge of the bed and taking Jennifer's hand in hers. "How did you get here?"

"Sevil jumped me here from London. We landed on your roof. "He wants my soul." Jennifer shivered. "When I refused, he said I'd regret it, just as Miranda will regret not pledging hers."

Jennifer grabbed Kacy's arm. "I'm scared, Kacy, really scared. Can't you summon your guardian angel to help me?"

"I've tried, but Rey must be busy because I've failed."

"Sevil wants the opal, too. But I can't give it to him. The stone belongs to Drake, and it guided me to him and protected me when I fell out of the sky."

"You're lucky you survived. That you're still alive."

"That's what Drake said."

It occurred to Jennifer that he might be worried about her disappearance. She started to sit up. "I need to send word to Drake…"

"Clay sent a stable lad with a message after we found you last night."

"Did you send him to Stonemeade or London?"

"London."

Jennifer lay back down. Her throbbing head demanded it. "Thanks, Kacy."

"You're welcome."

Tears puddled in Jennifer's eyes as she thought about her baby and worried that something might happen to him… or her.

"Talk to me," Kacy said. "Tell me what's wrong."

Needing to unburden herself, Jennifer explained everything—about Drake standing her up at the dressmakers, coming home late, smelling like he'd tried to drink a pub dry, then admitting he'd been with Prudence.

"All couples go through difficult times," Kacy consoled. "I guess we have to, but I don't know why."

"Me either," Jennifer moaned, mopping her tears with a corner of the sheet. "I'm all right now, Kacy. But I'm hungry. I didn't eat last night."

"I'll have Cook fix something, and I'll bring you a clean gown. Would you like a bath?"

"I'd love one."

Kacy smiled. "I'll be back in a jiff."

Alone, Jennifer recalled clinging to the rooftop while she listened to Sevil's repeated demands last night. She didn't know how long they argued. She'd been too stunned to think straight. But his words, *I will have your soul,* still rang in her ears. Her refusal had infuriated him. How would he retaliate?

~ * ~

Drake watched Clay's stable lad hurry up the walk. "I be Timthee, an' I have a 'portant message frum the Earl. It be 'bout the Duchess."

Drake ushered Timothy inside.

As the Jacob closed the door, the lad extended a folded parchment.

Drake ripped the seal open and read:

Drake,

Jennifer is with us at Havenhurst. We found her unconscious in the rain, near our front door. I've summoned my physician. She doesn't appear to be well.

Clay

"Th' earl asked me ta bring a reply," the young lad, who looked as though he had neither eaten nor slept for hours, said.

"We'll travel to Havenhurst together, lad."

Looking at the butler, Drake ordered, "Have someone fetch food for the lad." As he hurried away, Drake spied Bevins, near the staircase.

"Pack a valise for me. Instruct Teeny to pack one for the Duchess. Tell Winslow to have a carriage put to."

As his valet hastened to obey, Drake hastily scribbled instructions for Josian.

When the butler returned, Drake said, "Have the Earl's horses unhitched, fed, allowed to rest in the stable all day, and driven back to Havenhurst tomorrow, along with his carriage."

In a matter of moments Drake and Clay's stable lad were on their way south, with Winslow wending the ducal carriage through London's busy streets.

For Drake, every minute of the journey was torture. The words in Clay's message repeated themselves again and again. *Jennifer. Unconscious. In the rain.*

Had the wizard Sevil harmed her? How had she traveled to Havenhurst? Had the wizard dropped her from the sky? If so, what had that done to their unborn child?

Twenty

Reconciliation

Night had long since fallen by the time Drake and Clay's sleepy stable lad reached Havenhurst. Drake left his horses and carriage in the stable, and sent the tired lad off to bed. Then he knocked on the mansion's wide front door.

"Everyone, including the Duchess, hath retired," Clay's aging butler said.

"Is she in the guest room where we slept before?"

The butler nodded.

Too impatient to wait for the slow-moving butler to lead him, Drake hurried up the grand staircase alone.

In the guestroom, an oil lamp on the small bed table provided adequate light for Jennifer to read. She glanced up from her book, and closed it while Drake shut the door.

He thought she looked drowsy. So why was she reading?

"How do you feel?" he asked.

"With my hands," she quipped, setting the book aside.

He sat beside her and gathered her close. She let him hold her, but only for a few moments. Then she jerked away and yanked the bed covers up over her shoulders. Now she looked wide-awake. Alert. Ready to fight. Never had she looked more adorable. And never had he felt more repentant.

"I'm sorry if you worried about me, Drake, but I think we should get a divorce... or an annulment. Whatever people get when they haven't been married very long."

"No!" he all but shouted.

"Yes. I won't share you with Prudence... or any other woman. If I'm not enough for you, you can have them, but you can't have me, too." Jennifer clamped her lips together and folded her arms across the bedcovers.

Remorse gushed through Drake. "Jennifer." He reached for her, but she scooted across the bed.

"Don't touch me." She hiccupped, and looked mortified. "I can't— bear it." Her voice broke on a sob.

Drake was willing to do anything to please her. Except give her up... And stop touching her. She was his wife. His. And he must hold her, or die in the attempt.

In spite of her teary protests, he finally managed to gather her, bed covers and all, close again. He kissed her temple, then pleaded, "Don't cry, Jennifer. Please don't cry."

She didn't stop. He felt like crying himself. Did she truly want a divorce?

Not knowing what else to say, he explained. "I apologize for misleading you about Prudence. Like Miranda, she's my charge. She's also a widow. I set her up in a flat because her husband left her penniless. Although she and Miranda don't get on, Prudence was hurt when Miranda banned her from the wedding."

He paused, but Jennifer said nothing, so he continued. "Presumably you know I haven't seen Prudence since we wed. And apparently my failure to reply to all of her letters made her fear I intended to withdraw my financial support. Yesterday when I went to see her, she fell apart. It took hours to calm her. I should have sent a message to the seamstress shop. That I didn't, shames me. It won't happen again. Please forgive me, Jennifer."

"I can't," she whimpered, fresh tears sparkling in her eyes.

Startled, he demanded, "Why the devil not?"

Instead of answering, she pulled free, lay down, and let her tears have their way.

Drake felt helpless. But he couldn't give up. He didn't know how to accept failure. He touched her shoulder. When she didn't object, he lay beside her and drew her close again.

"You must forgive me, Jennifer. Otherwise, I'll be nothing more than an empty shell of a man."

"You'll never be an empty shell," she disagreed in a muffled wail.

He felt empty when he thought about losing her. Even now, holding her, he felt such remorse, it galled him. She must forgive him. And he must understand her actions.

"Why did you instruct my solicitor to prepare divorce documents?"

"What?" She jerked away and sat up, staring at him like he had two heads. "I didn't. I wouldn't. Not without first consulting you."

From her stunned outburst, he believed her. But if she hadn't given the instructions, who had? He hadn't bothered to look at the letter, but he would. He knew Jennifer's penmanship and would know if whoever sent it had tried to duplicate hers.

She swiped at the tears running down her cheeks. "You don't believe me, do you?"

"I believe you."

She looked startled and skeptical. "You do?"

"Yes."

He pulled her close again. As he held her, memories of other lives floated through his mind. At first they lapped at him like a gentle wave, then with more force, they surged, rushing through him in a gigantic deep swell that struck with a force so powerful, it rocked him from the top of his head to the soles of his booted feet. His body jerked, as though he had actually been hit, and the bed rocked. He damned near fell off and took Jennifer with him.

"Is something wrong?" she asked, staring at him again.

"No. For the first time in years everything feels exactly right."

"It does?" She looked doubtful.

He nodded, gazing into her concerned eyes, ready to admit what his heart must have always known. "I've loved you forever," he said quietly.

She studied him in silence. Finally she asked, "Do you remember me? Us? Do you really remember?"

"Yes." His mouth cut off further comment.

The kiss worked it usual magic. Jennifer melted in his arms, and Drake let her allure and mystique consume him.

Somehow, between heated kisses and caresses, and their eagerness to rid themselves of her borrowed bed gown and his clothes and shoes, she managed to say, "I've loved you forever, too, Drake."

"Thank God!" he murmured, running his hands through her hair. "I want this all over me. Over us."

Gently, he combed his fingers through the long strands. As it flowed around them, he spread it from her shoulders to his own, making a cocoon wherein lovers could play. At the same time he brought her body tight against his.

But he prolonged their love play, wanting to pleasure her as he never had before, and to absolve himself for doubting her and giving her the wrong impression about Prudence.

~ * ~

Jennifer loved Drake's touch. And she loved what his touch did to her. His desire kept her body shaking. He kissed and nipped all the places that turned her insides to jelly. She reveled in her ability to explore him, to tongue his nipples, tease them with her teeth, and to nip his flesh in other erotic zones.

Never had their lovemaking been more tender, more sweet.

Nor more wild, exciting, desperate, fulfilling.

Through it all, Jennifer tasted the hunger in his mouth, his urgent breath against her temple, her breasts, her throat. The heat of his body branded hers, and straining need drove them both to the brink of mindlessness.

Finally he positioned himself atop her.

"Yes, oh yes!" she breathed raggedly. Staring up into his eyes, she saw his hunger. His need.

"I want you," he said, his voice husky. "I want you more than life itself."

When he plunged, Jennifer writhed beneath him, meeting thrust for thrust until they floated beyond themselves to that special place where lovers dwelt.

And after they returned to sanity a long time later, she marveled at the wonder of their lovemaking. Too satiated to move, her arms around him went limp.

Drake rolled onto his side, pulling her with him.

"Drake?"

"Hmmm?" With his finger, he traced a line from her chin to her lips.

She took a slow, fortifying breath, preparing to tell him what they were up against. "I know what Sevil wants," she said.

"What?" Drake asked,

"My soul."

He hiked an eyebrow. "Your soul?"

Jennifer nodded. "If I don't promise to give him my soul when I die, he might take me away, back to the future."

Drake's arms had relaxed, but now they tightened. "You cannot promise your soul. We must find a way to defeat him and keep you here."

"I wish we could," she said.

"We will. We must." His hands slid to her waist and he kissed her forehead, before he reached to extinguish the lamp. Then he curled her close and held her in his protective embrace.

Secure in his arms, Jennifer basked in his love even as she envisioned Miranda with Catharine in the future watching *Independence Day* on the VCR, eating a batch of Aunt Rachel's homemade fudge, along with microwave popcorn and Pepsi. And laughing about the fun they'd had ice skating at a heated indoor rink. The nightly visions were now such a habit, Jennifer couldn't sleep until they came.

Pleased that Miranda liked the future and wanted to stay there, Jennifer snuggled closer to Drake's warmth. This is where she belonged, where she wanted to be for the rest of her life.

But what about Sevil? How could they defeat him, and keep him from taking her back?

Twenty-one

Christmas Cheer

After breakfast the next morning, Clay drew Drake aside.

"If you love Jennifer, I suggest you tell her before it's too late. I didn't declare my love for Kacy soon enough. That's why she was taken from me for that horrendous time. Don't let fate or a wizard decide your future."

"I've told Jennifer I love her many times," Drake said, touched by Clay's concern. "Our problem is devising a way to defeat the wizard. He wants her soul."

Clay frowned. "Surely she won't promise it."

"No. We're agreed. She won't. However, I must find a way to protect her and keep her with me."

"If there's anything Kacy or I can do, you'll let us know, won't you?"

"Of course," Drake said. "Thank you."

Outside, sometime later, Drake helped Jennifer into the ducal carriage, then climbed in behind her and waved goodbye to Clay and Kacy as Winslow drove the carriage away.

Worried about the wizard, Drake folded Jennifer between his arms. "We cannot allow the wizard to part us."

She buried her face against his shoulder and clung as though afraid. "I'm glad you feel that way, Drake. I'd give just about anything to stay with you."

What wouldn't she give? He didn't ask. He wasn't sure he wanted to know what might tempt her to return to her own time and leave him behind. He dreaded the thought of living without her.

"Let's talk about something pleasant," she suggested.

"What do you have in mind?"

"Christmas and Boxing Day. I bought a lot of gifts, but I still have more shopping to do."

"Can you shop in Kent? Or must we return to London?"

"Kent will be fine. But we'll need to have the things I've already bought sent to Stonemeade."

"I'll see to that."

"You won't leave me alone at Stonemeade, will you?"

"No. Not as long as the wizard poses a threat."

Afraid that if he let Jennifer go, even for a moment, she might disappear, Drake held her close throughout the entire journey.

~ * ~

When they arrived at Stonemeade, he led her inside, then into his study. When he released her, she sat down on a chair in front of his desk. He sat behind it, then wondered if he should be at her side. The wizard had abducted her from her own bedchamber in London. Presumably he could abduct her any time, from any place.

"I think I'd like to write in my journal." Jennifer stood up.

Drake darted around his desk and clutched her arm. "I'll have your maid fetch it." He pulled a cord to summon a servant, then moved his chair to sit beside his wife.

Later, while she wrote in her journal, Drake considered penning a message to Josian in London, instructing him to engage a team of husky bodyguards to protect the Duchess. But if the wizard froze them, what good could they do?

Before their marriage Drake had abandoned the idea of engaging a companion-chaperon because he didn't want to share his wife. He wanted her all to himself. But because he didn't know how to protect her all the time, he penned the letter to Josian. A team of bodyguards might not help if the wizard froze them, but hiring them made Drake feel better. They might, in some small way, hinder the wizard. And, as promised, Drake also instructed his secretary to send all of the Duchess's purchases to Stonemeade.

After he finished the letter and sorted his correspondence, he looked up and asked, "What did you buy for the servants?"

Jennifer smiled. "I bought each one of them something sensible, as well as something frivolous. Whether I'm here or not, Christmas should be a joyous time."

Drake frowned. "You must be here." And she would be, he silently vowed, even if he had to chain her to his side.

~ * ~

Jennifer wanted Stonemeade's Christmas decorations to be elegant, yet simple. After much deliberation she chose a color scheme of red, silver and white.

Under her direction, servants decorated every room on the ground floor, as well as the master suite and two guestrooms on the second floor, which they referred to as the first. When everything, including the tall pine tree in the lounge, had been decorated to Jennifer's satisfaction, she wandered through the mansion with Drake at her side.

Red berry-covered holly branches, along with red and silver bows draped the banister of the grand staircase as well as fireplace mantles in every room. Vases of fresh red and white flowers graced tabletops, stands, nooks and shelves.

"Stonemeade has never looked lovelier," Drake said, pausing at the entrance to his study and glancing up.

Jennifer looked up and laughed. "Is that mistletoe dangling up there?"

"It is, " Drake confirmed, grinning.

"Who put it there?"

Drake's grin grew. "One of the servants, at my behest."

"That seems like a strange place. Not very many couples will come in here, will they?"

"Mistletoe hangs in more than one place."

Jennifer grinned. "It does? Where?"

"I expect you may discover where during the days to come." He bent his head and kissed her. When he slid his hands down her spine to the small of her back, the quick bolt of awareness he always brought to her, stole her breath. Her heart flipped crazily, and she wondered if she could contain her happiness.

~ * ~

On the afternoon of December 23, Boyden and Charlotte arrived. Jennifer and Drake waited in the gaily-decorated lounge to greet them. Boyden entered on crutches.

"How wonderful to see you out of the wheelchair," Jennifer exclaimed, coming to her feet. "Your recovery is one of the best parts of the holiday."

"We have more good news," Charlotte confided almost timidly.

"What is it?" Jennifer matched Charlotte's hushed voice.

"I am with child."

Jennifer smiled. "I am, too."

"How marvelous." Charlotte returned her smile. "How do you feel?"

"Very good now. For a fortnight, however, morning sickness plagued me day and night. How about you?"

Charlotte glanced at their husbands, who both listened with amused, indulgent smiles. "I am still a bit queasy in the mornings."

"Then we won't do anything early," Jennifer promised, before she turned to Boyden. "Will that chair be comfortable? Or would you like another?"

"This one is fine, Duchess. Thank you for having us."

"The pleasure is ours," Drake assured him.

Charlotte looked around the lounge. Her gaze lingered on the tall, imposing evergreen decorated with hundreds of red and silver ornaments and matching bows. "Stonemeade looks lovely," she said.

"Thanks to the Duchess," Drake smiled.

"I say," Boyden said with a grin, "is that mistletoe hanging up there by the entry?"

"It is," Drake said. "I claim responsibility for that."

Jennifer smiled, thinking how often the servants had caught them beneath it and scurried away so as not to embarrass them.

"Come, Charlotte," Boyden invited with an engaging smile, as he anchored his crutches under his arms. "We must take advantage of the mistletoe."

~ * ~

Kacy, Clay, and the twins arrived the next morning. After Jennifer fussed over the babies, a servant led the nanny and twins up the stairs to their room. When the four friends were alone, Jennifer hugged Kacy. "This is such fun."

"Yes, it is," Kacy agreed, smiling. "Your tree is gorgeous. Who decorated it?"

"The Duchess," Drake said, with a bit of help from the servants."

"With a lot of help from them," Jennifer clarified. "I didn't want to endanger the baby by climbing the ladder." She glanced at the tree, then added wistfully, "I wanted to put candles on the branches, but I was afraid that might create a fire hazard."

Kacy winked. "I know the feeling. I didn't either."

"The tree could not be lovelier," Drake said.

"You're right," Clay said, then cleared his throat. "Have you seen the wizard?"

"No, thank goodness." Jennifer uttered a silent prayer that he wouldn't show up and spoil Christmas.

Hearing voices in the hall, she changed the subject. "I think Boyden and Charlotte are about to join us. Have you met Drake's cousin and his wife?"

Kacy shook her head, but Clay nodded.

Drake smiled at Boyden and Charlotte as they entered the lounge. "We're about to have tea. Will you join us?"

"With pleasure." Boyden sat down on the settee, and set his crutches aside. Charlotte sat beside him, smiling.

After introductions, they discussed the weather and the lack of snow. "Now that you've all arrived safe and sound, let the snow begin," Jennifer said, hoping for a white Christmas.

On Christmas Eve, after their guests retired to their respective rooms, Jennifer and Drake wandered around the mansion, once again admiring the decorations. In addition to the red berry-covered holly branches, and red and silver bows, mistletoe hung beneath three different doorways, to tempt couples to kiss. They took advantage of all three before they entered the lounge.

A Yule log had been laid in the fireplace, ready to be lit on Christmas morn. By the row of tall windows stood the Christmas tree decorated with red and silver. Candles glowed throughout the room. In the windows, the tree reflected on panes of glass as though it stood before a huge mirror.

"The tree looks like it was decorated by professionals," Jennifer said, delighted that her idea had turned out so well.

"It's beautiful," Drake said, "as are you."

"Thanks for indulging me and letting me decorate the way I wanted."

"The mansion has never looked lovelier."

"It looked beautiful on our wedding day."

"Yes," Drake agreed, smiling. "However, now we have more than flowers, and I like your choice of colors. Red, silver, white, and green, brighten every room. Thank you."

"Decorating was a pleasure." Basking under Drake's praise, she added, "All the gifts have been wrapped. We need to bring them downstairs and place them beneath the tree."

"Jacob is instructing the servants to carry them down as we speak."

Jennifer splayed her hands on Drake's chest. "I've never been this happy, ever before."

"Nor have I."

"It almost frightens me."

"Fret not, my love. If the wizard Sevil shows his face, he'll have to deal with Clay and I, and the ropes and weapons I auspiciously hid in every room."

"And those burly bodyguards you hired, too. They follow me everywhere I go, but I suspect they don't believe Sevil is real, or a threat."

"Fortunately, he hasn't yet shown his face. Let us hope for his continued absence, and consider ourselves blessed."

"Sounds good to me." Jennifer heard the rustle of feet and the sound of voices in the hall. "I think the servants have arrived with the gifts."

A minute later she busily arranged packages under the tree. "Now the picture looks complete," she said as she stood.

"Everything looks perfect," Drake agreed, nodding at the window.

Jennifer looked outside. And felt her bubble of joy might burst. "It's snowing!"

"Now we have everything you wished for."

"Almost everything." With a smile, she urged him to the doorway, beneath the mistletoe. "When you kiss me, I'll have everything I wished for."

Drake didn't waste time. He crushed her against his chest and kissed her thoroughly. She heard giggles and knew servants watched, but she didn't care. She was too lost in the magic of Drake's kiss.

And when he picked her up and carried her to the stairs, she felt she had found paradise on earth.

~ * ~

On Christmas morning a loud knock awakened them. Both nude beneath the covers, Jennifer scrambled for her new red velvet robe, shoved her arms through the sleeves, and tied the sash as she hurried to the door.

Kacy's maid stood in the hall. "Me mistress wishes to know at what hour ye wish her and me lord to join ye downstairs."

"The duke's cousin and his wife are late sleepers, and I'm sure the Countess will wish to have the babies fed and dressed so they can be with us when we open our gifts. Please tell your mistress not to rush. She has at least two hours. I'll send word when I know the Duke's cousin is up and about."

"Very good, Yer Grace." The maid bowed away.

Jennifer shut the door, then turned. Drake lay on his side, his elbow propped on a pillow, his hand supporting his head. The covers had fallen below his waist. With his hair mussed, his gaze lazy, his torso bare, and the opal dangling from the chain around his neck, he looked so sexy he took her breath away. She wanted to crawl right back in bed and seduce him.

When he smiled, she smiled, too.

"How do you feel this morning, my lady wife?"

"With my hands," she flirted, using words she often used to tease him. "Would you like me to demonstrate, my lord husband?"

"Yes." With a wicked gleam he tossed the covers aside. Without clothes he looked strong, handsome and virile.

Jennifer wished they didn't have to rush, that on this special day they could stay in bed as long as she wanted, and make love over and over again.

With a quiet sigh, she turned to get dressed.

But when Drake wrapped his arms around her from behind, she leaned against him and savored the contact. He moved her hair aside and placed a gentle kiss below her ear before he turned her in his arms. To her surprise and delight, he untied her sash, parted her robe, then knelt, and planted a kiss in the middle of her bare stomach.

Looking up, he asked, "Do you still feel well?"

"Yes. Very."

Drake stood, gathered her in his arms, and kissed her forehead. Thrilling tingles fluttered along her nerve endings and she trembled, awed by what she saw in his eyes. She arched up, nudging his head down, so she could kiss him. As soon as she ended the kiss, he started another, kissing her with such exquisite tenderness, it made her weak in the knees.

She hated having to withdraw so they could dress. But it would be rude not to be downstairs to greet their guests when they came down. She started to pull away.

Drake tightened his hold. "I'd like to give you one of your gifts before we dress."

Jennifer grinned. "I had the same thing in mind."

With his arm around her waist, he guided her to his bulky bureau. From the top drawer he withdrew a silver box, topped with a tiny bright red bow, and extended it.

Her heart fluttering, Jennifer lifted the lid. A sparkling necklace made of rubies and diamonds with matching earrings, winked up at her.

"They're gorgeous," she whispered, too choked up to speak out loud. She'd never seen anything like them. All she'd ever owned was costume jewelry, and nothing even close to these.

"Red is your favorite color," Drake said. "I thought you might wish to wear them today with your new red gown."

She nodded, tears brimming in her eyes. "They'll look exquisite."

"You'll look exquisite," he corrected. "You always do." He kissed her again.

Her heart pounded with love and joy and gratitude. She had intended to wait until they were both dressed before she put the necklace and earrings on, but when she felt his arousal pressing against her, she changed her mind. "Drake?"

"Yes, love?" he murmured, his mouth driving her mad as he trailed kisses down her throat.

"Would you fasten the necklace for me before we go back to bed?"

His nostrils flared when he raised his head. "Take the robe off."

Happily aroused herself, she let the robe slip off her shoulders and fall to a velvet puddle on the floor. Then she turned while he fastened the necklace. She melted in his embrace when he turned her back to face him.

~ * ~

A long time later, sitting on the edge of the bed with Drake beside her, she opened the drawer on the small bedside table. She withdrew one of her gifts for Drake and extended it.

"It feels like—thick pages of paper," he said, flexing the package slightly.

"Open it. You might be surprised."

Drake unwrapped the book, turned it over and read the title—*Reincarnation—The Missing Link in Christianity.*

"Tis unlike anything I've ever seen."

"It's a paperback," Jennifer explained.

"Where did you get it?"

"From Kacy. It came from the future, and her fairy godmother provided it. Kacy gave one like it to Clay sometime ago. For obvious reasons, they keep his locked in his desk. Although their servants don't read, they don't want them or anyone else to see something from the future."

Drake opened the book and saw the first and subsequent publication dates...1999 and 2003. If he'd had any lingering doubts that Jennifer came from the future, he had them no more.

~ * ~

When they were finally dressed, he led her from his chamber. Instead of guiding her to the stairs, he steered her to the music room.

"A grand piano!" she said, shocked by the huge instrument that now dominated the room, yet moving closer as she asked, "However did you get it in here and up the stairs without me seeing it? You've barely let me out of your sight."

"Clay supervised the delivery yesterday whilst you and I, and Boyden and Charlotte, visited Grandmother at the dower house."

Almost reverently Jennifer ran her fingers over the black and ivory keys.

"Play something for me." Drake pulled the round stool out for her.

"What should I play?"

"How about some Christmas music?"

"In a minute. First I'd like to play something special, just for you. For us. Would you close the door?"

As soon as he did, she played and sang very softly, *"Lay your head upon my pillow..."*

When she finished he put his hands on her shoulders. "I remember. That was our special song."

"Yes." She smiled up at him. "Do you remember our lives in the future?"

"Not entirely. However, somehow I know that song was very important to us."

"Maybe someday you'll remember why."

"If not, you can tell me."

Jennifer didn't comment. If she told him and left, he might suffer more than if she said nothing.

"You can open the door now, if you'd like. I'll play some Christmas music, if you'll tell me what to play."

"I'll do better than that." Drake produced sheets of music.

"This is great. Now I'll know what's popular in this time, and what hasn't yet been written."

After the first song, Boyden, Charlotte, Kacy, Clay and the twins joined them. All the adults sang, their rich voices mingling and complimenting every song Jennifer played.

When they finished *Deck The Halls*, they heard applause. Jennifer turned her head. The Dowager and Olvan stood together just inside the room.

"Now Christmas is complete." Jennifer smiled at them.

"Please don't let us stop you," Lucilla said.

"We should go down to breakfast," Drake announced. "The Duchess and Charlotte need nourishment, now they are eating for two."

Jennifer resisted the urge to say the babies would take what they needed, and eating for two was an old wives tale.

~ * ~

After breakfast everyone repaired to the lounge. Candles had been lit, adding cozy warmth to the gaily-decorated room.

When all the gifts had been opened and exclaimed over, Jennifer said, "This is the merriest Christmas ever!" She prayed it wouldn't be her last.

"I'll drink to that." Kacy raised her goblet.

The others did likewise. All eight adults grinned. As the ladies sipped juice and the men sipped wine, the twins crawled around, playing with discarded wrapping paper, seeming to enjoy the noise it made more than they enjoyed their new toys.

After a while, Jennifer said, "I'd like to go out to the stable for a few minutes."

"Why?" Drake glanced at Boyden whose crutches lay at his feet, half covered with gift-wrap.

"Don't be difficult," Jennifer teased. "Come out with me and see. I'm sure our guests won't miss us for a few brief minutes."

"On the contrary," Boyden reached for his crutches. "We'd like to join you." He glanced at Charlotte. "Wouldn't we?"

"Yes, of course." She smiled.

"We'll join you as well," Lucilla said, and Olvan nodded.

"So will we," Kacy added, and Jennifer silently blessed her. She felt there would be more safety from Sevil in numbers, even though she knew he had the capacity to freeze an entire room full of people.

Everybody donned coats, boots, scarves and hats. Delighted by the newly fallen snow, they made their way noisily across the snowy white ground. Clay led the procession with Kacy at his side, as though they could protect Jennifer if Sevil appeared.

In the stable, they immediately saw Jennifer's reason for wanting to come out in the cold.

"A pure white mare!" Drake exclaimed. "What a remarkable specimen of horseflesh. To whom does she belong?"

"To you." Jennifer smiled. "Merry Christmas. I thought you might wish to mate her with Quicksilver."

"Where did you find her?"

Jennifer glanced at Clay. "I had a lot of help."

She hadn't wanted to use Drake's money. Neither had she wanted to use Sevil's. Kacy and Clay had agreed with her, and Clay had purchased the mare at Tattersall's, and brought her with them yesterday. And he'd refused to accept money or consider Jennifer indebted. Could anyone else have such wonderful friends? Jennifer seriously doubted it.

Twenty-two

The New Year

A week after the new year, Jennifer sat in the dower house with Lucilla. They both sipped hot creamed tea. Beyond the window of her cozy sitting room, fluffy snowflakes fluttered to the already white ground.

"Snow always delights me," Lucilla said. "The landscape is so beautiful covered with white."

"Yes it is." Jennifer set her cup and saucer on the small table before them. "I should probably leave before the snow gets deeper."

"Nonsense," Lucilla said. "Drake will come for you."

Jennifer didn't disagree. She knew Drake would come, also that she'd feel safer walking from the dower house to the mansion with him, than she would feel with the bodyguards.

"Has Drake ever spoken to you about his first marriage?" Lucilla asked, surprising Jennifer.

"No, although he said Helen was pretty enough to launch a thousand ships."

"Pretty as a poisonous snake," Lucilla said dourly. "No one liked her, except Albert, Drake's brother."

Jennifer cleared her throat, then said delicately, "I heard a rumor that Albert and Helen had an affair."

"It was more than a rumor." Lucilla picked up the sterling silver teapot and refilled their cups. "Helen had ambitions... high ones. She married Drake because their fathers arranged it, however, she seduced Albert mere weeks after her marriage to Drake. 'Tis my belief Helen expected Albert to find her so irresistible he would divorce Alisha and marry her... After Helen obtained a divorce from Drake."

"Did Drake suspect they were—?"

"Carrying on? Goodness no." Lucilla poured cream and spooned sugar into her tea. "The servants knew, but Drake and Albert's wife didn't know until the accident."

"When did the accident happen?"

"Coming on four years, next June." Lucilla sipped her tea, a faraway look in her eyes. "Drake saw them riding towards the woods together, and thought they were merely out for exercise. When they didn't return after several hours, he went to look for them. At the far end of the woods stood an old crofter's cottage, abandoned years before, and refurbished quite lavishly at Albert's behest. He often went there. 'Tis where I suspect Helen first seduced him."

Lucilla set her cup and saucer down. "In any event, Drake saw smoke rising from the cottage and assumed it came from the chimney until he neared and saw the roof in flames. Albert's and Helen's horses were tethered outdoors. Drake risked his life by going inside the burning inferno. He found them in bed, naked and unconscious, and managed to drag them out. However, he arrived too late."

A vision flashed. Jennifer saw the first Drake die when the burning roof collapsed on him. Then she saw Dirk's spirit transported from the future to the past; saw him assume the first Drake's body, along with his life and memories.

"It was terrible for Drake," Lucilla continued. "Albert's Duchess, Alisha, avoided the scandal by killing herself."

"How—did she—do it?" Jennifer had to force the words out because the vision had stolen her breath.

"Jumped from the attic window," Lucilla said. "Drake hasn't been up there since. He had not one moment of peace during the formal year of mourning. The day he became a duke, ladies flocked to him, vying for his attention. You were the worst of all, badgering him to marry you. He finally sent you off to a finishing academy. Do you recall any of that?"

Jennifer shook her head, prepared to tell Lucilla what she and Drake had decided she should know. "I'm not Miranda."

Lucilla looked shocked. "Of course you are, my dear. You merely lost your memories when you had that nasty fall."

"That's what Drake told you before he realized I'm not her."

"But you married him using her name."

"Because I didn't know what other name to use. You see, I wasn't born in this time. I'm from the future. The wizard Sevil took Miranda there, and brought me back here."

"He switched places with the two of you?" Lucilla asked, her faded blue eyes ripe with incredulity.

Jennifer nodded. "I'm sorry if my news distresses you. But Drake and I thought you should know the truth, and the reason he hired bodyguards."

"Why did he?"

"To protect me from the wizard. Sevil wants my soul. I can't promise it, and I'm afraid he might take me back to the future."

"That would be a catastrophe," Lucilla objected, some of the shock fading from her eyes. "For the first time in his life, Drake's happy... with the babe on its way, and all."

"I can't express how happy I am either," Jennifer said.

"You need not try. It shows in your eyes, and the things you do and say."

"Are you upset—that I'm not Miranda?"

"Goodness no. I may not comprehend all of what you've told me, but I don't doubt you believe it's true. And Drake loves you. But Miranda, what will become of her?"

"She's quite happy in the future. I was orphaned at a young age and grew up with relatives. They think she's me, and she has access to my trust fund, so she isn't penniless."

"But she has none of your memories, just as you have none of hers."

"That doesn't seem to be important. She's living with my roommate, Catharine, who is also from this time."

Lucilla pressed a hand to her forehead. "How did this Catharine get to the future?"

Jennifer smiled. "A guardian angel took her there."

Once again Lucilla looked shocked. "An angel?"

"Yes." Jennifer nodded. "The Countess of Havenhurst's guardian angel. I've met him twice."

Lucilla picked up her tea and swallowed a long gulp. Cup and saucer still in hand, she said, "Presumably the Countess is also from the future?"

"Yes. She and Catharine agreed to switch places some time ago."

The dowager set her saucer down. "Is anyone else from the future?"

"No. No one that I know about." Jennifer sipped her tea. "I understand both Miranda and Catharine attended a finishing academy together in this time. When the wizard told Miranda where Catharine had gone, she asked him to take her there and make the switch."

"How do you know this?"

Jennifer thought she had shocked Lucilla enough for one day, so she decided not to mention her visions. "Sevil, the wizard, told me."

She glanced out the window again. The storm had turned into a blizzard. When Drake came, she wanted to stop by the stable and check Mordora. Even though she didn't ride now because she didn't want to harm her unborn baby, Jennifer visited the mare every day, always accompanied by Drake, and often flanked by bodyguards as well.

"I'd like to prepare to leave, Lucilla," Jennifer said. "That is, if you're all right."

"I am fine. You have given me much to contemplate."

"I hope you don't think too unkindly of me."

"No. Of course I don't. I think you're a dear. Now go." She fluttered her hands at the door. "I believe I hear Drake in the corridor."

Jennifer stood, then bent to kiss Lucilla's soft, wrinkled cheek. "I'll see you tomorrow."

"Yes. Tomorrow." Lucilla took another sip of tea.

In the hall, Drake smiled at Jennifer. "Did you tell her?"

"Yes."

"How did she take the news?"

"I think she's still in shock, but she isn't unhappy with me."

"Should I go in?"

"No. I think she'd like to be alone with her thoughts for a while."

"I'll talk to her tomorrow."

As Drake helped Jennifer bundle herself in her cloak and hood, she said, "I expected you sooner. Were you detained?"

He nodded, unwilling to explain Prudence's urgent letter that requested he travel to London at the soonest possible moment. He had written back that a trip would not be convenient, and invited her to Stonemeade—if she didn't wish to write about the matter troubling her, and felt she must talk with him.

If Prudence came to visit, he'd have to be on guard. He didn't want her to upset Jennifer, nor to ask questions she couldn't answer.

He turned a smile to Jennifer before he opened the door. With their arms hooked at the elbows, they made their way through the heavy, drifted snow, stopping at the stable. While Jennifer petted Mordora, and chatted to her, Drake looked in on Quicksilver, Awesome and the new white mare he had named Opal.

Soon they braved the storm again. A few feet from the stable, Sevil jumped before them. Dressed all in black, the wizard spread his cape-covered arms and clapped. Drake's legs froze in mid-stride, and a chill, frostier than the snowflakes landing on his face, turned his blood cold. He couldn't move. But he could see as he had seen at their wedding, and now he could hear, too. Why? Because he wore the opal? Was it magic as Jennifer suggested?

"What have you done to him?" she demanded.

"Rendered him incapable. At the moment he can neither see, nor hear us. I shall remove the spell after we talk."

"What about?"

"You know my desires. Have you made up your mind?"

Jennifer nodded. Sevil hopped gleefully from one black-booted foot to the other as snow swirled around them.

"I will have the opal... and your soul."

"No, Sevil, you won't."

His gleeful hopping ceased. A stunned expression froze his weasel face. "You won't give me the stone and promise me your soul?"

"No."

"Not a wise decision, my dear," he argued ominously. "You owe me. I gave you what your heart desired. I brought you here to see your dearest friend. I kept Miranda in America so you could wed the man you love. If you don't give me what I want, your regret will be immense and most difficult to bear."

Jennifer didn't flinch. Drake was proud of her, and wished he could speak to cheer her on, but he was frozen and mute.

"I hope that isn't true," she said.

"But my dear, it is," Sevil screeched, waving his arms wildly. "I am powerful, and I shall make your life miserable if you don't give me what I want."

His black eyes turned cold. When Jennifer did nothing more than stare, his appearance changed to the creature Drake had heard described, but never seen. A one-piece white oilskin jump suit that looked like slick fish scales covered his skeletal torso. A clear bubble enclosed his head, and his pawed hands did indeed terminate in sharp claws as Jennifer had said.

Jennifer latched onto Drake's arm, stiff and frozen at his side. He could only stare, unblinking.

Sevil pointed a claw at Jennifer's stomach and flicked his wrist. A streak of lightning sent her to her knees. She kept hold of Drake with one hand, but her other flew protectively to her stomach. Sevil grabbed Jennifer with his claws and tried to drag her away. She clung to Drake, but he felt her grip weakening. Frantic, he summoned the strength to blow through his lips. And then he could move. In a flash he stooped and wrapped both arms around Jennifer.

Sevil shrieked in frustration.

Torn between protecting her and strangling the wizard, Drake ordered, "Leave us or regret it."

With a screeching, hissing howl, Sevil bounded away, leaping the tall jumps Jennifer had described.

His heart thundering, Drake held her close. "Did he harm you?"

She shook her head and trembled in his arms. "But he might come back. Let's dash for the mansion."

"You shouldn't run in your condition." Drake picked her up to carry her. She flung her arms around his neck and clung, her body shaking all the way.

Drake carried her inside the library, helped her out of her wrap, gloves and boots, then removed his own, before he sat in a chair near the fireplace with her on his lap.

"I heard your conversation. Sevil wants the opal." Drake pulled the stone from beneath his shirt. "This isn't worth the fear he instills in you. Nothing is." Drake raised the chain over his head, but when he tried to slide it over Jennifer's, she objected.

"I can't take it, Drake. I gave it to you, just as you gave me these rings." She raised her left hand to indicate the betrothal and wedding rings, and the small ruby she also wore. "You don't want me to give them back to you, do you?"

When he shook his head, she slid the chain back over his head. The stone warmed as it rested against his chest.

"Besides, it might have been what brought you out from under Sevil's frozen spell."

Considering her suggestion, Drake tucked a wayward strand of hair behind her ear. "I dislike suggesting that you stay inside, but I know of no other way to keep you away from the wizard."

Jennifer laid her head on his shoulder. "I'll do whatever you think best, Drake."

He thought about their marriage, or non-marriage, and wondered how Jennifer viewed it. "Does it bother you to pretend you're Miranda?" he asked.

Jennifer shook her head.

"Will it bother you if you have to pretend to be her for the rest of your life?"

"Not at all, if I can live with you as your wife."

"Then let us speak no more on the subject. You're my wife... my Duchess. And I won't allow harm to befall you."

"I love you, Drake. Even if you never remember the memories we shared, I'll always believe you're Dirk, the man I loved in many lives and married in the future."

"I'm your husband in this life. That's what matters now."

"Yes. My husband, and my Duke." She smiled up at him.

He lowered his head and kissed her.

"I'm so glad you want to keep me here," she said afterwards.

"You must share all your fears with me, so I can decide how best to protect you."

"I will," she promised. "I can't spend eternity under Sevil's dominion. And we can't give the opal to him. He might use it for sinister purposes." A shiver trembled through her.

"Perhaps you should wear the opal to protect you and the babe." Once again Drake raised the chain over his head.

But Jennifer stubbornly refused to accept it. "It's yours, Drake. Please keep it. As Dirk, your guardian angel gave it to you, and I believe it will protect you as it protected me when I fell from the sky after my traumatic journey through time."

"I think it's more important to protect you and the babe, than it is me."

For the first time, they strongly disagreed.

Drake gave in finally, but Jennifer knew he wasn't happy about it.

~ * ~

That night, as though to make up for their disagreement, they made love almost until dawn. In the morning, to Jennifer's further delight, they spent most of the morning in bed, hugging, kissing, and talking. Drake had lots of questions about the future, and she happily gave him answers.

In the afternoon when she went downstairs, she saw smiles on the servant's faces. But Josian scowled when she passed him in the hall. Everyone, it seemed, was delighted Drake had spent half the day in bed with her; everyone, that is, except Josian. Jennifer wondered if anything ever delighted or pleased him.

Twenty-three

Mischief Brewed

A few days later, while Jennifer wrote in her journal, Josian knocked on her door. When Teeny opened it, Josian said, "The Duke wishes the Duchess to join him in the stable."

Although Jennifer thought the request odd, she didn't doubt Josian. "Thank you," she said.

After Teeny closed the door, Jennifer looked out the window at the snowstorm. "Summon the guards to accompany me outdoors."

"Yes, milady."

Moments later, Jennifer met the bodyguards downstairs at the front door.

As soon as they stepped outside, Sevil appeared and snapped his fingers.

Jennifer found herself in the woods, unable to move, talk or cry out. But she could think. Was Josian in cahoots with Sevil? Had Drake truly summoned her to the stable? Had the bodyguards been frozen? Or could they tell Drake she had disappeared? She imagined his concern. What if he came looking for her and couldn't find her?

The harder the snow fell, the colder she felt and the more worried she became.

It seemed hours passed. She felt as cold as an icicle.

Finally Sevil appeared again. Without warning he jumped her back through the woods and left her near the clearing by the dower house.

She stumbled through the snowstorm, past the stable, to the mansion.

"Your Grace," Bevins said the instant she entered, "The Duke, he went to search fer ye."

"How long ago?" Jennifer asked as she shucked her damp cloak and grabbed another.

"Two hours or more ah'd say."

Jennifer hurried out to the stable. "Tell Olvan I need him." she ordered the first groom she saw. Her heart in her throat, she added, "And please saddle Mordora."

"Yes, Yer Grace." The groom dashed away.

Olvan entered the stable, followed by Josian.

"We need to organize a search party," Jennifer said.

"For whom?" Josian asked.

"The Duke." Tears threatened, but Jennifer fought them. She had to be strong. "He's been gone more than two hours."

"I believe he went looking for you," Josian said, a sneer on his face.

Again wondering if Josian was behind Sevil's mischief, Jennifer said, "We're wasting valuable time, Drake could be hurt."

"We will find him," Olvan vowed.

A stable boy had saddled Mordora, and Olvan helped Jennifer mount. They headed for the woods, their progress slow, hindered by the snow. Josian and a dozen stable boys followed, as did both bodyguards.

"I'm so worried," she fretted to Olvan.

"The Duke be a strong, healthy man," Olvan consoled, as they rode deeper into the woods.

The farther they went, the more worried Jennifer became.

"There he be." Olvan called.

Jennifer bit her lip to keep from crying. Drake lay in the snow, inert and unconscious. She dismounted, and bent beside him, across from Olvan, who examined him.

"'Peers he has some broken bones," Olvan announced.

Jennifer dabbed at her eyes. "Fetch two thin logs, sturdy ones," she ordered two stable boys.

As they hurried off, she said to six others, "Take your shirts off and give them to me."

The lads didn't argue, but Josian said, "Surely their coats would keep the Duke warmer than their shirts."

Already removing her own wool cloak to cover him, Jennifer said, "I don't want their shirts to warm him. They're newer than their coats, and the material is sturdy." She didn't add she didn't want the boys to get sick from exposure, although that concerned her. "We need to make a stretcher, or we might harm him more than he already is," she explained.

"How ever can we do that?" Josian demanded as the two boys returned with two sturdy-looking poles.

"Break the limbs off," she said to Olvan, ignoring Josian.

Olvan grabbed his knife. The others merely watched curiously while the old Scot whittled the branches off. As soon as he finished one pole, Jennifer started to thread it through the sleeves of a shirt. When she had threaded both poles through the sleeves of all six shirts and buttoned them to hold the stretcher together, she said, "Roll the Duke onto my cloak, Olvan. The men can use it to help ease him onto the stretcher."

After they had Drake on the makeshift stretcher, she tucked her cloak tenderly around him. "Lift him, but please be careful."

It seemed an eternity passed before they got him home, up the stairs, and in bed.

Jennifer ordered everyone except Olvan from the room, but Josian and Bevins both refused to leave. Using the scissors she'd grabbed from a drawer, she cut Drake out of his cold, wet clothes, then moved aside so Olvan could examine him again.

"I fear his shoulder be broken, lass. I dinna think his leg be broken, though. Jest bruised. But a possible concussion from the fall."

Jennifer swallowed a lump of fear. "What about frostbite?"

"Ah dinna think he has that, lass. I see no spots ta worry yerself about."

At least they had that to be grateful for. It occurred to her that the opal should have protected him. Then she realized he didn't have it on.

"The stone I gave him. It's gone." *What had happened to it? Had he somehow given it to Sevil without telling her?* She swallowed another lump of fear. *If so, what evil things would Sevil use it for?*

Across the room, Bevins picked something up from the top of the bulky mahogany bureau. "Is this the stone, Yer Grace?"

Jennifer nodded. *Why had Drake taken it off?* She took it from Bevins and slid it over her head to keep it safe, worrying about Drake. Did he have internal injuries? She would have put the stone around his neck, but didn't want to hurt him further by any unnecessary movements.

~ * ~

An hour later the physician confirmed Olvan's diagnosis. Drake had a broken shoulder, possible concussion, and a very bruised leg.

"The Duke is young and strong," the doctor said. "We can hope for a full recovery."

But Drake didn't regain consciousness. Jennifer feared he might have a brain injury. *Would he wake up? If he did, would he be all right?*

She spent the night at his side, praying he would recover, fearing she might lose him again. Drake was an excellent horseman and she wondered whether Sevil was responsible for his fall. And why had Drake taken the opal off? Why couldn't she convince him it would protect him? Did he think he was invincible?

~ * ~

Jennifer passed the night in deepest darkness. By the time morning arrived her heart felt near the breaking point. And then Drake's breathing changed. It sounded normal.

She heaved a sigh of relief, and prayed he would wake up.

Finally, shortly after the sun came up, Drake opened his eyes. Relieved, Jennifer leaned close and asked, "How do you feel?"

He tried to move and grimaced. "Like my horse threw me." Then he asked, "Are you all right?"

"I'm fine, now that you're awake."

"How long have you been here?"

"All night." Gently, she touched his good arm. "You have a broken shoulder, Drake. You must have landed on it when you fell."

"Something spooked Quicksilver. Is he all right?"

"I don't know," Jennifer said. "We didn't see him, and as far as I know he didn't return to the stable. I'll send the stable boys to look for him."

She raised her fingers to the base of her throat and touched the opal. "Why did you take this off?"

"I didn't wish to tarnish the chain when I bathed."

"It would have protected you."

"Now that I am injured, I'd like you to wear it."

Worried about Sevil, Jennifer nodded and kept the chain around her neck.

With his uninjured arm, Drake reached for a lock of her untidy hair. "You look all in. For the babe's sake, if not your own, you should go to you own room and rest."

"I don't want to leave you."

"Come back after you've rested. I'll be here," he promised.

~ * ~

A few hours later, after a nap and a bath, she dressed in clean clothes, then returned to Drake's chamber. The only person with him was Olvan.

"The physician just left," Olvan said. "Drake hath sprained or broken his ankle as well."

"Does it hurt?" she asked Drake, filled with compassion and concern.

"It hurt like bloody hell when I tried to stand on it," Drake said.

"But it's all right now." He smiled. "Come here and kiss me, my lady wife."

Happy to comply, Jennifer smiled and leaned over. While she kissed Drake, Olvan quietly slipped out of the chamber.

Jennifer and Drake spent the rest of the day talking, savoring each other's company and sharing the food brought up to his room at meal times.

It was late when he said, "You should sleep in your own chamber so I don't disturb you in the night."

Touched by his concern, Jennifer kissed his cheek before she left. Extremely tired, she fell asleep immediately.

~ * ~

Prudence, wearing too much rouge and perfume, arrived the next day. Jennifer recognized her from her visions.

"I am not here to see you," she announced haughtily. "Drake invited me, and I must speak to him in private."

"Allow me to lead you to his chamber," Josian said, startling Jennifer when he appeared so quickly behind her in the hall.

Without comment, she watched them march up the stairs.

Taking pity on Drake for having to endure Prudence's strong perfume after she had a quick vision of him fanning his hand in front of his nose, Jennifer instructed a maid to serve tea in his room.

The maid knocked on the door.

Drake called, "Enter."

Jennifer followed the maid inside.

"You must be travel weary," he said to Prudence. "Show Mrs. Bennet to her room," he ordered the maid.

Prudence pursed her lips in a pout, but she followed the maid without comment.

As soon as she left, Jennifer opened a window to air out the room. "Am I expected to entertain Prudence?"

"No." Drake grimaced when he shifted his weight in the chair. "I need you to entertain me, wife. Come here and let me taste your sweet lips, and smell your fresh scent."

More than happy to obey, Jennifer leaned down, but Drake pulled her onto his lap. "I don't want to hurt you," she protested.

"You won't unless your refuse to kiss me."

Delighted by his husky suggestion, she wrapped her arms around his neck and kissed him, gently at first, then with more passion when his lips parted and demanded.

His eyes smoldered when she pulled back to ask, "Can I do something to make you more comfortable?"

"No. All I need is time to heal, and your company while I do." He kissed her again, and she gloried in the taste of his mouth, the feel of his uninjured arm holding her close, and his masculine scent that never failed to thrill her.

A little later, still on his lap, she asked, "Would you like me to get you something to read?"

"I'd be grateful. Otherwise, I might sulk because I cannot ravish you as I'd like."

Jennifer kissed his cheek before she left his chamber.

When she found Prudence in the library with Josian, they jumped apart.

"What do you want?" Josian demanded.

Annoyed with his curt tone, she said, "A book for Drake."

"Make haste." Josian's superior attitude raised her hackles, and she barely restrained the impulse to say something to put him in his place.

Back up in Drake's room, she explained what had happened. "I have bad vibes—feelings about Josian and Prudence. They're up to no good. I'm sure of it."

"Don't fret, Jennifer. Josian and Prudence have known each other for years. I'm sure you just startled them."

"I hope you're right."

"Come sit beside me. Let's take turns reading to each other."

Jennifer grinned. "Sounds like a winner."

Later, she said, "I should go talk with the cook about the evening meal."

"Hurry back," Drake said.

In the hall, as she approached the stairs, she heard Prudence walk up behind her. "Drake didn't want to marry you, and your marriage won't last."

Startled, Jennifer turned and looked into the cold, bitter, calculating eyes of the patronizing brown-haired woman, who still reeked of strong perfume.

"I know you're increasing, however, the babe will not be Drake's heir."

"I beg your pardon," Jennifer said, stunned.

Arms outstretched, Prudence pushed Jennifer. Shocked, she grabbed for the banister, trying to break her fall. But all she caught was empty air. She fell and still she tried to grab hold of something. But she tumbled down the stairs. At the bottom she hit her head and blacked out.

~ * ~

Hours later, Jennifer awakened in her bed. Her hands went to her stomach. "My baby," she moaned to Teeny, sitting on a chair beside the bed. "Did I lose my baby?"

"Yes, my lady," Teeny nodded, her eyes sad and red-rimmed. "I fear ye did."

Tears ran down the sides of Jennifer's face, soaking her hair. Teeny's pity didn't help. When the maid tried to coax Jennifer to eat, she had no appetite.

Unable to get out of bed to go see Drake, she knew he was in no condition to come to see her. For hours on end she lay in bed wondering why he didn't find a way to visit her or send a message.

Finally, late that night he hobbled in, one crutch under his good arm, and glared down at her. "You fell down the stairs and lost the babe."

"I didn't fall. Prudence pushed me."

Upset, she touched the opal around her neck, wondering if she might have broken her neck if she hadn't been wearing it, and wishing it had protected the baby... that she hadn't miscarried.

To her surprise, Drake reached for the stone. She didn't try to stop him. He eased the chain up over her head, then threw both stone and chain across the room. They smashed against the wall and the stone shattered in two.

Jennifer gasped. "The opal brought me to you, and I think it protected me from getting killed."

"That rock has no power. 'Tis nothing more than a worthless stone."

Jennifer's heart froze. What had happened to the warm, wonderful man she'd married? Who was this frigid, remote stranger who stared down at her with harsh features and ice-cold eyes? A shudder of fear swept through her. Had Sevil cast a spell over him? Or had somebody else taken over his body?

"You erred when you told Prudence you didn't wish to be increasing."

"I didn't tell her that. She lied if she said I did."

Drake looked drained, and in spite of feeling shattered herself, Jennifer's broken heart went out to him.

"You must be under some kind of spell that's making you act like this."

"I am under no spell." He turned and hobbled from the room, slamming the door behind him.

Jennifer lay absolutely still, too shocked to cry. And for a few minutes, too shocked to think. Then she slid out of bed. Her body hurt as much as her heart as she made her way slowly across the room to retrieve the opal, split in two, with the chain still attached to both stones.

She limped back to bed, crawled under the covers, and clasped the broken opals to her aching heart. Had the stone lost its power when it broke in two? She clutched it more tightly. The stones remained cold. Tears trailed down her cheeks. She'd lost the baby who had been so dear to her heart; the baby who had been created by their love. She sniffed through her tears, wondering why Prudence had pushed her. Because she felt threatened by the baby and wanted her to miscarry? Or had the push been an attempt to kill her?

Shivers, cold and frightening, trembled through Jennifer. When she recovered, she'd go to Havenhurst and stay with Kacy until Prudence left and Drake returned to his normal self. But what if he didn't? What would she do then? What if Sevil had cast a spell over him, a spell that would endure unless she agreed to pledge her soul to him?

Weary and heartsick, Jennifer set the broken stones on the table beside her bed. Then she wiped her tears. She had to believe Drake was under a terrible spell. Otherwise she might not survive. She might shrivel up and die.

Twenty-Four

Fear, Doubt, Remorse

With the baby's demise, all pleasure left Jennifer's life. She couldn't get out of bed for at least a fortnight... Doctor's orders. Misery over losing the baby was a constant torment. All she had left were raw sores in her empty heart.

Other than Teeny, Jennifer had no visitors. But she had a constant companion... tears. Her eyes actually hurt from crying so much and so often. And her soul felt as barren as her empty stomach. Not only had she lost the baby, Jennifer had lost the closeness she'd shared with Drake. To make matters worse, Sevil appeared every night to taunt and threaten.

After a few awful days with nothing to fill her time except idleness, Jennifer got up and dressed without Teeny's help. Stiff and sore, Jennifer made her way to Drake's chamber.

Josian stood guarding the closed door. "The Duke does not wish to see you," he announced.

With injured dignity, Jennifer turned away. Could she believe

Josian? Was he acting under Drake's orders? Or had he taken it upon himself to make that decree?

Miserable and unsure, Jennifer fretted, as she had for days. Had Drake cast her aside because she lost the baby? He couldn't feel worse about that than she did. Or was it because Sevil had cast some sort of spell over him?

She hadn't seen Drake since the night he'd shouted at her. No one told her if he was on the mend or worse.

Determined to see him later that day, she returned to his room. Josian was no longer guarding the door. Buoyed up, Jennifer pushed the door open, then she heard Drake say,

"Send her away. I don't wish to see her just now."

Hurt again, Jennifer stumbled away, bewildered by the turn of events. A week ago she'd been on top of the world. Now her world had fallen apart.

At bedtime, with Teeny's help, Jennifer changed to a nightgown. When someone knocked, she grabbed her robe and jammed her arms through the sleeves before Teeny opened the door.

Josian stood in the hall. He looked from her to Teeny before he said, "The Duke wishes to see the Duchess."

A surge of relief raced through Jennifer. "Thank you."

With wild hope dancing in her heart, she limped to Drake's chamber. Without knocking, she opened the door.

And gasped in shock.

Bare-chested in the huge bed, Drake had his unbandaged arm around Prudence whose bed gown had slipped over her shoulders. And they were kissing.

"What the bloody blazes?" Drake stared beyond Prudence, straight into Jennifer's tormented eyes.

She screamed before a new swirl of emotions tightened her chest. Clenching her fists, she blinked back tears, then turned and fled. Not back to her own room, but down the stairs, out the front door. She ran all the way to the stable, her feet in flimsy slippers, her new ivory robe billowing behind her.

She found Olvan all by himself.

"What is it, lass? What be wrong?"

"I have to leave. I must go to Havenhurst."

"Why, lass?"

"Drake. He's—in bed—with Prudence."

"That canna be, Jennifer lass. The lad loves ye."

"If he does, I'm not sure I want his kind of love." In panic, she added, "Please help me, Olvan. If you won't, I'll go alone, even if I have to walk."

Too devastated to think of anything except getting away from Drake and Prudence, Jennifer turned to flee through the woods.

But Olvan grabbed her arm. "I'll take ye, lass. Dinna ye wish to dress and pack first?"

"No. I can't bear the thought of going back inside."

"Ye've no cloak, and no shoes, lass. 'Tis cold, near to freezing."

"There must be lap robes in one of the carriages," she cried, unable to stop the tide of tears streaming down her cheeks.

Olvan nodded. "Yea. There be."

He summoned a groom and stable boys to prepare a carriage. Then he fetched lap robes.

When Olvan started to climb inside the carriage with her, Jennifer said, "Please stay here, and continue the search for Quicksilver."

Olvan nodded, and instructed John to take her to Havenhurst.

Weak and sore from the fall, and still hemorrhaging from losing the baby, the journey felt like the longest and bleakest of Jennifer's life. Tears leaked from her eyes all the way. She tried to convince herself that Drake must be under a spell. Even so, she hurt like she'd never hurt before, and she felt as if she'd been betrayed by her trusted soul mate.

Finally they reached Havenhurst. She knew she must look a sight when Clay's bent butler answered her knock and bade her enter.

"The Earl an' Countess be in London," he announced.

"I have to see them," Jennifer moaned, shivering.

"On the morrow," the kindly butler said. "Tonight you must rest, Yer Grace. Ah'll give yer driver a bed, and show ye to the guest room ye shared with the Duke in December."

Alone in the familiar bed, Jennifer cried and cried, her heart broken, her spirit crushed. She knew she might never see Drake again. As long as Sevil wished her harm, she couldn't return to Stonemeade. Her presence there would only hurt Drake more. And maybe he didn't want her now. Maybe he wanted Prudence.

~ * ~

"What the devil are you doing?" Drake barked at Prudence while he tried to force the murky fog from his brain and only half-succeeded. He'd been asleep when she came to his room. At first he thought she was Jennifer, and welcomed her into his bed. Wanting her near, he wrapped his uninjured arm around her before he realized his mistake. Although Prudence wore Jennifer's faint perfume, she smelled nothing at all like Jennifer. Neither did her presence soothe nor excite as his wife's did.

Shocked by the kiss Prudence forced on him, he saw Jennifer in the doorway and recoiled. "What the bloody blazes?" he had demanded. To his horror, Jennifer screamed and fled.

He had to go explain what she'd seen wasn't what it seemed. He jerked away from Prudence.

She slid closer.

"Get out," he growled, shoving her away again.

"You don't truly wish me to leave, do you Drake?" Prudence reached beneath the bedcovers and slid her hand up his bare thigh.

Repulsed, he grabbed her wrist with his uninjured hand.

"I know you're unhappy with Miranda and..."

"I'm not unhappy with her." Although he'd never struck a woman, he was sorely tempted now. "Get out, or I'll toss you out on your backside."

Prudence's smug, satisfied smile remained. "I don't think you have enough strength to follow through with that threat," she purred.

Drake lunged at her. Momentum carried them over the edge of the bed and dumped them on the floor. Drake broke the fall with his good arm, but the jolt to his injured shoulder sent pain shooting through him. The pain cleared the fog as anger couldn't. Suddenly he felt more alert than he had felt in days. What had caused the grogginess? Had he been sedated without his knowledge?

Josian thrust the door open. "What happened?"

Anxious looks passed between him and Prudence. It dawned on Drake that they had planned this mischief to brew trouble between him and Jennifer.

"Out!" he roared. Jumping to his feet, he wrapped a bed sheet around his naked hips. "Get out of my home, and out of my life!"

"Drake," Prudence pleaded, "you cannot mean that. You're upset..."

"Bloody damn right, I am upset! I should have booted both of you out ages ago." He limped to the door that separated his chamber from Jennifer's. She wasn't in her room.

"Where's the Duchess?" he bellowed at Teeny.

"The Gaffer, he said ye wanted ta see her," the maid said.

Drake glared at Josian. Prudence had suggested he hire Josian when he became a duke and needed a secretary. Although Drake had taken her advice, he'd never been particularly happy with Josian. Now he realized the two had taken advantage of his wealth, his good will and tolerance. But they had overstepped their bounds once too often.

"Which part of my order didn't you understand?" he barked.

"There's been a misunderstanding," Prudence started to say.

"Get out!" Drake roared, "or I'll throw you out."

Heads bowed, they left. As he watched them go, he vowed their spirits would be cowed before he finished with them.

Jennifer's words slammed through his mind. *I didn't fall. Prudence pushed me.* A tight fist clamped around his heart as he recalled his cruel response. What had possessed him to say such awful things? Surely Jennifer had been heartbroken, and he'd only added to her misery.

With a grimace he pulled the bell chord. Had the wizard cast some sort of evil spell over him?

Bevins arrived within moments.

"Instruct the servants to find the Duchess. As soon as you finish, come back and help me dress."

"Aye Yer Grace." Bevins bowed out of the room.

Moments later, fully dressed, Drake scowled when Bevins announced, "The Duchess canna be found anywhere in the mansion. Jacob said he saw the Her Grace run outside to the stable in her bedclothes a'fore ye summoned me."

Drake grabbed his crutch and stormed outside as fast as his injuries allowed. Not only did he and Jennifer have the wizard Sevil to contend with, Prudence and Josian had conspired against them as well. Drake cursed himself for not realizing their treachery sooner.

"Have you seen the Duchess?" he asked the first stable lad he saw.

"Aye. She be gone, Yer Grace."

A tight band wrapped around his heart and squeezed. "When did she leave?"

"A'fore Th' Gaffer an' Mrs. Bennet went. The Duchess, she begged the Scot to have a carriage readied, an she left, wearin' nothing more'n her bedclothes an' slippers."

Guilt slashed through Drake, tormenting him with razor sharp claws. Disgusted with himself, he ordered, "Summon Olvan." Then Drake went back inside his mansion where he sat in his study, facing the dark window, willing Olvan to come.

While he waited, Drake cursed himself anew. He shouldn't have wasted valuable time untangling himself from Prudence, and getting dressed. He should have followed Jennifer without delay, stark naked. At least he could have stopped her.

His thoughts returned to Prudence and Josian. Not for an instant did he doubt they had conspired to push Jennifer down the stairs. And they must have put something in his food or drink that fogged his mind, too.

Time dragged. Olvan didn't arrive. Drake cursed Prudence and Josian again, and planned his revenge. He would file a formal accusation of attempted murder, and have them imprisoned.

When the hours continued to drag, and Olvan still didn't appear, Drake hobbled up to Jennifer's chamber. He found the opal, broken in two, and pocketed both stones. But he found nothing else in the room to comfort him.

Dawn arrived before Olvan did. By then Drake was near the end of his rope. As Olvan entered Jennifer's room, Drake came unsteadily to his feet without using his crutch, and faced the Scot.

"Where did Jennifer go?"

"To Havenhurst."

"You shouldn't have helped her leave."

"I couldna stop her. If I dinna agree to prepare a carriage, she woulda gone on foot. With my help, she had some protection."

"Why didn't you go with her?"

"Because the lass thought it best for me to stay and help the lads search for Quicksilver."

Drake almost choked on remorse. She'd seen him in bed with Prudence, endured the bitter words he'd hurled at her, and still she worried about Quicksilver.

"I followed the carriage to Havenhurst," Olvan surprised him. "Tis why I couldna be summoned last eve. The wizard dinna accost her. Jennifer lass, be safe."

"Thank you. Now I must fetch her."

Spurred into action, but unfit to ride, Drake dashed out to the stable as fast as his broken ankle allowed, and ordered a carriage put to. Winslow went with him, but Drake rode atop the carriage and drove, pushing the horses as fast as he could.

~ * ~

Early in the morning, dressed in clothes borrowed from Kacy's wardrobe, Jennifer instructed John to drive her to London. Her heart felt like a raw, open wound, and hurt almost beyond endurance.

While the carriage covered the miles, her mind asked and answered the same questions over and over again. Did Drake love her? He'd said he did. But if he did, why had he invited Prudence to his bed? Did Sevil have anything to do with them being in bed together? Or had Prudence acted on her own?

Jennifer decided not to stick around long enough to find out. Life would only get worse, unless she promised her soul to Sevil, and that she couldn't do.

When they reached the London hotel where Kacy and Clay were staying, Kacy took one look at Jennifer and welcomed her with outstretched arms. After listening patiently to the weeping account, Kacy sympathized. "You've been through a lot."

With no tears left to shed, Jennifer tried to be brave. "Have you seen your guardian angel?"

Kacy shook her head. "I've tried to summon him, but so far nothing I've done has worked."

"I need to leave," Jennifer said. "I want to go home. Back to my own time. I'm desperate to get as far away from Drake and Prudence as possible."

"I hate the thought of your going," Kacy said. "I'll miss you. It's been so nice having you here."

"I'll miss you too, but if I stay, I'm afraid Sevil will make life miserable for Drake and unbearable for me. And I don't ever want to see Prudence ever again. She tried to kill me, and made me lose the baby. I loved my unborn child." Jennifer's voice broke on another sob as the pain of losing her baby slashed through her again. "I can't forgive Prudence. She's awful. She's evil. So is Josian. Drake would be better off without him."

Twenty-five

The Guardian Angel and The Wizard

"The Earl and Countess be in London," Clay's aging butler announced after Drake pounded his uninjured fist on the front portal.

"Is the Duchess here?"

Montfort shook his head. "She left fer London early this morning, Yer Grace."

Furious with his bad luck, Drake exchanged horses, and hurried to London, cursing unfortunate delays all the way.

The only people at Clay's town house were the workmen refurbishing it. He questioned them repeatedly, but no one knew where the Earl had taken accommodation for his stay in London.

Drake engaged an investigator to locate them. Then, with time and guilt weighting him down, he instructed Winslow to drive him to White's and settled back inside the ducal carriage. Maybe some of his fellow members knew where Clay was.

The sudden appearance of a strange little man with brilliant white hair and a well-trimmed beard, dressed in a pure white vested suit, shocked Drake. He blinked at the apparition across from him. "Who are you?"

"I am Rey," the plump man said. "Your guardian angel. Do you not remember me?"

Drake started to shake his head, but memories of a far distant time emerged. "I had forgotten you, Rey. I knew you in another time; another life, just as I knew Jennifer..."

"In several other lives," Rey finished.

"Why are you here?"

"To help you. To tell you Jennifer will attend the Haymarket Theater this evening, accompanied by the Earl and Countess of Havenhurst."

The angel floated across the aisle and sat beside Drake. "Now I shall heal your injuries."

The constant pain he had endured since Quicksilver threw him disappeared as soon as Rey touched him. Not quite able to believe he was free from pain, Drake rolled his shoulder and put weight on his ankle. When he remained pain free, he asked, "How can I thank you?"

"Your thanks is unnecessary, however, I appreciate your asking." The angel smoothed his fluffy white beard, his gaze serious. "The wizards are at war. Tonight is Sevil's final test. You may wish to be with Jennifer when he approaches her."

With that Rey winked, and vanished.

Still stunned by the angel's appearance and what he had said and done, Drake rapped on the carriage front. When Winslow stopped, Drake instructed him to take him to his Chelsea townhouse. Once there, he spent the remainder of the afternoon reliving the memories of his life in the future that now flooded him. He had no idea how he had come to be a duke after he'd been killed in a car crash in the twenty-first century, but the title meant nothing without Jennifer in his life.

Impatient by nightfall, Drake arrived at the Haymarket early, and went directly to Clay's empty booth.

As soon as Jennifer entered with Clay and Kacy, Drake said, "I must take my wife. Please forgive me for not explaining more just now. Time is of the essence."

He picked Jennifer up and started to carry her away.

"Put me down," she ordered. "You'll hurt yourself."

"I'm fine," he said, pleased she didn't fight him.

"You're making a spectacle of us," she said crossly.

Unable to ignore the pointed stares and whispers, Drake damned the apologies he would have to make, just as he dammed the wizard Sevil, and Prudence and Josian for interfering in their lives. He hated scandal. But he would endure anything to keep his wife close and safe.

After he settled her on his lap in the carriage, Winslow drove them toward his Chelsea home. Jennifer didn't say anything. She merely accused with her green-speckled eyes.

Drake ached to ease the tension he felt in her body, but he didn't know where to begin. He owed her an apology. Would she listen with an open mind and believe what he said?

He didn't recognize her clothes. She must have borrowed them from Kacy. The cloak had parted and the gown's scoop neckline afforded a glimpse of Jennifer's lovely cleavage. Drake chastised himself for staring.

Although his injuries were healed, hers weren't. She'd lost the baby and bruised her body as well when she tumbled down the stairs. He must protect her, defend her, and keep her safe. Silently praying they would defeat the wizard, so they could spend the rest of their lives in peace, he said, "I'm sorry for all you've suffered."

Expecting the wizard to appear any moment, Drake tightened his arms to hold Jennifer closer. She tried to resist. He didn't let her. For a few moments they dueled in a silent battle of wills. Finally she stilled, and he relaxed slightly.

"The wizards are at war. Tonight is Sevil's final test."

Her eyes grew large and round. "How do you know?"

"My guardian angel told me."

"When?"

"This afternoon. After I arrived in London. He thought I might want to be with you when the wizard approaches you, as indeed I do."

Jennifer looked frightened and Drake hurriedly said, "I owe you an apology. I love you, and never meant to hurt you. It's my fault Prudence pushed you. My fault you lost the baby."

Tears clouded Jennifer's eyes. "And it's my fault you broke your shoulder and sprained your ankle."

Drake hugged her closer. "No. I suspect the wizard spooked Quicksilver, and is responsible for my accident. However, my guardian angel healed my injuries." Drake flexed his shoulder to prove it no longer hurt, then he touched Jennifer's cheek tenderly. "I wish he could heal yours as well. I think the wizard must have cast some sort of spell that made me lash out at you as I did. I should have been prepared for such trickery and prepared..."

A flash of jagged silver lightning slashed through the carriage. And then Sevil appeared on the seat opposite them.

Jennifer wrapped her arms around Drake. He reached beyond her, trying to grab the wizard. But Sevil clapped his hands, and Drake froze in a stiff, rigid posture. He knew the carriage had stopped, and wondered if Winslow was as helpless as he. Although Drake couldn't move, he could see and hear, and he listened intently, the broken-open stones warming inside his trouser pocket.

With Drake's warning fresh in her mind, Jennifer had a feeling this might be her final confrontation with Sevil. She hoped so, but feared the outcome.

Furious with him for all the trouble he'd caused, she said, "If you harm Drake again, you'll regret it."

"Do not threaten me," the wizard said.

"I regret ever having seen you," she snapped.

"I will ignore that statement because I feel magnanimous tonight."

"If you do one more thing to hurt Drake, I'll find a way to repay you, so help me, God."

Sevil blanched, then hissed, "I warned you not to threaten me. And you must not invoke the name of the Deity in my presence."

"I'll do what I want. I'm sick and tired of you and what you've put us through."

"Then promise me your soul."

For half a second she was tempted, just to get him to leave them alone. But if she gave in now, she would be under his control forever.

"No."

"I must have it now. Tonight." He sounded desperate, but he looked arrogant. Confident, too.

"I've told you repeatedly that I won't promise you my soul, or anything else. Not now. Not tomorrow. Not ever."

"An unwise decision, Jennifer. And most ungrateful. I gave you great joy by bringing you here and depositing you in the Duke's lap."

"You intended for me to land in Paris where Kacy was, but the opal guided me to Drake."

"How dare you question me?"

"I dare plenty, you obnoxious toad."

"I am not obnoxious." He looked and sounded indignant. "I am powerful. I can give you any—"

"I don't want anything from you."

"Not even the Duke and his love?"

Jennifer's throat went dry. Was Sevil threatening to separate her from Drake? It was what she'd expected and she had to be brave. "Not if the only way I can have him is through you. Don't you know forced love holds no appeal for humans? Now get out of my life, and never show yourself to me again. You sicken me and I can't stand the sight of you."

The whites of Sevil's eyes glowed red.

"You hate me, don't you, Jennifer?"

"No, even though you're a horrible creature. I can't believe God had a part in your creation."

Sevil blanched again. "You do hate me." The whites of his eyes glowed a more brilliant shade of red. "Admit it." Cunning glittered in his terrible eyes. "Hate is such a powerful tool."

Jennifer sensed the best way to foil him was to stay calm. She forced herself not to react with heat or anger, or fear. "You're not worth that much emotion, Sevil."

He leapt off the seat. Bent over, he jumped up and down on the narrow carriage floor, yelling, "You hate me. You hate me. Tell me you hate me!"

Amazed at the calm settling over her, Jennifer said, "You disgust me, and I'll never do anything you ask or suggest. When will you be smart enough to understand that?"

Sevil stopped jumping. "Sevil lives. Sevil is smart," he raged. "Sevil lives. Sevil is powerful, and you must do as he says. Now."

"You're nothing more than a palindrome."

"What?" For a split second he looked astonished.

"Sevil is lives spelled backwards. And that's all you are. Nothing more than a twisted, backward demon—freak. Can't you exist without preying on decent, innocent people?"

Sevil flinched. "I am powerful. You must obey me."

"You're wasting your breath," she said in disgust.

"You must!" Sevil raged. "You must!"

"No."

He flicked his fingers at her.

A noxious fog filled the inside of the carriage.

Jennifer tightened her arms around Drake.

But the noxious fumes made her dizzy, faint, sick to her stomach. Afraid she might barf, she clapped her hands over her mouth. And knew her mistake the instant she let go of Drake.

The carriage door opened. A flash of wild grief ripped through her as a whirlwind swept inside. Before she could react, the wind spiraled around her; whirled her off Drake's lap and outside, up into the black, star-studded sky.

Jennifer knew she was going back even before she heard Sevil's shrill voice wailing, "You dared to deny me. Now suffer the consequences."

Through the fog she saw him fade. And disappear.

Then she spun into orbit. Inside the noxious, foggy whirlwind, her heart dived to her stomach and tears streamed down her eyes.

Would she ever see Drake again? Her sense of loss was beyond tears.

~ * ~

The instant Jennifer flew out of the carriage, Drake came out from the spell. He lunged after Sevil as he jumped through the open carriage door, but a hand on Drake's shoulder stayed him.

He glanced around and saw his white-haired guardian angel. "You will not find her."

"Why not?" Drake asked, still determined to jump.

"She has returned to her own time."

"No-o-o," Drake protested in a loud shout as the carriage started to move again.

Rey motioned at the door, closing it without touching it.

"Can you bring her back?" Drake asked, his heart hopeful, his remorse painful.

The angel shook his head. Drake knew he would always remember the sympathy in Rey's eyes, just as he would remember the emptiness in his own jagged heart.

"I cannot undo the wizard's spell. He used the last of his power to send her back."

Numb with loss, Drake couldn't make himself believe the truth. Denial was easier to handle.

"That furious act was the wizard's last," Rey said. "Sevil has been cast into outer darkness and will not bother humans again for a long period of mortal time."

Drake didn't care a fig about the wizard. He wanted Jennifer, the woman he loved, the woman he would love forever. "I want my wife. I can't live without her."

"You must live," the white-haired, wingless angel said. "It is not your time to die."

Wracked by an aching hollow emptiness, fear clouded Drake's thinking. His brain couldn't accept the possibility that he might not see Jennifer again in this life. For a few seconds hopelessness settled in his chest. Then he forced optimism.

"I will find her. I must find her. She's my heart. My soul mate."

Twenty-six

The Return

In the living room of the small house near Denver University that she had shared with Catharine before her unexpected journey to the past, Jennifer stood in stunned disbelief. Outside the living room window snowflakes fell on the barren winter lawn. Inside the cozy room she felt as cold and numb as if the January snow fell on her bare flesh.

Unable to believe what she'd just heard, she gasped, "Would you repeat that?"

Fresh tears sparkled in Catharine's blue eyes. "I said Miranda died in a car crash last night and her, or rather your funeral, is already being planned."

Still in shock from being thrust back to the twenty-first century, Jennifer asked, "Who was driving?"

"Miranda."

"Was she alone?"

"Yes."

Jennifer's heart wrenched, and she nearly choked as she asked, "How are Aunt Rachel, Uncle Mac and Tyler taking her—my death?"

Tears rolled unchecked down Catharine's cheeks. "Pretty bad, as you might imagine."

Jennifer reached out and hugged her. "I'm sorry, Catharine. Miranda's death must be a shock to you, too."

"It is," Catharine sniffed. "I asked her not to drive, but she was so sure nothing would happen to her, she rarely took my advice."

Jennifer's old cat, Mordora, circled her ankles, her soft fur rubbing against Jennifer's shins. After five months in long gowns, it felt strange, almost indecent to be dressed in a sweater and jeans.

As Jennifer loosened her embrace, Catharine backed a little away, and shoved her long blond hair behind her shoulders. Tears still trickled down her cheeks.

Miserable herself, Jennifer bent down, picked up her cat and started to pet Mordora. Pain and loss twisted cruelly through her. Still in shock after losing Drake, Jennifer could barely think, but as she stroked her cat, she asked, "Where did the accident happen?"

"On I-70, northwest of downtown, by the Mousetrap."

"Was anyone else hurt?"

"No." Catharine wiped her wet cheeks with a tissue she pulled from her skirt pocket. "Apparently your car skidded on what the police called black ice. When it hit a rail, Miranda plunged to her death."

Jennifer swallowed. Had Sevil known Miranda was dead? She'd probably never know the answer to that. She'd seen him fade, and hoped she never saw the wizard again.

"I feel so helpless and out of place," she said. "I don't know what to do."

"I suppose you could tell Tyler, and your aunt and uncle that the girl who died wasn't you," Catharine offered a solution. "I don't know if you could convince them though. Miranda did a pretty good job of imitating you. Your relatives might think you're the imposter."

Jennifer still couldn't believe what had happened. Her thoughts in turmoil, she wondered if she had a right to try to prove Miranda was an imposter... to put Aunt Rachel, Uncle Mac and Tyler through that kind of upheaval.

A feeling of doom settled on her shoulders. She didn't belong in the past, but she didn't belong here either. How could things change so much in so short a time? She'd only been gone five months—a lifetime in some ways. Now she had no life here or there. Worst of all she'd lost Drake. Forever? Would she see him in another life? And how could she live without him in the meantime?

Shaken and missing him with all her heart and soul, she said, "This is bizarre."

"Yes, it is," Catharine agreed. "It's wonderful to see you again, Jennifer. I'm so pleased you're alive and well. But I need to leave." She wiped her tears again. "Your aunt and uncle asked me to come over this morning to discuss the funeral arrangements, and I promised to be there by nine."

Still in a daze, Jennifer couldn't move. One thought kept repeating itself. She'd lost Drake.

Now her relatives were lost to her, too.

Without her identity, she couldn't claim her inheritance, or use her social security number so she could work. And what about college graduation? She'd missed half of her last year. Even so, she wouldn't have missed the time she'd shared with Drake for anything.

"I hate to leave you." Catharine picked up her coat, put it on, and shoved her long hair behind her shoulders again before she opened the door.

"I'll try not to be gone too..." she gasped and gaped.

A tall, handsome, very blond man, dressed in a three-piece navy blue suit, white shirt and paisley tie, stood in the hall outside their apartment.

"May I come in?" he asked. "I must talk to Jennifer."

"I don't know. That is, I—What I mean is..."

"Don't be alarmed, Catharine," Jennifer came to her aid, although she felt shell-shocked herself when she saw Drake. How had he gotten here? "I know him."

Because she was afraid to believe her eyes, Jennifer decided she must be hallucinating.

To her surprise her hallucination stepped inside.

Her chaotic insides quivered. She gave him the once over with eyes as wary as his.

"How did you get here?"

She blinked when her hallucination answered. "My guardian angel brought me."

Jennifer took a step forward, then changed her mind and backed up. "Are you real?"

"Very."

"Wh—hy are you here?"

"Because we have to talk."

Jennifer had been through too much to believe her hallucination could be real.

"I guess I'll go now," Catharine said, drawing her attention.

Jennifer swallowed. She'd forgotten all about Catharine when she saw Drake, but she knew Catharine didn't drive, and was actually afraid of cars. "Is Tyler coming for you?"

"No. He offered, but I told him I could ride the RTD."

"You like to ride the bus, do you?" Drake asked, his attention also shifted to Catharine.

"No. I don't like to ride in any vehicles be they car, bus or airplane, but I am—adjusting." Then to Jennifer she said, "Miranda used your credit cards and spent a lot of your money, but she left this." Catharine removed a small box from her purse, which she extended. When Jennifer opened it, a beautiful old-fashioned diamond solitaire sparkled at her.

"Miranda took it off when she arrived in this time," Catharine said. "It must be quite valuable, given its age."

"I wondered what happened to it," Drake said, then, "You may keep Miranda's betrothal ring, Catharine."

"No. I cannot." She backed away.

"Of course you can." Jennifer handed the ring back. "It'll be a nice reminder of the time you spent with Miranda."

Catharine finally smiled, her eyes red-rimmed and swollen from her tears. "You won't leave or do anything serious without letting me know your plans, will you, Jennifer?"

"No."

Catharine embraced Jennifer. "I'll go now. Goodbye, and good luck."

I'm going to need it, Jennifer thought, turning her dazed gaze back to Drake—her hallucination. Nothing seemed real, least of all him. But, oh, how she wished he were.

"She really does look like Kacy," Drake said after Catharine closed the door behind her.

Jennifer nodded. Pain twined around her bruised heart. She might as well talk to her hallucination, and pretend he was real. "Miranda's dead," Jennifer said, her voice dull and flat.

The guilt that hurtled through Drake's eyes jolted Jennifer like an electric shock. Maybe he wasn't a hallucination. Her heart pumped with jubilation. Had he come after her?

"How did Miranda die?" he asked.

"In a car accident—last night. You know what a car is, right?"

He nodded.

Jennifer blinked, fighting the urge to cry, aching to be gathered close, yearning to be reassured that he loved her, that Prudence meant nothing to him.

But Drake didn't reach for her. Instead he said, "Sometimes you remind me of a frail, porcelain faced doll, Jennifer. But the pale freckles on the bridge of your nose make you look far more touchable than a doll." His eyes roamed over her jeans and bulky red sweater. "I'll never tire of looking at you, any more than I'll tire of being near you."

Touched by his words, Jennifer didn't reply. She couldn't. She was too choked up to say a single word.

"May I hold you?" he finally asked.

She shook her head. Why did he ask? Why didn't he just do it?

He frowned. "I don't intend to leave without you. You're my wife, and in my heart you always will be."

Jennifer licked her dry lips, and somehow found her voice. "I'm not your wife. I was a proxy for Miranda, remember?"

"I thought we settled the fact that you're my wife, no matter what name you used."

When she didn't argue, he asked, "Can you forgive me for all the pain I caused you?"

"I don't know."

"You must." He looked startled, yet he had a determined gleam in his blue eyes. "Please say you forgive me."

Jennifer wrung her hands, too distraught to think clearly. He hadn't said he loved her.

"Why?" she asked.

He wrinkled his forehead. "Don't you know?"

She shook her head.

Drake reached for her clenched hands, and tugged them up to hold near his heart. Hers was beating a frantic tune. His was too, she discovered.

"I'm Dirk."

"But you have none of his memories," she objected.

"Yes I do." He grinned. "I have all his memories now, as well as Drake's. I wasn't born Drake, although we share the same birthday—in different centuries. After I died in this time I somehow took over his life in the past. It started the day Helen died, the same day I died here. Apparently when Drake tried to save her and his brother's lives, he inhaled too much smoke himself. I wasn't actually married to Helen. She was the first Drake's wife—not ever mine. But I married you in this century, so you are truly my wife, Jeni."

Afraid to believe he was really here, she trembled as she asked, "Do you have—all Dirk's memories?"

He winked. "You bet. There have been times when I didn't feel like Drake at all because I dreamed of my own memories—Dirk's that is. I didn't regain all of my memories... Dirk's, until my guardian angel told me I'd find you at the Haymarket Theater last night. Now they're as much a part of me as Drake's are."

Afraid she'd succumb to Drake the instant he kissed her—if he kissed her, Jennifer forced herself to say, "I'm not going back with you."

"Then I'll stay here with you."

A spark of perverse satisfaction forced a reluctant grin. "You can't."

"Why not? I'd sooner die than live without you."

Jennifer saw the familiar glint in his wonderful eyes... And more. The love that had defied time. But why didn't he say he loved her? And then she knew why. Because he feared rejection.

Her heart skipped a beat when he slowly laced her fingers with his. Tiny shivers of excitement darted up and down her spine, energizing the lethargy that had bogged her down. As they stared, she lost track of reality, and felt her eyes grow wide with anticipation. Somehow her subconscious knew without the words that he loved her. Always had. Always would.

Mesmerized, she let love shine through her eyes.

His mouth came down on hers, more gentle and tender than ever before, as though he could wipe away all past hurt and seal their future for all time and perhaps beyond to another life. Forever.

The shrill ringing of the telephone jerked them apart. "Don't answer it." He pulled her close again.

"I didn't intend to."

"I won't give you up," he groaned against her cheek. "Tell me where you want to live. In the nineteenth century or here?"

The hesitancy in his voice made her love him even more, if that were possible.

When she said nothing, he said, "I can't right the wrongs, Jennifer, but I can ask you to forgive me until you do. And I can plant another child deep inside you, and love you until time ceases to be."

The hint of finality created a warm spot way down deep inside, and a merry tune in her head. Too emotional to speak, Jennifer swallowed.

"And," Drake added, "I've cursed myself time and again for the harsh words I uttered after you lost the baby. I should have held you in my arms and allowed us to share our grief. Some kind of demon must have possessed me to say such appalling things. You must forgive me so I can forgive myself."

She tried to say, *I do forgive you, and I know Sevil was responsible for most of our problems,* but the words got stuck in her throat. Somehow he knew how bad she felt for losing the baby.

"All I can say is that I love you. I've always loved you." He paused and when she still didn't say anything, he said, "Say you love me, too, Jennifer. I need to hear you say the words."

"I love you, Drake," she managed in a trembling voice.

He smiled... And what a smile. It lit up her heart and made her tingle all the way from the top of her head to the tips of her toes.

"You're not only my wife, Jennifer, you're my life. After I assumed Drake's identity, I observed life. I didn't truly live until you came to me."

She knew she startled him when she asked, "Where do you want to live?"

For a few seconds all he did was stare. Then he said, "I've won. You've forgiven me." He looked astonished.

Jennifer smiled. "We've both won, Drake... Dirk. Good grief. I don't know what to call you."

"Drake—if we're going back. Are we?"

"Yes. Unless you prefer not to."

"I have obligations there, Duchess... and so do you. But I'll stay here and find a way to make a living, if you prefer to live in this century."

"I want to live with you. Where, is your decision."

"No. It's our decision, Jennifer. We're partners, and you'll share in all our decisions. What would you like to do?"

"Go home—to Stonemeade. That's where we belong. And your grandmother—Lucilla, will miss us if we don't return. I'll miss her too, as well as Kacy and Clay, Olvan, Teeny, Bevins, Jacob, John and all your servants. Won't you?"

He nodded. "Our servants, Duchess. Ours, not mine."

"What about Prudence?" Jennifer asked then. "Will she try to interfere again?"

"No. I sent her and Josian packing. When you saw Prudence with me, I thought she was you. She wore your perfume. That's why I allowed her in my bed. I discovered immediately that she wasn't you, but you fled before I could push her away. I think she and Josian drugged my food or drink, and conspired to push you down the stairs."

When Jennifer trembled, Drake kissed her temple. "If they haven't left England, I intend to press charges for attempted murder."

Jennifer shivered, remembering her fear when she'd wondered if Prudence wanted to kill her. She had killed their baby. Drake tightened his hold, then kissed Jennifer's lips. Gently at first, and when she responded, with more passion.

She felt as if she were in a daze, floating off the floor in a happy stupor. His tongue tasted delicious, like peppermint. And he smelled as good as ever. Maybe better. His fresh piney scent transported her back to his lodge and the first time he had kissed her in the past. But as the kiss continued, memories converged with other kisses in other lives. They too, had left her wanting more, and feeling unfulfilled. But she sensed now and hoped with all her heart, that they would fulfill their love for many years to come.

Finally the drugging kisses ended. And Drake said, "I know now that Josian and Prudence concocted the letter that instructed my solicitor to prepare the divorce documents in December. Rey confirmed my suspicions while we traveled through the colorful, spiraling time tunnel."

"Rey is the name of your guardian angel?" Jennifer asked, her heart hopping .

Drake nodded.

"That's Kacy's guardian angel's name, too."

"And yours as well, Jennifer."

She shook her head. "I don't have one."

"Then who do you think is responsible for your visions?"

A quick vision flashed, revealing that Rey was indeed her guardian angel.

"He restored me to my wife," Drake said, "and I'm relieved to have her in my arms."

To Jennifer's delight, Drake hugged her again, and kissed her soundly, too.

"I love you," he murmured against her mouth, against her cheek, her temple and hair. "I love you so much it hurts, Jennifer."

"I love you, too, Drake."

Their lips merged again, and her heart pounded with love and joy for what she knew they would share in the days and weeks and years to come.

Drake ended the kiss, and held her slightly away while he reached inside his pocket and removed the broken opals.

"Rey smoothed these for us, and added a chain so we could both wear one. Mine guided me to you... Twice. And it guided you to me once. I think it may have saved your life too, when Prudence pushed you down the stairs. May I place yours around your neck so it can live near your heart?"

Jennifer nodded solemnly and stood still while he did. Then he drew her hand to his chest. Beneath his shirt and tie she felt his half of the opal.

"Have they lost their power, now that they're split in two?

"No." Drake drew her hands to his mouth and kissed each one reverently. "Rey said their power is in the belief. Drake smiled tenderly. "Rey also said Quicksilver has been found and returned to the stable."

"That's wonderful. Oh, Drake, I'm so happy!"

"I am, too. I plan to spend the rest of my life pleasuring you, spoiling you, treasuring you. And I vow no one, including the wizard will ever bother us again."

Jennifer smiled up at her husband. "The only important thing in the world is being together."

He nodded. "Long ago we met and started on a journey that will last forever."

"As will our love."

"As will our love," he agreed.

Then he lowered his voice, and repeated the words he had spoken to her after they eloped, when they were alone in their room.

"I will love, honor and cherish you forever, my darling Jeni."

And, although it sometimes proved difficult, the man known as Dirk and Drake, and a number of other names, kept his solemn word. Forever.

Meet Evanell

Born in Utah, Peggy Parsons writes under the pseudonym Evanell, which is her middle name. She graduated from Orem High School, attended Brigham Young University and the University of Utah. After working as a secretary for several years, she moved into the oil and gas industry. In addition to Utah, she has lived in Colorado, England, Nevada and Arizona. She served as Treasurer and later as President of the American Women's Club of London, and wrote articles for the London Bridge, a magazine for American women living in the U.K. While in England she often traveled to Europe. She has also visited Mexico, Russia and Australia.

When her husband took early retirement, they traveled around the U.S. for four years, towing a 40' fifth wheel. She now lives in Arizona during the winter and spends the summer months at her cabin in Utah. Peggy/Evanell took up golf in 1992 and served as President of her Women's Golf Club in 1999. She has three sons and nine grandchildren. She lost a twelve-year old grandson in 2000. Married to her current husband for twenty-five years, she also has four stepchildren and three step- grandchildren.

She has always loved to read and vowed to give the characters in her head their own written stores some day. Her hobbies include golf and Mah Jong.

Works From The Pen Of Peggy P. Parsons & Evanell

Written as Evanell

Glimpse of Eternity

    Startled, and still on the bed, his gaze level with hers, he said, "If you like my kisses, why did you stop me?"

    "Because that's not why I'm here. And I'm sure my guardian angel wouldn't approve if we did anything more."

    Clay breathed in and out, slowly. "Why then, did you thank me?"

    "For the reunion."

    Puzzled, he frowned. "The reunion?"

    She nodded. "I think we've known each other before. In prior lives. But I don't expect to stay in this century. So I don't think we should kiss again. I He wanted to kiss her again. Giving in to the impulse, he lowered his head.

    She thwarted him by scooting off his lap, jumping to her feet. Instead of dashing away, she stood before him, her mouth swollen from his prolonged kiss, her eyes blazing with unfulfilled passion. And then to his utter amazement, she said, "Thank you."

    need to try to help solve your problems, not complicate them, so I can go home."

Glimpse of Forever

    Having loved and lost Drake in other lives, including her current life in the twenty-first century, Jennifer is delighted when she finds herself catapulted into his life in the middle of the nineteenth century. Mistaking Jennifer for his intended, Drake finds her much easier to deal with after she falls from a tree in his woods. Although he thinks she tricked him into agreeing to wed her, he plans to have a marriage in name only. Now he discovers he wants her to be his wife in every way.

With her gift of sight, Jennifer knows Drake's charge is impersonating her in the future. When she convinces Drake she isn't his intended, he promises they will fight the evil wizard who wants her soul together. Then he is thrown from his horse and wounded. Fearing the wizard will never let them live in peace, Jennifer returns to the future only to discover the girl impersonating her is dead and she has no life to reclaim.

Glimpse of Never Ending Love

Still standing close but no longer touching, Catharine said, "Tyler?"

"Yes?"

"Will being together be this exciting if we are married?"

"Yes," he promised. "We'll make it this exciting or more."

Neither said another word, but both knew a commitment of sorts had been made.

He reached inside his breast suit coat pocket and removed the betrothal ring. "You'll let me know when you're ready to wear this, won't you?"

She nodded, staring at the huge diamond solitaire sparkling up at her.

Written as Peggy P. Parsons

One Stolen Night

Having broken up with her high school sweetheart after graduation, Pamela Tate follows her dream of attending the University of Hawaii where she meets the legendary Robin, who steals more than her bruised heart.

Yours Till Niagra Falls

Embarrassed by her attempt to warn Jade about a conniving college classmate, Kia flees to her beloved Camp in the Adirondack's to mourn the loss of her family. When Jade shows up uninvited and unexpected, she agrees to let him stay in one of her log cabins. Although she isn't ready for love, she wants to trust Jade, but his association with her unscrupulous ex-boyfriend, makes it difficult to believe he isn't there for a sinister reason.

Paper Marriage

Chandler's eagle gaze checked Analyn's compact living room. "Is your whole apartment decorated in red, white and blue?"
"What if it is?" He'd broken her heart. Would he insult her taste, too?

Yesterday's Secrets

Story begins with Janalou boarding a bus in Spartanburg, SC. She meets seven people and they form a friendship and stay together after they transfer to a different bus. That evening Janalou has an attack of appendicitis and is rushed to the hospital, then ends up traveling by car across the country with Kree to give her body and her facial bruises time to heal before she meets his family and starts to work with them.
When Janalou discovers her father/papa and stepmother have been arrested for her murder (even though no body was found--there was blood in the house), she feels compelled to return to Spartanburg. The next day at the court house she meets her real family, including her identical twin, and discovers she was kidnapped when she was four. Her twin tells/reminds her that for their last Christmas together they were given twin dolls, and dresses in their own size to match the dolls.

Letter to Our Readers

Enjoy this book?

You can make a difference

As an independent publisher, Wings ePress, Inc. does not have the financial clout of the large New York Publishers. We can't afford large magazine spreads or subway posters to tell people about our quality books.

But we do have something much more effective and powerful than ads. We have a large base of loyal readers.

Honest Reviews help bring the attention of new readers to our books.

If you enjoyed this book, we would appreciate it if you would spend a few minutes posting a review on the site where you purchased this book or on the Wings ePress, Inc. webpages at: https://wingsepress.com/